I dove toward the phone. "Hello?"

"Happy birthday, Princess," my dad said. "Penny and I are on our way to see you!"

Terror seized me. "What does that mean?"

My dad laughed. "We're surprising you on your birthday."

My father could not see this place. No, no, no. I'd lose everything. If, after last night, I had anything left to lose.

"That's great, Dad," I forced myself to say. "So . . . where are you exactly? Did your plane just land?"

Please let them still be at the airport. I could make this house look presentable in an hour.

"Nope. We should be in Westport in twenty minutes."

Twenty minutes?!

There was groaning from the couch. Brett flipped onto his back and said, "It's eff-ing freezing in here."

"April, there's not a boy over, is there?" my dad asked.

I sliced my hand through the air to tell Brett to shut up.

"What? Of course not! Vi's mom is listening to NPR."

"We just passed the country club. We're making better time than I thought. Can't wait to see you, Princess."

"You too," I choked out, and hung up. I closed my eyes. Then opened them.

Two half-naked boys in the great room. One in a tiara. More half-naked boys in the bedrooms. Empty liquor bottles and trashed cups.

And Vi's mom nowhere in sight.

I was a dead princess.

SARAH MLYNOWSKI

ten things we did
(and probably shouldn't have)

HARPER TEEN
An Imprint of HarperCollinsPublishers

HarperTeen is an imprint of HarperCollins Publishers.

Ten Things We Did (and Probably Shouldn't Have)
Copyright © 2011 by Sarah Mlynowski
www.epicreads.com

Library of Congress Cataloging-in-Publication Data
Mlynowski, Sarah.
    Ten things we did (and probably shouldn't have) / Sarah Mlynowski.
— 1st ed.
        p.   cm.
    Summary: Sixteen-year-old April, a high school junior, and her
friend Vi, a senior, get a crash course in reality as the list of things they
should not do becomes a list of things they did while living parent-free
in Westport, Connecticut, for the semester.
    ISBN 978-0-06-170126-9 (pbk.)
    [1. Conduct of life—Fiction.   2. Interpersonal relations—Fiction.
3. Self-reliance—Fiction.   4. Connecticut—Fiction.]   I. Title.
PZ7.M7135Ten   2011   2010045556
[Fic]—dc22   CIP
                                                             AC

12 13 14 15 16   LP/RRDH   10 9 8 7 6 5 4 3 2 1
❖
First paperback edition, 2012

For Farrin Jacobs,
brilliant editor and true friend.

ten things we did

(and probably shouldn't have)

saturday, march 28

THE MORNING AFTER

I bolted awake. A siren.

The police were outside my house. Ready to arrest me for underage partying, excessive flirting, and an overcrowded hot tub.

But wait.

My brain turned on. No, not the cops. Just my phone—my dad's ringtone.

Which was even worse.

I rummaged around the futon. No phone. Instead I felt a leg. A guy's leg. A guy's leg flung over my ankle. A guy's leg that did not belong to my boyfriend.

Oh God. Oh God. What did I do?

WEEEooooWEEEooooWEEEoooo!

Upstairs. The siren ring was coming from upstairs, the main level of Vi's house.

Maybe I should just go back to sleep . . . No! Phone ringing. In bed with not my boyfriend. I managed to get myself out of the futon without disturbing him and—um, where were my pants? Why was I in bed with a guy who was not my boyfriend without any pants?

At least I had underwear on. And a long-sleeved shirt. I looked around for some pants. The sole item of clothing within grabbing distance was Vi's red dress that I wore last night for the party.

That dress was trouble.

I ran up the stairs bare-legged. At the top, I almost passed out.

It looked like a war zone. Empty plastic cups littered the wooden floor. Half-eaten tortilla chips were planted in the shag area rug like pins on a bulletin board. A large blob—punch? Beer? Something I'd be better off not identifying?—had stained the bottom half of the pale blue curtain. A white lace bra hung from the four-foot cactus.

Brett was in surfer shorts, face-planted on the couch. He was using the purple linen tablecloth as a blanket. Zachary was asleep in one of the dining room chairs, wearing an aluminum foil tiara on his lolled-back head. The patio door was open—and a puddle of rain had flooded the carpet.

WEEEooooWEEEooooWEEEoooo! Phone was louder. Closer. But where? The kitchen counter? The kitchen counter! Nestled between a saucer of cigarette butts and an empty bottle of schnapps! I dove toward it. "Hello?"

"Happy birthday, Princess," my dad said. "Did I wake you?"

"Wake me?" I asked, my heart thumping. "Of course not. It's already"—I spotted the microwave clock across the room—"nine thirty-two."

"Good, because Penny and I are on our way to see you!"

Terror seized me. "What does that mean?"

My dad laughed. "We decided to surprise you on your birthday. It was actually Penny's idea."

"Wait. For real?"

"Of course for real! Surprise!"

My head was spinning, and I felt like vomiting and it wasn't just because of the many, many, definitely too many glasses of spiked punch I had consumed last night. My father could not see this place. No, no, no.

Oh God. I'd violated 110 percent of my dad's rules. The evidence was all around, mocking me.

This wasn't happening. It couldn't happen. I would lose everything. If, after last night, I had anything left to lose. I took a step and a tortilla chip attacked my bare foot. *Owww*.

Mother friggin' crap.

"That's great, Dad," I forced myself to say. "So . . . where are you exactly? Did your plane just land?"

Please let them still be at the airport. It would take them at least an hour to drive here from LaGuardia. I could make this house look presentable in an hour. I would find some pants.

Then I would toss the bottles and cups and cigarette butts and vacuum the tortilla chips and maybe the bra, maybe even Brett and Zachary—

"Nope, we just drove through Greenwich. We should be in Westport in twenty minutes."

Twenty minutes?!

There was groaning from the couch. Brett flipped onto his back and said, "It's eff-ing freezing in here."

"April, there's not a boy over, is there?" my dad asked.

I sliced my hand through the air to tell Brett to shut the hell up.

"What? No! Of course not! Vi's mom is listening to NPR."

"We just passed the Rock Ridge Country Club. Looks like we're making better time than I thought. We'll be there in fifteen minutes. Can't wait to see you, Princess."

"You too," I choked out, and hung up. I closed my eyes. Then opened them.

Two half-naked boys in the great room. One in a tiara.

More half-naked boys in the bedrooms.

Empty liquor bottles and trashed cups.

And Vi's mom nowhere in sight.

I was a dead princess.

number one:
lied to our parents

THREE MONTHS EARLIER

"How would you like to finish high school in Cleveland?" my dad asked me out of nowhere during Christmas break of junior year.

Fine. Maybe it wasn't completely out of nowhere.

THREE MONTHS, ONE MINUTE, THIRTY SECONDS EARLIER

"April, can you sit down? We need to talk to you about an important issue."

This should have tipped me off that something disconcerting was about to take place. But at the time, I was too busy multitasking to pick up on the signals. It was Thursday night, nine fifty-five, and Marissa had just dropped me off before my ridiculous ten o'clock (even during Christmas holidays) curfew. I was standing in front of the fridge debating between grapes or an apple for my evening snack *and* contemplating if tomorrow night was finally the right time to have sex with Noah.

I was leaning toward the apple. Even though what I really wanted was chocolate fudge cake. But since Penny didn't eat junk food, especially chocolate junk food, the likelihood of finding chocolate fudge cake in our fridge was about as high as finding a unicorn in our backyard.

As for the other thing . . . the one that made me want to jump on my bed and hide under the covers . . . it was time. I loved Noah. He loved me. We had waited long enough. We had planned on doing it over the break, but my brother, Matthew, had been here until this morning. Tonight, Noah had a party he had to go to with his parents and on Saturday he was leaving for Palm Beach.

Tomorrow was the only time. Plus, my dad and Penny had a dinner party in Hartford, an hour away, so that would leave me an empty house from about six to midnight. Sex would not take six hours. Would it?

I guessed it would take thirty minutes, tops. Or an hour. Or three minutes.

I was ready. Wasn't I? I'd told Noah I was ready. I had convinced myself I was ready. Ready to have sex with Noah. Noah who had dimples when he smiled. Noah who'd been my boyfriend for over two years.

I grabbed the apple, rinsed it, then took a large bite.

But was it a bad idea to do it the night before he left for a week in Palm Beach? What if I freaked out the next day and he was at the bottom of the country?

"You're dripping," my stepmom said, eyes darting back and forth between the offending fruit and the white-tiled floor. "Pretty please, use a plate and sit down?" Penny was obsessed with cleanliness. The way most people carried around a cell phone, Penny carried around hand-sanitizing wipes.

I took a plate and a seat at the table, across from them. "So what's up?"

"And a place mat," she added.

Then came my father's contribution: "How would you like to finish high school in Cleveland?"

The question did not sound like English. It made zero sense to me. I wasn't going to Cleveland. I'd never been to Cleveland. Why would I be going to school there? "Huh?"

My dad and Penny stole quick glances at each other and then refocused on me. "I'm starting a new job," he said.

The kitchen was suddenly a hundred degrees. "But you already have a job," I explained slowly. He worked for a hedge fund right here in Westport, Connecticut.

"This is a better job," he said. "A very lucrative job. Very."

"But—why do you need two jobs?" In retrospect, I *was*

being dense. But they were throwing massive information bombs at me. Cleveland! New job! Place mat!

"I *don't* need two jobs," he said slowly. "That's why I'm quitting Torsto and taking the job at KLJ in Cleveland."

My brain was refusing to process this information. "You're moving to Cleveland?"

"*We're* moving to Cleveland," he said, sweeping his right hand to include all three of us. My dad, Penny. And me.

I choked on a piece of apple.

What? Me? In Cleveland? No. No, no, no. Not happening. I gripped the arms of my chair. I was not moving. They would not, could not, make me let go of this chair.

"We're all moving to Cleveland," Penny piped in. "On January third."

Nine days. They wanted me to move in nine days? Wait. But. "You asked me *if* I would like to finish high school in Cleveland. My answer is no. I would not."

They looked at each other again. "April," Penny said. "My folks have already found some terrific schools for you to . . ."

As she rattled on, panic grabbed hold of my throat and tightened its grip. I wasn't going to Cleveland. I wasn't leaving my life. I wasn't leaving Marissa. Or Vi. I wasn't leaving Noah. I wasn't leaving Westport smack in the middle of junior year. Not happening. No way. "No thanks," I managed, my voice squeaky and weird.

Penny giggled nervously and then added, "We found a very nice house in . . ."

I took another bite of my apple and willed myself not to hear her. Lalalala.

If I didn't leave Westport to move to *Paris* with Mom and Matthew, I wasn't leaving to move to *Cleveland* with them. And why Cleveland? Penny's parents were there so we had to be there too? Was it all about her? My head started to spin.

". . . wonderful because you're right in time for the new semester—"

"I. Am. Not. Moving," I said with as much force as I could muster.

They stared at me again, obviously unsure how to react. Penny reached over and played with the tip of my place mat.

I couldn't leave. I couldn't, *I couldn't.* I tried to blink away the black spots that were suddenly dancing before my eyes. There had to be a way out. An escape. "I'll stay here," I said quickly. "I can stay here, can't I?" Yes. That was it. They could go. I would stay. Ta-da! Problem solved.

"You absolutely cannot stay here by yourself," Penny said.

I could, I could, I could. Please?

My dad leaned forward, resting his elbows on the table and his chin in the palm of his hand. "We're going to rent out the house until the market gets better and then we're planning on selling it."

"Don't rent it! Or rent it to me! I'll stay!" Not that I had any money. But it was all I could think of.

"You are not staying here without us," my stepmom told me. "That's ridiculous. And it's not safe."

Wait a sec. I caught my breath, anger pushing out the panic. I narrowed my eyes at my betrayer of a father. "This is why you two were in Cleveland last month?"

He nodded, a bit sheepishly.

"I thought you were visiting Penny's parents. Why didn't you tell me you were interviewing?" I had been oblivious, enjoying the weekend with Marissa's family. Lalala clueless me.

Another look with Penny. "We didn't want to worry you."

Yeah, why would I want some time to get used to the idea? Much better to spring it on me like a knife-wielding jack-in-the-box. "But now it's all set?"

"Yes," he said. "I gave my notice yesterday."

So Penny, Penny's parents, and my dad's *company* knew before I did. Way to make a daughter feel important. Did Matthew know too? Did Mom know?

"It's a beautiful city, April," Penny said, rubbing her hands together like she was washing them. "I loved living there. And it's very culturally interesting. Did you know the Rock and Roll Hall of Fame is there?"

The panic set in again. "I can't move," I said, struggling for air. "I just can't."

"Is this about Noah?" she asked.

"No, it's not about Noah." Of course it was about Noah. Noah, who had filled my room with fifty helium balloons on my sixteenth birthday. Noah who helped me lug all my suitcases and badly taped boxes from my mom's to my dad's. Noah who had the softest hands I'd ever held. Noah who called me his cutie.

But it was not *just* about Noah. It was about Marissa and Vi and my whole life. I couldn't leave everything—everyone—behind. My dad and I were close, but now he had Penny, and Penny and I . . . we didn't have much of a relationship. She tried to connect, I tried to connect, my father tried to connect us, but it was like we had walkie-talkies that were on different frequencies. Moving to Ohio with them would be lonely. Too lonely.

"You'll meet lots of new boys," Penny said.

"It's not about Noah," I repeated, louder, over the sound of my pounding head. What was I going to do? I could *not* move to Cleveland in ten days. I needed a plan. Fast. They were four seconds away from packing me up and tossing me halfway across the country. "I have friends here. I have . . ." What else did I have? "Soccer. School." I was grasping at straws, but I needed to get through to them. I had only recently started to feel settled again. I couldn't just move. Breathe. Breathe. Breathe.

"You'll make new friends. And soccer season is over," Penny said, reaching to pat me and then apparently deciding not to. "You can play on a new team next year in Cleveland. And you can still keep in touch with everyone back here."

I didn't want to *keep in touch*. I knew all about *keeping in touch* and I hated it. And now I'd have to do it with Noah and all my friends. Were Cleveland and Connecticut even in the same time zone? Where was Cleveland exactly?

The black spots returned to the corners of my eyes. If I moved to Cleveland, I'd wake up every morning wishing I was still in Westport. I'd wake up every morning in the big black hole. I couldn't let that happen. There had to be another way. Someone I could stay with here. Marissa? I sat up straighter. Yes! Maybe. No. In theory, her family would be happy to have me, but they really didn't have the space. Marissa already shared a room with her sister. I couldn't exactly sleep in her trundle bed for the rest of the year.

Noah? Ha. Sure, I loved him, and I got along with his parents and siblings, but I wasn't ready to share a bathroom with any of them.

And that left . . . Vi.

Wait. That was it. "I can live with Vi!" Yes, yes, yes!

"You want to live with your friend Violet?" my dad asked.

"Yes!" I exclaimed. My ribs expanded as hope poured in. "I can move in with Vi."

"You can't live with a *friend*," Penny said, emphasizing the word *friend* like I had said "family of anacondas."

"Not just a friend," I rushed to explain. "A friend and her mom." This could work. It could really work. Vi had a funky house on Mississauga Island, right on Long Island Sound. From her living room windows you could see right onto the water.

"I don't think it's appropriate for you to move in with

another family," my dad said. "And I doubt Vi's mother would agree to it."

Well, I didn't think it was appropriate—or fair—for them to yank me out of school in the middle of my junior year. "Vi's mom will be completely cool with it. Last year they volunteered to host an exchange student but it didn't work out. Suzanne's really laid back."

Dad's eyebrows went up.

"Not too laid-back," I added quickly. "Plus, the basement is already set up like a bedroom. Has its own bathroom and everything. I could at least ask, couldn't I? And then we could talk about it some more? We could at least consider it?"

Penny wrinkled her nose. "You want to move into a basement? Basements are cold and drafty."

"I don't mind." A basement in Westport was better than any room in Cleveland.

"I don't know," Penny said, shaking her head.

It's not up to you, I wanted to say but didn't. I pointedly looked at my dad, and did my best to appear reasonable and mature. Speaking slowly, I said, "There's no point in me moving all the way to Cleveland now. I have six months left of the year. Let me finish it here. At Hillsdale. I love Hillsdale. I'll be fine at Vi's. She'd love to have me."

A furrow formed in Dad's brow.

"Please?"

"But what about next year? Isn't Vi a senior?" my dad asked.

"Let's deal with this year first. If I have to move next year, I'll move next year." There was no way I was moving next year either. But who knew what the situation would be by then? Once upon a time I lived with my mother, father, and brother at 32 Oakbrook Road, but that had changed too. "Who knows? Maybe you'll hate Cleveland and want to come back. Or maybe Vi will still be here next year." Yeah, right. Vi had big plans and they involved colleges far, far away from Westport. "Can't we try Vi's for this semester? Please?" By the final *please* I had tears in my eyes and a quivering lip.

No one spoke.

I wasn't sure what I expected. I kind of doubted they were actually going to let me move in with a friend. *I* wouldn't have let me move in with a friend. When the pause continued, I thought I was done for.

"I guess we can talk to Violet's mother," my dad said at last.

I jumped out of my chair and threw my arms around him.

TINY COMPLICATION

I left two messages on Vi's cell on Thursday night but she didn't call me back. She was probably busy with some sort of party. We're Jewish, so to me it was the Day Dad Told Me He Was Moving, but to the majority of the world it was Christmas. I hadn't told her the details, only that I needed to talk to her.

She called me back Friday morning at eleven.

"Everything okay?" she asked. "I just called in for my messages. My mother borrowed my cell yesterday and can't remember where she left it."

I filled her in, then held my breath. What if after all this Vi didn't want me there?

"Of course you can live with me! Of course my mom won't mind! I absolutely cannot let you move to Cleveland! Hells no!"

Whoosh—I exhaled with relief.

"We're going to be housemates!" she squealed.

I would have used the word *roommates* myself, but Vi was a *housemates* type of girl. *Housemate* sounded sophisticated. *Roommate* was for kids. Vi was also the type of girl who hated being called a "girl." She was a woman, thank you very much. She drank wine, wore her hair in a short black bob, worked out every morning, edited the school paper, and read the *New York Times* daily. "Girl" would not do. Vi rocked.

Vi and I went to the same preschool. Back then the classes were mixed, three- and four-year-olds together. Vi and I bonded. Our moms bonded. Eventually Suzanne and my mom lost touch, but Vi and I stayed friends over the years even though we weren't in the same grade, even though we didn't run in the same crowds. Sometimes we overlapped— like the night of The Incident. But usually we stayed to our own social circles. We always stayed friends though.

"We're going to have a blast," she continued.

We would have a blast. Living with Vi and Suzanne would not be like living with my dad and Penny.

Let's take a second to compare, shall we?

Every bed in our house was required to have hospital corners. I was told to please use a pillow if I was going to lean against my linen headboard. Vi and her mom, on the other hand, both had water beds. I'd never seen Suzanne's water bed made. Vi's house smelled like cinnamon incense. Mine smelled like hand wipes with a splash of Lysol. Due to The Incident, my curfew was ten P.M. Suzanne did not believe in curfews. Anyway, they'd be tough to enforce since her shows usually went until eleven and she herself was never home before one at the earliest.

One more Suzanne/my dad comparison: Suzanne was spontaneous. She had last-minute potluck dinners and marathon movie nights. My dad and Penny scheduled sex. Every Tuesday and Saturday at eleven. I tried to be asleep. It wasn't like it was on the calendar, but I could hear the Barry Manilow playing like clockwork. Can you imagine . . . scheduling sex? Could anything be less romantic?

Okay, so Noah and I were trying to schedule sex—tonight?!—but clearly, that was for a different reason. We couldn't spontaneously get a place to ourselves.

"This is perfect," Vi continued. "You have no idea how perfect. My mother was just offered the lead role in the traveling production of *Mary Poppins*."

I laughed. "Your mother is playing Mary Poppins?"

"Yes. I see the irony."

"For how long?"

"It's a six-month contract. The show starts in Chicago

for six weeks and then moves around the country. She'll be relieved if I have someone to hang out with."

Holy crap. "The two of us . . . in your house?" The two of us. In her beach house. With no parents.

"Hells yeah! Isn't that perfect?"

"Your mom is fine with leaving you alone?"

"Darling. Finding work is tough these days, and my mom's not getting any younger or any thinner. She's twice the size she used to be. If she's offered Traveling *Mary Poppins*, she's taking Traveling *Mary Poppins*."

Suzanne had been a midlevel Broadway star. Then she'd gotten knocked up by a cute Brit. Then, cute Brit dumped her for a cute Australian. Suzanne moved back home to Westport so her mom could help with baby Violet, and Suzanne became a waitress and did community theater. When Vi started high school, Suzanne started acting again in the city. The roles hadn't been great. A lead role was huge. So I should have been happy for Suzanne—and I was—but if she was going to be Mary Poppins in Chicago . . . then I was going to be Le Misérable in Ohio.

I fell back on my bed. "Vi, my dad is not going to let me stay at your house without your mom there."

There was silence on the other end of the phone. "Why not?"

"My father is a big believer in supervision."

"But we'd have so much fun."

"So much fun," I answered forlornly. "Oh God, I'm going to have to move to Ohio." The black spots were returning. I covered my eyes with my hands. "Why is my father ruining my life? Whose parents get up and move to another city?"

"Mine."

Right. "Why don't we have normal parents?"

Another pause. "Maybe my mom can convince your dad to let us try it out."

"Vi, my dad is never going to let me stay with just you. He won't let me live without a responsible adult on the premises. I don't even think it's legal."

"I would hardly call my mother a responsible adult. Last night she had at least thirty actors over, all drunk and singing show tunes."

"Telling my dad that will not help my case either. I'm screwed."

"No, come on. Just explain that it's not a big deal. My mother will call him when she wakes up."

"It's eleven."

"She went to bed late." She let out a long, pondering sigh. "Perhaps putting my mom and your dad on the phone together is not our best move. My mom tends to overshare. So here's what we're going to do: Let me talk to him."

"You're not going to be able to talk him into this, Vi." She was good, but not that good. Last year, she'd won the school's public-speaking competition. Her topic had been "how to win a public-speaking competition." She was very convincing.

"What if he thinks I'm my mother?"

18

"Scusies?" My toes curled in my socks.

"He calls the house phone. He thinks I'm her. I tell him that I'm delighted to have you live with us, and I just don't mention the traveling-around-the-country bit."

Huh. "We just don't tell him?"

"Exactly. What he doesn't know . . ."

"Omigod, that's insane. I can't do that." My breath grew shallow. I wasn't the kind of person who did something like that.

"Then move to Cleveland."

I could not move to Cleveland. Not now. Not eight days after I was about to do it with my boyfriend. Not in the middle of the year. Not ever.

I heard myself say, "What number should he call you on?"

THE INCIDENT

It was the beginning of sophomore year.

I was not yet aware how strong wine coolers were. Sure, they tasted like lemonade but before you knew it you were on the sand doing mermaid impressions.

Me, Vi, Marissa, and Vi's friend Joanna had gotten drunk on Compo Beach. Lucy Michaels had videotaped us with her iPhone, and shared the video with her mom.

Unfortunately, Lucy's mother was the new school guidance counselor.

After Mrs. Michaels told all of our parents—and showed

them the video—here's what happened:

Joanna went to Andersen High School, so it didn't matter.

Marissa was grounded for a week.

Vi's mother said, "So? They didn't drive home afterward, did they?" (We didn't. Vi's friend Dean had picked us up.)

But me? I was grounded for two weeks, plus I got a ten P.M. curfew—indefinitely.

Yes, I'd been the one rolling around in the sand declaring I was a mermaid. I was also the one who'd asked Dean to pull over so I could throw up, but my dad didn't have video evidence of that tidbit.

It probably hadn't helped that I had only moved into my dad's place six days earlier.

He and Penny had many closed-door conversations and then, eventually, it was decided that I would have to be home by ten P.M. every night, even on weekends, so I would not get into any more trouble. As if trouble only happened after ten P.M.

"Don't you realize how dangerous it is for a girl to be roaming around drunk?" my father asked, shaking his head. "I thought you had better judgment."

"I did," I said. "I do." I hugged my knees into my chest and tried to disappear into my bed.

His voice was spiked with disappointment. "I don't understand *why*. I know you didn't act out like this when you lived with your mother. At least I hope you didn't."

"I didn't," I said, which was true. I had always been good.

Sure, I'd had a few sips of alcohol before, but that night on Compo Beach was the first time I'd gotten plastered.

"Then why now?"

Because it had seemed like a fun idea? Beach! Wine coolers! Mermaid! Also, I was pissed at Noah (because of The Corinne Situation) and wanted to show him I could have a crazy, fun night without him. "I don't know," I said. "I'm sorry, Dad."

"Penny thinks you're acting out because you're mad at your mother for moving away."

I shook my head, but I didn't actually answer the question.

WHY LUCY MICHAELS RATTED US OUT

Who knows? She was always walking by herself, staring at people. She had big navy eyes that never blinked. You could watch her in class for fifteen minutes and those eyelids would not flutter. At the time of The Incident she'd been a sophomore like me, although she'd just moved to Westport and I'd lived there my whole life.

Ratting us out the first week she started at Hillsdale was not a brilliant strategy for making friends.

BACK TO CLEVELAND

My dad and I were sitting in the living room, on opposite sides of the suede couch, when he called "Suzanne."

I was dying to scoot closer to him so I could possibly hear what Vi was saying, but I decided that listening to the full conversation might spark cardiac arrest.

"Hello, Suzanne, this is Jake Berman, April's father. How are you?" my dad boomed.

I had a mini–heart attack even without hearing Vi's response.

"Great, great, so nice to hear . . ." he continued. "Yes, thank you. Now about April coming to stay with you—"

My hands started shaking, like I had overdosed on coffee. When I couldn't steady them, I decided I was better off leaving the room than giving myself away. If my dad suspected he was talking to Vi instead of Suzanne, it was over.

I hurried over to the kitchen and tried to shut out his voice.

"—inconvenienced in any way—"

La, la, la.

"—she'll have an allowance for food—"

Sounded promising . . .

"—Yes, responsibility—"

Don't listen. Pace instead. Yes, I told myself. Pace. Up and down the kitchen. But not too loudly. Sound busy. Very busy opening and closing the fridge. Hello, fridge. Hello, apples. Hello, grapes. Hello, low-fat mozzarella. Maybe I should wash my hands. Drown out the sound. I turned on the water, nice and loud, then lathered and rinsed. Then lathered and rinsed again. I couldn't believe I was doing this. Lying to my dad. Living with Vi was the right thing to do, wasn't it? What if my dad said no? What if he said yes?

When I turned off the water, there was silence. I wanted to run back into the living room but refrained.

"Dad?" I said tentatively.

No answer. Oh God. He'd figured it out. Vi had cracked. I was dead. I braced myself before entering the living room.

He was typing into his BlackBerry, but he stopped when I came in. "Well, Princess"—he exhaled as if he was slightly astonished—"looks like you can do it if you want to. You can stay with them to finish out the year. Suzanne said the best way to reach her is via email, so I'm sending her my contact details."

She did? You were?

"She's going to be in a production of *Chicago* this spring— she offered to get us tickets when we're back in town."

"How generous," I sputtered.

"Are you sure this is what you want to do?" he asked, looking up at me.

As our eyes met, I realized that now it would be me and him that would have to *keep in touch*.

Oh.

But I couldn't move to Cleveland. I just couldn't. Sure, I was bummed my dad was leaving but what I felt was mostly relief. I was staying. I looked at my hands and said, "Yes."

THE RULES

I reread Noah's IM—*Can't wait for tonight. . . . What time should I come over?*—before replying: *Don't come over. I'm so sorry, but we have to postpone. Again. Whole life in upheaval. Can we go somewhere easy? Burger Palace?* As I was typing the last word, my dad knocked, opened my door, and handed me a piece of paper. THE RULES was printed across the top.

I'll explain later, I quickly typed, then shut my laptop.

"One," Dad said, reading from his own copy of "The Rules." "You are to keep up your grades."

"Grades," I repeated, swiveling my chair to face him. "Keep up. Check."

Of course I would keep my grades up. I had a 3.9. I wasn't about to mess with that. Not this semester, when it mattered most.

"If your GPA drops *at all*, you're on the next plane to Cleveland."

"Absolutely, I understand," I said.

"Next," he continued. "No boys in the house."

I batted my eyelashes. "Am I supposed to stop Vi—and Suzanne—from entertaining gentleman callers?"

He laughed. "Don't be smart."

"It's hard to control."

"No Noah in your room. No you and Noah alone in the house." These were his house rules here too.

"So the rule is just for Noah. I can have as many other boys over as I want?"

He raised an eyebrow.

"Dad, I'm joking. No boys. Especially Noah. Keep going."

"Three. No drinking," he said.

"No drinking," I repeated, blushing. "I'm guessing mermaid

impersonations are out too?"

He smiled. "Yes. Rule number four: Your curfew will remain intact."

Was he kidding? He wanted me to keep my ten P.M. curfew even though he lived in another city? "Dad, come on—"

He shook his head, his expression stern. "I'm being serious. Your curfew stays. I discussed it with Suzanne."

I was sure "Suzanne" would take my curfew enforcement very seriously. "Okay," I relented.

"I trust you, April. You've definitely proven yourself in the last year and a half."

I nodded and tried to ignore the guilt creeping in when I heard the word *trust*.

He put his arm on my shoulder and squeezed. "You can tell a lot about a person not just by their successes, but by how they deal with their setbacks, and, April, I'm very proud of how you complied with your curfew. I don't think you've ever been late."

"I haven't," I said truthfully. Well, except when I stayed over at Marissa's. As long as she checked in via cell every few hours and kissed her parents good night when she got in, she didn't have a curfew. Her parents trusted her—and kept her close. They kept all five of their kids close. They had dinner together every night. Friday night, Shabbat dinner, included grandparents, cousins, and close friends. I had a standing invitation, in addition to a mom-crush on Dana, Marissa's mother.

So that was it? Keep up my grades, no drinking, no boys,

and my curfew? Doable. Or at least fakeable.

"What should I do about buying things?" I asked. "Like when I need new clothes."

He cleared his throat. "I'll deposit money into an account for you at the beginning of every month. Two hundred will be for rent and an additional two hundred will be for groceries. You'll give that money directly to Suzanne. Plus some extra for you."

"Oh," I said, surprised. "How much in total?"

"A thousand dollars a month."

Holy crap. Was he kidding? A thousand dollars a month? I knew my dad's job paid well . . . but that sounded like a lot of money.

He laughed at the surprise on my face. "It's not just for overpriced jeans, April. It's for rent, food, books, school lunches, entertainment, gas . . ."

"Gas? For what?" Wait. "Am I getting a car?" I squealed.

He squeezed my shoulder again. "It wouldn't be fair for you to have to rely on Violet and Suzanne for transportation."

"Yes! Yes! Thank you thank you thank you thank you!" I jumped out of my chair and threw my arms around him.

"Don't thank me." He kissed me on the forehead. "Thank Penny. She doesn't think you should have to depend on other people to get around. She offered to leave her car here for you," he said, glowing. "I'll get her something new in Ohio." My dad was always trying to prove to me how much Penny cared about me. But if she cared that much, she probably wouldn't be dragging my dad off to Cleveland.

Still. If she could give, I could give.

"Thank you, Penny," I said, and I honestly didn't care if she got a new car and I ended up with the ten-year-old Honda she'd had since before she married my dad. I was lucky to get any car. Even one that was bright yellow and reeked of disinfectant wipes. At least it was clean.

My own car! My own money-stocked bank account! My very own basement. With walls adjacent to no one! I felt like the luckiest girl in the world, and if I felt that twinge of guilt, well, I pushed it away. Far away. Like, to Cleveland.

"I expect you to send me a budget every month, tracking how your money is being spent. It will be an excellent learning experience for you. You're going to have to learn to be practical."

"Budget it is. So that's it?" I asked, feet dancing. "We're all set?"

"You're all set."

After my dad finally left the room, I opened my laptop to see if Noah had responded, but he hadn't. I knew he'd be disappointed that tonight would not be *the* night, but he'd cheer up when he heard the news. I hadn't told him anything about Cleveland or Vi's house yet. I had wanted to get it all sorted first because I hadn't wanted to worry him for no reason. Like father, like daughter, I guess.

I spun my chair back and forth. I couldn't believe it was all happening. That my dad was letting me stay. My dad had asked Suzanne to get together in person, but Vi had told him that they were off to L.A. for the rest of the holidays, but that they'd be back in time for the move and would talk in person then.

I couldn't believe he was letting me stay so easily. If I were a parent, I would . . . well, I don't know what I'd do. I know I'd never get divorced. Not that I can blame my father for that. But still. When I get married I'm going to make the marriage work.

Getting married is forever, no matter what my spouse does.

YOU SAY POTATO, I SAY PROPOSAL

"I like being a couch potato," I told Noah.

It was a Saturday, a year earlier, January of sophomore year. Outside it was freezing—it hurt to breathe. We were in his basement, on his brown suede couch, under an afghan. I was cuddled in the nook of his arm. His fleece sweater was soft against my cheek. Noah and I hadn't moved in two hours.

He played with a strand of my hair. "Let's stay here forever."

"We may have to eat eventually," I said.

"We'll order in."

"We'd have to get the door." I made walking motions with my fingers.

"My parents will answer it and bring the food to us."

"What about school?" I asked, closing my eyes.

"We'll homeschool."

"My dad might wonder where I am."

"Tell him we ran off and got married."

I laughed. "He likes you, but not that much."

He pulled me tight. "Could you imagine?"

My heart stopped. I opened my eyes. "Running off and getting married?"

"Yeah." He turned to face me. "I could spend every day with you. Right here. On the couch."

My whole body felt warm. Safe. Loved. I traced my finger from his nose to his chin. "I love you," I said. Part of me could do it. Run off and get married. But another part . . . another part of me wondered if I could really trust anyone. If *anyone* could really trust anyone. If all relationships were doomed.

I couldn't say this to Noah, though.

"But . . . there is the small fact that we're fifteen," I said, trying to lighten the mood.

"So?" His eyes lit up. "I love you too. That's why we should do it. It would be fun! And exciting!"

"And illegal. I think you have to be eighteen to get married." I lifted my hands above me to stretch. "We'd also have to get off the couch."

He pressed his hand flat against mine. "I bet we could get a rabbi to come here."

"I'm not sure I could get married in yoga pants. Maybe if they were white instead of black."

"Fair enough." He kissed me on the forehead. "I really would do it, you know."

I snuggled into the softness of his fleece. "So would I," I murmured, not wanting to let go.

"You're not going to believe what's happening," I said the second I got into Noah's car.

His dark hair was damp and wavy, just the way I loved it. Tonight he was wearing gray jeans and his puffy neon-yellow jacket that somehow looked cool on him. He was thin and self-conscious about his body—even though he didn't need to be—and liked to look bigger. He gave me a big kiss on the lips. "Let me guess. You're going to seduce me in the backseat?"

"Ha, ha, ha," I said. "No. Sorry. I can't deal with sex tonight. My life is too crazy."

"Okay," he said, sounding confused and a little disappointed.

"So yesterday, my dad sits me down and tells me that we're all moving to Cleveland. Cleveland! Not as far as France, but seriously. What is wrong with my parents?"

His smile drooped. "You're leaving?"

"Do you think I'd leave you? No way." I reached over and traced my finger over his knee. "I'm not going anywhere."

"So they're not moving?"

"No. They are. But they're letting me stay with Vi!"

"Vi?" He looked kind of shocked.

"Yes!"

"You're moving in with Vi?"

"Yes!"

"What about your dad and Penny?"

"They're leaving!"

"And leaving you with Vi. For how long?"

"For the rest of the school year. At least the rest of the school year. I'm staying in Westport!"

"You're staying in Westport . . . because of me?"

"Yes!" Wait. Kind of. I had been kidding, but now I didn't want to hurt his feelings. "Mostly you. But also Marissa and school and . . . you know. My life is here."

His mouth fell open. "Wow."

"I know! I'm going to live with Vi!"

He cocked his head to the side. "April, I know you think Vi is God incarnate—"

Huh? "I do not."

"Yeah. You do. But she's kind of intense. Are you sure you want to live with her?"

"Yes," I snapped. "She's one of my best friends. And anyway, I don't have that many options here."

"Isn't Vi's mom kind of a weirdo?" Noah asked.

"No, she's cool, but that doesn't even matter. Because that's the craziest part. She won't be there. She's moving to Chicago for a while. And then Tampa or something. Although my dad doesn't know that."

He shook his head in bewilderment. "Huh?"

I explained it all, my excitement building.

"So it's just you and Vi?" he said when I finished.

"Uh-huh."

"That's . . . amazing," he said, green eyes wide.

"I know."

"When are your dad and Penny leaving? When are you moving in with Vi?"

"January third, probably. The day you get back." I hated that he was going away. I hated that he was going over New Year's. He always left me over New Year's.

"This is all insane," he said, putting his arm around me. "But I still don't get why we can't have sex in your house tonight."

I rolled my eyes. "Because I'm freaked out. Because if for some reason my parents caught us, they would force me to move to Cleveland and I would never see you again. Because in eight days we will have a whole basement to ourselves."

He smiled. "A whole basement, huh? So we can do it anywhere in the basement?"

"Yes. But we'll probably do it on the bed." I pulled him by his jacket toward me, and kissed him. His lips were soft. Familiar. I kissed him again, harder, then pulled away. "We can still visit your backseat tonight. Just no sex. And not in front of my house. Can't risk my parents taking me away from you."

He took my hand. "Drive, then burger?"

"Let's do it. Well, not *it*. Love you!" I chirped, and blew him a kiss.

"So you keep telling me," he said in that way that sounded like a joke but I could tell wasn't.

I blinked. "I do!" Could he really think the reason I was

putting off sex was because I didn't love him?

"I *know* you love me." He shook his head. "I love you too."

"Eight days and I'm all yours," I said.

He nodded and put the car into DRIVE.

THE FIVE-STEP PROCESS TO LYING TO PARENTS

1. Create two fake pmail accounts.
2. Give Suzanne's fake pmail address to Jake.
3. Give Jake's fake pmail address to Suzanne.
4. Keep emails brief. Include vague details.
5. Get away with it.

EMAILS BETWEEN THE REAL JAKE BERMAN AND THE FAKE SUZANNE CALDWELL

From: Jake Berman <Jake.Berman@comnet.com>
Date: Fri, 26 Dec, 3:10 p.m.
To: Suzanne Caldwell <Suzanne_Caldwell@pmail.com>
Subject: Contact Information

Suzanne,

Here is my contact information: You can reach me anytime via email or on my cell, 203-555-3939. I can't thank you enough for taking April in this semester. With everything that's happened in the last few years, I think she feels very tied to Westport and her life here, so I understand why she's so reluctant to leave. I'm glad to have found this solution. I'll deposit money into April's bank account

by the first of every month, and she will give you four hundred dollars cash for rent and groceries. Thanks, also, for ensuring she follows my rules—especially obeying her curfew (10 p.m.). It's a dangerous world. And as we know, teenagers need structure.
Best, Jake

Sent From BlackBerry

————————

From: Suzanne Caldwell <Suzanne_Caldwell@pmail.com>
Date: Sat, 27 Dec, 12:15 p.m.
To: Jake Berman <Jake.Berman@comnet.com>
Subject: RE: Contact Information

Dear Jake,
April is a delight; we're truly happy to have her. And don't worry about a thing. If she's ever home even a minute after ten, I will contact you ASAP. However, just so you know, cell phone use is discouraged at the theater—if you have any questions or concerns, the best and fastest way to reach me is via email.
Best of luck with your move to Cleveland,
Suzanne

EMAILS BETWEEN THE REAL SUZANNE CALDWELL
AND THE FAKE JAKE BERMAN

From: Suzanne Caldwell <Primadonna@mindjump.com>
Date: Sun, 28 Dec, 2 p.m.
To: Jake Berman <Jake.Berman@pmail.com>
Subject: April

Jake—

Vi passed on your info—and I have to tell you I am so thrilled that April will be staying at our place while I'm traveling! She'll be great company for Vi and hopefully they'll keep each other out of trouble! Vi is really responsible, though. More responsible than I was at that age, that's for sure. You wouldn't believe the trouble I got into. Well, maybe you would—I got pregnant with Violet for one. Ha ha! But seriously, as I told Vi, no rent is required—I'm grateful that April will be around! Vi gets moody when she's alone for too long! Maybe they can take turns buying groceries or something? Call me anytime on my cell, 203-555-9878.

Cheers!

Suzanne

————————

From: Jake Berman <Jake.Berman@pmail.com>
Date: Sun, 28 Dec, 9:10 p.m.
To: Suzanne Caldwell <Primadonna@mindjump.com>
Subject: RE: April

Suzanne—

Thank you for your email. Congratulations on your upcoming project. *Mary Poppins* sounds like the perfect role for you. You're very generous about not requiring rent—we appreciate it! April can definitely pay for groceries and also her share of heat and electricity. I'll leave it up to Vi to figure out. It sounds like she's on top of it. And I can't imagine her being moody—she's always such a pleasure to be around. She's so smart and self-assured! You should feel lucky to have such a wonderful daughter. Please continue to contact me via this email address if you have any questions or concerns—it's the best and fastest way to reach me.

All best,

Jake

HOLY CRAP

Vi was an evil genius. A moody, self-assured, evil genius.

number two:
played I never

MOVING IN

"So that's it?" my dad asked after depositing, with a thud, the last cardboard box on top of two others on my new floor.

The ceiling was low, the walls were bright white (practically fluorescent), the room smelled faintly like spoiled yogurt, and the window looked onto the recycling bin. But it was mine. All mine. My stomach hadn't stopped fluttering since we got here early this morning.

My dad leaned forward, clasping his hands in front of him to stretch his upper back. "Are you sure you don't need help unpacking? I've got time, hon. I'm happy to do it."

"No, no, Vi and Marissa are here to help me. You get back to your own boxes." I swallowed. "I mean, the movers probably have questions for you." They were flying out tonight.

Vi gave me a discreet thumbs-up from her crossed-legged position on my new futon. She was wearing black skinny jeans and an off-the-shoulder green top. I shot her a small smile, but despite myself, I felt a stab of loneliness.

"I know, I know . . ." He pulled me into a hug. He smelled warm and musky, like always. "Oh, I'm going to miss you, Princess."

Then don't move to Cleveland, I almost said. But I didn't. Because, yes, I'd miss my dad, but he was choosing to go. To leave me. And besides, I was about to live a sixteen-year-old's dream. House on the beach. No parents. Parties whenever we wanted. Boyfriends whenever we wanted.

"I'll miss you too," I said.

"It's too bad I didn't get to talk to Suzanne," my dad said, his forehead crinkling. He glanced at the basement stairs as if hoping Vi's mom would suddenly appear, while Vi, Marissa, and I simultaneously looked at the floor. Very interesting floor. Old, beige, well-stepped-on, carpeted floor. "I was hoping to go over the logistics one last time," my dad said. "In person."

"I know," Vi said. "She felt *so* bad about not seeing you. But like I said, my great-aunt fell and broke her hip, and my mom had to take care of her."

"She's a good niece," my dad said.

"She really is," Vi said, nodding. "She told me, like, five thousand times to tell you how sorry she is."

"Please tell her I'm sorry to have missed her as well," my

dad said. He headed back up the stairs with the three of us trailing him. By the time I reached the top, I was light-headed, maybe from taking the steps too fast, but more likely because I was having an unexpected panic attack. A real one, with tight lungs and spots in front of my eyes and everything.

If my dad realized what we were really up to . . . ?

I grabbed the handrail to steady myself. Chill, I told myself. Breathe. The only way he's going to find out is if you let him find out.

"She's really good on email," Vi said. "Want me to tell her to check in with you as soon as she's back?"

"Sure," my dad said. He turned to me. "So this is it?"

Tears sprung to my eyes, throwing me off guard. I forced a smile. "This is it. Um, I really appreciate it, Dad. Your trusting me and all."

"Don't forget your curfew. And remember to start the car every day, or the engine can die. Especially in the winter. I put a flashlight in the glove compartment just in case. And you have your cell."

He was being so sweet. It was killing me. "Yes, Dad."

He gave me another hug before leaving. "Be good, Princess. Stay safe."

I nodded, because I was having a hard time with words. It'll be better once he's gone, I tried to tell myself, but this moment—him leaving, me staying, the truth of what I was doing an invisible purple elephant between us—was harder than I'd anticipated. If my dad found out I'd planned such a huge deception, he'd be furious. But worse? He'd be *hurt*.

I'd seen him cry only once, and that's what I found myself thinking about when I kissed him one last time, waved as he got in his car, and finally closed Vi's door as he drove away. In my mind I saw my dad's eyes welling up that one and only time, tears spilling down his cheeks like raindrops.

Marissa and Vi picked up on none of this, thank goodness. The minute the door closed, they launched into their own versions of a happy dance. Marissa's involved twirls, which puffed up her blue cotton dress, while Vi's was kind of like the front crawl. I snapped myself out of it. I would be fine, and so would Dad. He'd be happy in Cleveland. He wouldn't find out the truth. I wouldn't *let* him find out the truth. I could handle living on my own.

"You guys are so lucky," Marissa said.

Vi was already trotting back down the stairs. "Time to unpack—and I'm talking pronto, sister."

"Um, why?"

"Your housewarming soirée is tonight," she called up to us. "And it starts at seven!"

THE ONE TIME I SAW MY DAD CRY

We were at David's Deli. I was slurping my chicken soup. It was a day after my fourteenth birthday, March 29. My mom fidgeted with her fork. "April. Matthew. Your father is moving out." Her voice was calm. Too calm. I wanted to yell that she could at least pretend to be sad.

My dad made an "ah" sound and I turned to him, expecting him to say something. But instead of speaking, he was swallowing hard, like he was trying to hold down sobs. Tears dripped down his cheeks. He tried to wipe them away before we could see. As if that would work.

Except it did, I guess, because Matthew was clueless. "Is he going to sleep in the tent?" he asked. "Can I sleep in the tent too? Please, Dad?"

My dad shook his head. I knew that no matter what, my dad didn't want to move out. I wanted to jump out of my seat and throw my arms around him and tell him that everything was going to be all right, like he used to do for me.

I wanted to scream.

I wanted to cry.

I wanted to spill the chicken soup over my mother's head.

I wanted to tell my dad that even though his wife of over a decade had slept with someone else, even though she clearly no longer gave a shit about him, I still loved him.

But it hurt to look at him. So I glared at my mother instead and put my arm around Matthew. I kept glaring, until finally, her eyes filled with tears too and she looked down at her plate.

MARCH 28

Yup, believe it: I was born on March 28, yet my name is April.

I was supposed to be born on April 14, but I was two and a half weeks early and my mom decided that April didn't have to be literal. It could be metaphorical. A new season. A new family unit.

At least they hadn't named me March.

LOST IN TRANSLATION

> Matthew: You better call Mom back. She's trying to get in touch with you. Has bitten off all her nails.
> Me: Moving into Vi's today! Will call her later! xxx
> Matthew: U R?
> Me: Dad leaving 4 the Cleve
> Matthew: Oh right.
> Me: Didn't you tell Mom he's moving?
> Matthew: Forgot. Did u?

NOT THAT KIND OF MOTHER

Why didn't I consult my mother about my living situation?

In a traditional mother–daughter relationship, the daughter would probably call her mother to discuss a move like this. Although in a traditional mother–daughter relationship, a high school junior would live with her mother.

But my mother lived in Paris with her new husband, Daniel (pronounced "Danielle" *en français*). She'd been gone a year and a half, since the summer after freshman year.

The truth is, it hadn't occurred to me to consult her about my living situation.

Which I maybe shouldn't have mentioned to her in those exact words.

"How could you not have talked to me about this?" she asked on the phone, sounding slightly hysterical.

"It's not such a big deal," I said. "Daddy and Penny are moving to Ohio—they leave tonight—so I moved in with Vi."

"Wait—you moved? This happened already?"

I looked around my quickly and fully unpacked room. Vi is nothing if not efficient. "Yes. Today. My housewarming soirée is in a few hours. I just got out of the shower actually, so I don't have too long to talk. I think Noah is coming over."

"But–but—you can't just do that!"

"Actually, I can," I said, and if it sounded cold, too bad. I didn't actively *want* to be cold, but face it, my dad had custody of me. She had custody of Matthew. That's what they had agreed on when she decided to leave Westport to move to Paris and be with *Danielle*. She was thrilled to be done with child support, done with alimony, done with my father. "You have no idea how annoying it is to have to justify the cost of orange juice," she'd said to me. And you have no idea how many people you've hurt, I said back to her, but only in my head. Screw the orange juice.

"I think you lost your say somewhere over the Atlantic," I added.

There was a pause. "I'm still your mother. I still get a say." She sighed. "I wish you'd come live with us in France."

43

"Thanks, but no thanks," I said curtly. Then I felt bad so I added, "I would never be able to finish high school in French." For some reason, whenever I spoke to my mom, I felt guilty. But shouldn't she be the one to feel guilty? She was the one who left *me*. "I want to be here," I said, keeping my voice steady. "With my friends."

"I can't believe your father agreed to this," my mother said. "Suzanne's not the most responsible mother. I remember when she let the two of you walk to the Baskin-Robbins on Main Street by yourselves when you were nine. When you were nine!"

I hung my head upside down to scrunch my hair with gel. "Don't worry about Suzanne. She won't even be here. She's going to be traveling."

"What? What?"

I grimaced. Why had I said that? "She got the lead in Traveling *Mary Poppins*. Don't tell Dad." No, she wouldn't tell my dad. She didn't even talk to my dad. And anyway, she would never tattle on me. I was her *friend*. When your parents divorced and your mom started dating again, that's what happened. At least, that's what happened with us. Roles shifted. Moms need someone to dissect dates with and (inappropriate or not), tag, you're it.

"April—"

"What?" I snapped.

"I don't like the idea of you living by yourself."

"I'm not by myself. I'm with Vi. You're not going to be annoying about this, are you? It's not a big deal." Why had I even told her? Stupid. Did I want her to worry? Did I subconsciously want her to call my dad?

"I'm not going to call your father, but I don't like what you're doing one bit."

Relief washed over me. "Thanks, Mom. I appreciate it. We'll be good, I promise."

"I trust you, April, but promise to call me if you get into any trouble. No, before you get into any trouble."

The doorbell rang. Noah. I hoped Vi would let him in. "Listen, Mom, I gotta go. Noah's upstairs and I just got out of the shower. And isn't it, like, midnight there? Matthew's asleep?"

"Can you call me tomorrow please?" There was defeat in her voice, and it irritated me and made me feel guilty simultaneously.

"Yup. Give Matthew a kiss for me." He had spent a week with us in Westport over winter break and the second he got his Unaccompanied Minor butt back on the Air France plane, I'd felt like a part of me was missing. I cried when I said good-bye to him. I always did. Most sisters found their little brothers annoying, but not me, never me. I brought Matthew along with me everywhere. We used to play hide-and-seek and build forts out of cardboard boxes and speak to each other in pig Latin so our parents wouldn't understand.

"Really tomorrow, though," she continued. "Not like two weeks ago when you said tomorrow and then I call again today and discover your landline's been disconnected."

"Right. Sorry about that. I've been busy."

"Apparently." Another sigh. It was amazing how well I could hear the sighs despite the ocean between us. I said good-bye, hung up the phone, slipped on my jeans and shirt, and turned on the music, trying to drown out any concerns about my mother.

I needed to raid Vi's closet. She had tons of funky stuff. Cool shirts, sexy heels, and one red dress that was super-hot. Long-sleeved, low-cut, and short. It screamed Notice Me, among other things. Moving in with her came with the added bonus of borrowing whatever I wanted, right? And I wanted to wear that red dress. Not tonight, but soon.

There were three knocks on the basement door.

I tossed my cell on my bed. "Come in," I said, trying to make my voice sound light and fluffy.

"It's me again!" Marissa called, running down the stairs. She was in a gray knit dress and black tights and ballet flats. Marissa always wore dresses. She loved them. Winter dresses. Summer dresses. Tights. Bare-legged. Whatever. She was probably the only teenager who hated wearing jeans. She'd wear a dress to play soccer if she was allowed. "Did you miss me? I've been gone a whole hour. Did you see that Vi taped your dad's rules to the fridge? So funny."

"Oh, hey," I said.

"What, I'm not exciting enough for you?" she asked.

"No, you are . . . of course you are. I was just expecting Noah."

He had flown in that morning and I thought he'd have come over by now. Wouldn't tonight be the big night? First night back . . . first night in the new house . . . hello, first-time sex. It was new Independent Me. And Independent Me was a hundred percent ready for sex.

"Have you spoken to him yet?" Marissa asked.

"Not yet," I said. "I left him a message. I told him to come over for the soirée."

"I'm sure he's just crazed," she said, waving her hand.

I felt out of touch. Noah had called a few times from Palm Beach but it was tough to actually talk since he was staying with his whole family at his grandfather's.

I hunted for my black eyeliner and viewed my reflection in the full-length mirror we'd leaned against the wall. Not bad. My long hair was perfectly wavy instead of frizzy, and my skin looked smooth. I lined the inside rims of my lids, hoping to make my brown eyes pop.

"I don't know how you do that," she said crawling onto my futon.

"Penny taught me," I told her. The one thing we bonded over—makeup. "Want me to show you?"

"God, no. I'm getting heebies just watching."

Next up—mascara. "Sorry I'm taking so long. Almost done."

"No rush." She smiled dreamily. "I'll just lie here and pretend this is my room. I might nap."

"Happy to get a trundle bed."

"Wait till Noah sees your new digs. He's going to freak."

"We'll find out if he ever gets here." Where was he, anyway?

"He's probably getting you flowers or something. Something sweet. Do you know how lucky you are? You have an amazing boyfriend who lives ten minutes away, plus you have your own place." Aaron, Marissa's boyfriend, lived in Boston.

I applied my lip gloss. "You're forgetting one of the most important things."

"What's that?"

I smacked my lips together, then went over and hugged her, because I really did love Marissa. Without Marissa, I'd probably still be lying in a pool of my own misery. "I have you."

A KICK IN THE PANTS

Two and a half years ago, in September of freshman year, Marissa decided we needed to be on the soccer team.

"But we're not athletic," I reminded her. We were both around five foot five and small, and not particularly active.

"So? A sport would be good for us. Our confidence. Our morale. Our asses." We both knew what she really meant was, a sport might make you stop moping.

While soccer was fun, it didn't stop me from crying into my pillow at night over how my mom cheated on my dad and made him cry and how dinnertime was lonely and quiet and usually McDonald's and how my father was dating like a lunatic and my mother wanted to chat with me about the cute guys in her office.

Marissa thought it was awesome that my mom wanted to

hang out and gossip, but it just gave me a headache. Marissa moved to Plan B. "I told Noah Friedman to come to Burger Palace for lunch with us," she told me.

"Who?" I thought I knew who he was, but I wasn't sure.

"Noah. He's in my English class. You'll like him."

"Why?" I asked, leaning against my locker.

"He's cute. He's sweet. He's smart. I think you guys would be good together," she said.

The three of us met by the front door. He had wavy brown hair, green eyes. Taller than me, but not much. His cheeks were pink, like he'd run to meet us. He smelled fresh, like mint gum. We walked down the street to Burger Palace, Marissa in the middle.

The waitress came over and asked us for our order. Marissa got chicken fingers. I got a burger. Noah, sitting across from us, got a burger, fries, a side of mac 'n' cheese, and a milk shake.

"That's a lot of food," Marissa said.

"I'm a growing boy," he said.

"I'll share your fries," I offered. "So you don't explode."

He smiled at me. He had dimples. I wanted to reach over and touch one.

"Glad you're here to keep me under control. But where were you two weeks ago when I actually did explode at Bertucci's? I ate way too much pizza."

I laughed. Sitting there with Noah, I felt like I belonged. I forgot to be sad about my parents' divorce. I forgot to be angry.

The waitress came back to our table. "Sorry to tell

you, kids, but we're out of beef patties."

"But . . . this is the Burger Palace," I said.

She shrugged. "Turkey burger? Veggie burger? Lamb? We still got burgers."

"Um . . ."

"Sure," Noah said. "Turkey."

"And you?" the waitress asked me.

"Turkey burger, I guess. Thanks." I waited for the waitress to walk away before grumbling, "How does a burger place run out of burgers?"

"They have burgers, just not beef. You don't like turkey?" Noah asked.

"I do," I said. "But I can't just switch gears like that. I need to rearrange the expectations of my palate." I made an exaggerated lip-smacking sound. "There we go. Rearranged."

"Your palate, huh?" He laughed. "You're cute."

Now my cheeks felt pink. So are you, I thought.

Under the table, Marissa squeezed my hand.

BETTER LATE THAN NEVER

Noah showed up last to the soirée.

Vi was busy pouring beers and glasses of wine as the guests arrived, and Joanna handed them out. It felt odd watching them serve alcohol. Like we were old, living in an apartment in New York, having cocktails. Already Dean and his brother, Hudson, were finishing the last of the chips.

We'd left the door unlocked and I was refilling the chip bowl when I spotted Noah at the door. "Hi!" I said. I dropped the bag and pushed through the others to get to him as he smiled at me. It wasn't the private homecoming I'd been dreaming of—but at least he was here.

"Hey, everyone," he said, glancing around the room. He was looking adorable, like he always did when he came home from Florida. Slight tan, cheeks a bit burnt. He was wearing a new green top that his parents must have bought him on their trip. I'd never seen it before.

"What's up?" RJ called from the couch. RJ played center on the varsity basketball team with Noah. Compared to RJ's six-foot-three, wide, bulky frame, we all looked like dwarfs.

I wrapped my arms around Noah's neck, which was cold from outside. His cheeks were flushed. "Hi," I said again.

"Hey," he said softly, looking around.

I stood on my tiptoes and kissed him lightly on the lips. He was the perfect height for me, only a few inches taller. "I missed you," I said. He smelled like shampoo.

"I missed you too," he said. He kissed me again.

"Get a room!" Dean hollered.

Noah blushed. "So," he said, looking around again. "This is home."

"This is home," I repeated. I tried to make eye contact. "How was your flight?"

"No problems." He checked out the surroundings—the appliances from the seventies in the kitchen, the huge rectangular wooden dining room table, the purple tablecloth, the massive blue suede couch, the shag carpet, the clutter of lamps, and candles and stuff that did not belong to me. The water behind the windows and the lights across the way. "Crazy."

"I know." I was sure it was bizarro for him to see me in this new environment, this new home. It was weird for me to be in it. But what was also weird was why he hadn't called me when he'd landed. Why hadn't he come straight over? Why wouldn't he look at me?

Maybe it was all in my head. Maybe it was just that everyone was watching. Maybe it was because Corinne was watching.

"Come sit down," I said, leading him to the rest of the party.

I NEVER

"My turn," Vi said. "I've never kissed a girl."

All four guys—Noah, RJ, Dean, and Hudson—plus Joanna, drank to that one. But that was no surprise.

Dean put his arm around Vi. "If the rest of you ladies would like to try right now, don't let us stop you."

Vi punched him in the arm. "Yes, that's what we're going to do, make out with each other for your viewing enjoyment." The two of them were sharing a lounge chair.

"Excellent," Dean said, his loud laugh reverberating around the room. Dean and Vi had been best friends since they met freshman year. Now he had his hands on Vi's hip. He always seemed to be touching someone or something.

A ball, a cushion, a girl's hip.

I was sitting between Marissa and Noah on the couch, and Joanna was on the other side of Noah.

Joanna was a senior at Andersen. She was wearing vintage jeans and a lace shirt that you know she bought at an actual thrift store and not at Urban Outfitters like everyone else. Next year she was backpacking through Australia instead of going to college. She was also the only gay person I knew who had come out, and possibly the only gay person I knew, period. Last year she had brought her (now ex) girlfriend from Stamford to her junior prom. Joanna lived a few blocks away from Vi, also on Mississauga Island, but at the end, near the yacht club.

"My turn," Dean said. "I've never had sex." Then he drank. Dean had been the first guy in their year to lose his virginity, when he was in eighth grade, with a high school student. It had made him a bit of a legend. He had always been cute—he had shortish, shaggy brown hair, puffy cheeks, and a quick smile. But it wasn't his looks that got the girls—he was funny.

"Hells no," Vi said. "You can't say something you've *done* and then drink."

Dean swallowed. "Why not?"

"That's the rule."

"Your rule," he said.

"House rules," she answered.

"So should I be drinking here or not?" RJ asked, lifting his glass.

"That depends on whether or not you've had sex," Vi said.

He didn't drink. Neither did Corinne, who was sitting across the room, running her pale fingers through her red hair and watching us not drink.

Joanna, Hudson, and Vi drank.

No one else touched his or her glass. It was a clear division between juniors and seniors, my friends and Vi's friends.

I didn't know who Joanna and Hudson had done it with, but I knew Vi had lost her virginity to Frank, a hot college student who had a part in one of her mom's plays.

I'd been hoping to change my virgin status tonight. I kind of assumed that was the plan.

But . . . apparently Noah's plans were not the same as my plans.

TWENTY MINUTES EARLIER

"Okay, everyone, it's time to play I Never!" Vi had called, and started passing out cups.

"I'm driving," Noah said, waving his away.

"Hells no!" Vi exclaimed. "I assumed you would just crash here."

"No can do," he replied.

"Why not?" Vi asked.

Noah shifted uncomfortably. "Because."

"Because why?" Vi asked.

"Because my parents want me home," Noah said.

She turned to me. "Is he a mama's boy?"

I wanted to laugh, but I didn't because Noah looked annoyed. But he was a mama's boy. Noah's mom was the kind of mom who knew every detail of her two boys' lives from their upcoming tests to what underwear they were wearing. Fine, maybe not the underwear. She wasn't creepy. But she knew when they needed *new* underwear because fresh boxers would appear in their rooms. "A little," I said.

"A guy who treats his mom well treats his wife well," Marissa said.

"He definitely treats his girlfriend well," I said, kissing him on the cheek.

"You can still *play*," Vi said. "I'll just give you something else to drink." She put the glasses down on the coffee table and headed back to the kitchen. "How about . . . soy milk?"

Noah shrugged, still looking annoyed. He shifted away from Vi and put his arm around me. Since Vi's and my friendship was so separate from my everyday social life, Noah and Vi had never spent much time together. I had assumed they'd get along. Why wouldn't they? I liked them both.

"Soy milk? That's disgusting," Dean said. He was fingering one of the seven candleholders that were also on the coffee table.

"That's all we have. April, we really need to go grocery shopping tomorrow. How about water?"

"Whatever," Noah said.

"Water it is. Chardonnay for everyone not driving. Thank you, Mom, for leaving me a stocked liquor cabinet."

"Dude," Dean said, looking at Noah. "You've never done it? That's going to change. Your girlfriend has her own house. Speaking of . . ." He lifted his glass. "I've never had my own house."

Vi and I drank.

I put my hand on my hip, the alcohol making me feel tough. "You didn't want to say, I've never been abandoned by my parents?"

Dean blushed and shook his head.

Marissa squeezed my shoulder.

Hudson laughed.

I looked over at him and smiled. "At least someone thinks I'm funny."

Hudson was also a senior. Which was weird because he was ten months older than Dean but still in the same grade. Hudson was hot, while Dean was more of a cutie. Hudson had dirty-blond hair, crazy cheekbones, and blue eyes that were right now popping from across the room. He looked nothing like his brother. And as far as I could tell, Hudson kept his hands to himself. He kept most things to himself. He dated Sloane Grayson for most of last year but they broke up during the summer before she left for college. He was a possible drug dealer. Probably a rumor but supposedly he'd bought a brand-new Jeep with no help from his parents. Also, he was always "working" yet no one would say what he was doing.

"I can't believe you guys get to live together," Joanna said. "Lucky bitches."

"My parents would have *made* me move," Corinne said.

"Our parents keep hoping we'll move," Dean said. "Vi, why couldn't April just move into your mom's room instead of the basement?"

"My mom is going to come back for a weekend or so," Vi said. "This is still her house."

She was?

"It's kind of like April has her own apartment," Marissa said.

"But, April, won't you, like, miss your parents?" Corinne asked, looking not at me but beside me in Noah's direction. She definitely wasn't concerned with my feelings. She wanted me on the next plane to France or Ohio. Or anywhere not here. She licked her lips after she spoke. She always licked her lips. Maybe she thought it made her look sexy. Or maybe her lips were just dry and scaly and in desperate need of moisturization.

In a way I felt bad for her. It must be hell to be so obviously and publicly in love with someone else's boyfriend for all of high school. Not bad enough for me to hand him over. Sorry, Cor. Keep licking those lips.

"She's going to have too much fun to miss anyone," Marissa said.

RJ stretched his right arm, making it pop. "What happens if

April's dad Googles Vi's mom and sees that she's in Chicago?"

Silence.

"Then I'm screwed," I said. I took a sip of wine.

"Let's get back to the game," Marissa said, bumping her knee against mine. "I've never worn a tie."

All the guys drank.

RJ looked at Corinne. "Never have I ever worn a bikini," he said.

Vi snorted. "Never have I ever?"

"That's how we do it," RJ said.

"It sounds ridiculous," Vi said. "But since I have worn a bikini, I will drink."

RJ watched Corinne as she sipped. He was probably trying to get her drunk so he'd have a chance with her. He'd been obsessed with her since the beginning of the year. He invited her everywhere. But if Corinne liked him back, she would have hooked up with him already. Clearly she was still interested in Noah.

"I've never been to Europe," Hudson said.

I drank. Noah drank. Corinne drank. Awesome. Maybe the three of us should take a trip together. Or not.

"I've never been to Disney World," Joanna said.

I drank again. I hated Disney. More specifically, I hated Epcot. The burn down my throat helped wipe out the memory.

Marissa bumped my knee again. She knew all about my Epcot story.

"I've never been to Danbury," Corinne said.

I laughed into my glass. Seriously?

Joanna looked incredulous. "How is that possible? It's forty minutes away."

Corinne shrugged. "No reason to go."

"What about the Danbury Fair Mall? That should be reason enough," Marissa said.

Corinne shook her head and licked her lips.

Hudson's cell rang. He picked up the phone, looked at the call display, and muttered, "Excuse me." He took the call in the bathroom.

"Who's he talking to?" Joanna asked Dean. "Why so secretive?"

"You'd have to ask him," Dean said with a smile.

I wondered if he was still seeing Sloane or if it was something sketchy.

"Is he making a delivery?" RJ asked in a fake whisper.

"Yeah. To your mom," Dean responded. He refilled all the empty glasses and then squeezed himself between Marissa and the end of the couch.

"Um, hi there," she said, scooting away from him and laughing.

Vi rolled her eyes. "Try not to molest the newcomers," she scolded him. "And Marissa has a boyfriend."

"Then where is he?" Dean asked.

"Boston. We go to camp together."

"Clearly you need a Westport boyfriend too," Dean said.

Hudson returned to his spot.

"My turn," Vi interrupted. "I've never gotten dumped."

"You've never been in a relationship," Dean said, drinking.

"So? I've still never been dumped."

Corinne, Joanna, RJ, and Hudson drank too.

I wondered whether it would be Noah or me who would have to drink to that eventually.

"Who dumped you?" Joanna asked Hudson. "It wasn't Sloane, was it?"

"That's a personal question," Hudson said, leaning back.

"It's a personal game," Joanna answered.

"We should make it *more* personal," Dean said. "Let's play strip I Never."

"I'm in." RJ looked at Corinne.

"Not happening," Vi said. "Keep your pants on. Why do guys have such one-track minds?"

"We don't," RJ said. "We care about beer too. And Fantasy Football."

"Don't listen to him," Dean said to Marissa. "I'm a Renaissance man. I care about lots of things. Like flowers. And orphans."

We all laughed, but Vi wasn't done with him. "Please," she said. "Even if you were in a relationship, you wouldn't kick a hot, naked lady-stranger out of your bed."

"I would too," Dean cried, holding his hands to his chest in mock hurt.

"I love you, babe, but you wouldn't."

Noah rolled his eyes.

"Let's move on," I said, my neck tensing. "Who's next?"

"Something's ringing," Corinne said.

In the distance I heard a cell ringing. My cell. Crap, it was downstairs. All of my friends were here. Which meant—my mom, dad, or Matthew. But my mom and Matthew were probably sleeping . . .

I excused myself and ran down the stairs.

The phone was no longer ringing by the time I reached it. I checked the call display. My dad. Three times. Uh-oh. I was about to hit REDIAL when it rang.

Him again.

"Hi," I said.

"I was about to get back on a plane. Is everything okay?"

My heart jumped into my throat. "No! Yes! I mean, everything's fine! I was just upstairs. I didn't hear the phone."

"I think you should always have the phone on you. So you can reach us. Or so we can reach you."

"You want me to get one of those cell-phone belts? People will think I'm a drug dealer." And, hey! Speaking of drug dealers, there's one sitting upstairs! Maybe.

"April, that's not funny. If I call and get no answer, I get worried. I'm a dad. I'm allowed."

"Okay, okay. I'll keep my phone with me."

"Next time you don't answer I'm calling the police."

"Dad! That's insane. What if I'm in the shower? I don't want the police barging into the house."

"Then answer the phone."

WHY I MADE MY DAD'S RINGTONE A POLICE SIREN

See above.

BACK TO I NEVER

Two minutes later I was once again in my seat on the couch between Noah and Marissa. Joanna, who was still sitting beside Noah, had her glass lifted. "I've never had a pet," she said.

"Does a mouse count?" Dean asked.

Hudson groaned. "Michelangelo the mouse. He lived in your closet for six months."

"You couldn't trap it?" Vi asked.

Hudson laughed. "And kill his pet?"

Vi slapped her hand against the couch. "Shut up. Why have I never heard this story?"

Dean sighed. "It was before your time, my sweet."

"Noah has the cutest dog," Corinne said, and I hated her a little.

"Thanks," he said. He put his hand on my knee. "April had a very cute cat too."

"Had?" Hudson said. "That sounds . . . sad."

"Oh, Libby didn't die," I said quickly, placing my hand over Noah's. "When my mom moved to Paris she couldn't bring her along 'cause of customs issues. And my stepmom isn't a cat person, so . . . we gave her away."

"Still sounds sad," Hudson said. I looked up and realized he was staring at me. Those eyes. Wow.

"It was," I said, wondering if he meant my mom taking my cat, or my mom moving to Paris.

Noah turned his palm up so our fingers were pressed together. My hand was sticky from the wine.

Dean lifted his glass again. "I'll follow the house rules now, okay? I've never hooked up with anyone in this room." He scooted closer to Marissa. "Perhaps I can drink to that later in the evening?"

Everyone laughed, including Marissa. Marissa is too head over heels for Aaron to take Dean seriously anyway.

Noah drank. I drank.

Corinne drank. And smiled.

Noah turned pink.

THE CORINNE SITUATION

It happened the summer after freshman year when I went with my mom to France. They were moving. I was visiting.

Noah and I had "the talk" before I left. We weren't breaking up, but we agreed that if something happened over the summer, it wouldn't be the end of the world. It had made sense at the time. At least to me. Noah and I had been together for less than eight months, I was going to Europe for two months, and I assumed there would be cute

European boys to flirt with. I wanted to have an adventure. Since we were only fifteen, it seemed silly to stay exclusive for the summer. We would only resent each other, et cetera, et cetera.

Obviously when I had made the suggestion to potentially see other people, I had imagined it would be me who would see the other people. Not him. And especially not someone we went to school with.

I hadn't planned on missing him as much as I had.

I had thought, France! Romance! Chocolate! French boys who'd kiss me on the Eiffel Tower! I hadn't expected to feel so out of place. I hadn't expected the language barrier to be so tough. I hadn't expected my mother—and my brother—to be so consumed with setting up their new lives that they had no time for me. I hadn't expected my emails and phone calls to Noah to feel like a lifeline. Since we spoke every night, I assumed he was twiddling his thumbs waiting around for me, that he was just as lonely as I was. In retrospect, I always spoke to him before I went to bed, which was only around five his time. But not once during any of our phone calls had he said, "Oh, by the way, you'll never guess where my tongue just was! In Corinne's mouth!"

We had plans for the night I flew home.

Penny had unpacked all my stuff from my mom's while I'd been away. My clothes. My books. My ceramic pen holder. All nicely put away in my dad and Penny's furniture. I sat on the canopy bed Penny had picked for me when they'd first moved in and looked around the room, feeling out of place and comforted all at once. Then I jumped into the shower to get ready.

When Noah pulled his bike into my driveway, I ran outside and kissed him before he could even get off.

We met our friends on Compo Beach. Corinne was there. I was oblivious. I was nice and sweet and triumphant in an "I just got back from my über-glamorous trip to France, and what did you do this summer? Hang out at the mall? How original" way. I had tossed my styled-in-Paris hair and let my glowing skin speak for itself. Maybe I hadn't had a French fling, but I had managed to come back from France looking hot. While my mother and brother were setting up their lives I was sitting in the backyard taking in the sun, or walking through the neighborhood. My skin was tanned, I'd had a great haircut, and I was skinny, despite the pounds of bread and Brie I consumed. French women don't get fat, you know.

I flounced around Compo Beach like an idiot.

That must have been what Corinne thought—that I was a clueless idiot. She kept licking her lips and playing with her hair and I couldn't help but wonder what was up with her.

Later, back on my porch, I said to Noah, "I didn't see anyone in France. I just want you to know."

I waited for him to say, "Of course I didn't either—I am

crazy in love with you!" Or a simple "me neither" would
have sufficed.

Instead, he looked down at his sneakers and flushed, and
then fidgeted with his fingers. And I knew. I knew who
it was too. I was almost more pissed that he didn't tell me
immediately—for letting me go out in public clueless—than
I was about what happened. Almost.

Come on! He stood by while I asked Corinne how her
summer was! She had an incredible summer. She was hooking up with my boyfriend!

Tears streamed down my cheeks as he told me the story.

"You're making *me* cry," he said, his eyes welling up.

"Good!"

"I'm sorry," he said. "I'm a dumbass! I just assumed you
were hooking up with French douches . . . and Corinne was
there. . . . Shit. I'm sorry."

"Are you?" I asked. I felt as if my world had flip-flopped,
as if everything I trusted had been turned upside down, and
not for the first time. "Would you even have told me if I
hadn't brought it up?"

"Yes!" he said, looking at his shoes. "I *was* going to
tell you."

"Tonight?"

"Yes . . . maybe . . ."

"Maybe?"

"I'm just so happy you're home!"

"Whatever. You're probably going over to her house next."

"No, of course not! April . . . you're the one who said we should see other people."

I pressed for details. It seemed like a good idea at the time.

What did you do exactly? (Just kissed.) No under-the-shirt action? (A little, but not much.) A little was enough. Anything below the belt? (No, no, nothing.) Why should I believe you? (I wouldn't lie.) How many times did it happen? (Not many.) How many times *exactly*? (Two, maybe three. Four tops.) Where did it happen? At your house? (At the beach.) Compo Beach? Where we just went? (Yes.) Every time? (Mostly.) So not always. Where else? Your house? (No. Never. Her house.) You were in her house? Her room? (The living room.) What, did her family meet you or something? (Just once.)

The black spots danced in front of my eyes. My heart hurt. I was sinking, sinking, sinking.

I hadn't been back to France since. Obviously I'd have to go at some point. My mom and Matthew lived there. And I would visit. Soon. It wasn't just because I didn't want to leave Noah unattended, I swear. My brother spent Christmas in Westport, so it hadn't made much sense for me to go there. And my mom and brother came here last summer to see me. She wanted me to visit this summer. She expected me to visit this summer.

And maybe I would. I wasn't sure. I had a lot going on. You know.

And it wasn't that I didn't trust Noah. Because I did.

When we'd first started dating, I'd asked him if he'd ever cheat on anyone.

"I'd never," he said. "You?"

"Never," I'd told him. Never would I ever.

number three:
skipped school

THE DIABOLICAL TWINS

We didn't skip school on the first day of the winter semester, but we *were* extremely late.

Why?

Because—as it turns out—there is a difference between Seventh Generation dish soap and Seventh Generation liquid detergent. You wouldn't know this from looking at the bottles. Both are white. Both feature green-and-blue photographs of grass and sky. To the casual observer (well, to me), they might look like identical twins. The kind of identical twins who wear matching outfits just to screw with you.

Before the soap fiasco, I was taking my sweet time getting ready for school. I had woken up at the crack of dawn. Partially because while the basement had blinds, it did not have blackout shades, partially because it was all still new to me—new house! New bed! New ceiling!—partially because I could hear Vi stomping on the floor above me, and partially because I'm the kind of geek who finds the first day back to school exciting.

I even had a back-to-school outfit laid out on my desk—one of Vi's low-cut gray sweaters, her crystal necklace that hung on a rope of black suede, and my favorite jeans.

Upstairs, Vi was still in gym clothes, putting a bowl into the dishwasher. "Morning!" she said. "Will you run the dishwasher when you're done?"

"Of course," I said. "Were you working out?"

"I do the HardCore3000 videos. Have you ever tried them? Incredible. You should do it with me tomorrow morning."

"Um . . . maybe." I tended to sit on my ass whenever it wasn't soccer season. But maybe Vi's athleticism would inspire me. Or not. "Is there anything to eat for breakfast?"

"Not much," she said. "There's some cinnamon raisin bread in the freezer. We really need to go grocery shopping after school."

We'd been planning on shopping the day before, but it had snowed all day. Well, that and we'd been too hung over to leave the house. Not hung over in a sick way—just tired and happy. Saturday night had been so much fun. Sure, it had been a bit weird with Noah—since he'd driven people home, we never got any alone time. But there'd be plenty of time for that.

"Should we meet back here around five and go together?" she asked. "I have an *Issue* meeting after class or else we could take one car to school."

"Yeah, let's meet here then." *The Issue* was the school paper. Every month they chose a different theme and all the articles had to be about that. Last semester they'd done Family, Sports, Health, and Holidays. "So what are your next issues?"

"No January issue, but February is bullying, and I'm thinking March will be sex," she said and then disappeared into her bathroom.

Sex? I guess I wouldn't be the cover story.

After I finished eating, I loaded my plate into the dishwasher and scoped out the situation. I had never actually *run* a dishwasher before. That was something my mom did, and then Penny or my dad. I was more of the unloading type.

How hard could it be?

First, the soap. Probably under the sink. Yes! Seventh Generation Dish Soap! I took out the white container, squirted it into the welcoming square, closed the door, and pressed START. All right, then. I headed back downstairs, where I brushed my teeth, put on makeup, and grabbed my car keys.

And then.

I got to the top of the basement stairs to find Vi on the kitchen floor on all fours with a dish towel, surrounded by a flood of white, foamy bubbles.

"What happened?" I asked.

"I think you used the wrong soap," she said calmly.

"I am *so* sorry." My cheeks burned and I felt like a complete idiot. "Let me get it. Where are the paper towels?"

"Under the sink. But I think a towel-towel would work better."

I grabbed the other dish towel and crouched down beside her. We mopped up the rest of the mess in silence. Great start to the year, April!

After we were done she said, "Will you just put these towels in the wash? I'll run it when I get home."

"I can run—" I started but she gave me a look and I decided that having a brief seminar on all the appliances was not a terrible plan under the circumstances. "Okay."

By the time I hurried down to the washing machine (which was in my bathroom downstairs), and then back up, Vi had almost contained the situation. "You better go on. It's going to take you a while to clean off your car."

"Right. Thanks," I said. It was a one-car garage and my car was just outside in the driveway. "I'll see you at school."

I stepped into my boots, zipped up my coat, and braced myself for the cold. And there it was. Penny's car. My car. Buried under two feet of snow. Excellent. I wiped the snow off with my gloves, then used the scraper on the windows. Once my gloves were soaking, my wrists were frozen, and I was done, I tossed my schoolbag into the passenger side, and climbed in. It felt strange to sit in the driver's seat of Penny's car. When I drove—which I hardly ever did—I always took my dad's car. A blood relative would hate you less than an inherited one if you scratched his vehicle.

I stuck the keys in the ignition and turned. And turned again.

Nothing.

One more time for good luck.

Still nothing.

Agh! I banged my head against the steering wheel. My dad was right. I should have started the car over the weekend. What was wrong with me? How was I going to manage on my own if I couldn't even run the dishwasher or start my own car?

I took a deep, icy breath.

I could just go with Vi and get a ride back with Noah. Although this was the exact reason I had gotten the car in the first place—so I wouldn't have to depend on other people to get around.

If I called Noah now, then at least we'd get to talk. Last semester, he'd picked me up every day. But then I'd been on his way, and now I was not. Anyway, driving with Vi made more sense, since we lived together.

The garage door opened. Vi's car was running inside. I immediately spotted the problem with my plan to catch a ride with her. My car was blocking hers.

In her rearview mirror, I saw her slap her palm against her forehead.

Vi was going to rue the day she invited me to move in.

Vi called Dean and Hudson to come get us.

"I'm so sorry," I told them through Dean's rolled-down Jeep window.

"Are you kidding?" Dean asked. "This is the highlight of my day. I get to be the knight in shining armor!"

"Technically, I'm the knight," Hudson said. "Since I'm driving."

"Dean, get in the back, and let me sit in the front," Vi said. "Two guys in the front is ridiculously chauvinistic."

"It's our car," Dean protested.

"My car," Hudson said. "Technically."

"I don't care whose car it is," Vi said. She pointed to Dean. "Out."

"Fine," Dean said, popping open the Jeep door. "But if I'm in the back, so are you."

"Wahoo!" I cheered. "Shotgun!"

As we all climbed into our spots, I looked over at Hudson. Those cheekbones! Jeez. It was almost a shame to waste them on a guy. If I didn't have Noah, I don't think I'd be able to talk to Hudson without freezing up. "Thanks for being my knight," I told him.

He smiled. "My pleasure. Do you want me to try jump-starting your car? I have cables."

"Oh. Thanks. I don't want to make us even later, though. I'm really sorry about this. My dad warned me I should start it every day in the winter, but I was feeling rebellious."

"Rebelling against parents you don't even live with. I like it." He took the car out of PARK and headed down the street.

"It's easier to rebel when no one's around to see it. I'm wimpy like that."

He shook his head. "You seem pretty gutsy to me. I don't know that many girls who would move out on their own at sixteen."

I blinked. Gutsy? Me? I moved in with Vi because I was afraid of leaving my life behind. I was the opposite of gutsy. Instead of admitting that, I sat up straighter. "I'm not exactly on my own. I have Vi."

"And Zelda," Vi piped in.

"Who's Zelda?" I asked.

"Didn't I tell you about the ghost that lives in the oven?"

I turned around to face her. "No. You did not."

"Personally, I think the creaks are because the oven is from 1972, but my mother is convinced they're from a ghost. Zelda."

"Did someone die in the house or something?"

"No, my mother is just crazy," she said. "She was convinced we had a ghost. And that the ghost committed suicide in our oven, Sylvia Plath style. Which doesn't even make sense, because our oven is electric."

I wasn't sure why one couldn't kill oneself in an electric oven, but decided not to ask.

"Great to know," I said instead. "Whenever you're out

and I want company, I'll talk to Zelda."

"Why don't you get a parrot?" Dean asked. "At least he would talk back."

Vi slapped his knee. "Why would you assume the parrot is a male?"

He bowed his head. "I'm sorry. At least *she* would talk back."

I narrowed my eyes and gave an exaggerated wag of my finger. "Oh sure, if an animal talks a lot it must be female."

"Gutsy and funny," Hudson said, making me blush. "Vi, where have you been hiding her?" He looked over at me and smiled.

"In the oven," Vi and I answered simultaneously.

LATE

By the time we got to school, we were fifteen minutes late.

The front door was locked and we had to buzz. Once you had to buzz you were done for. We did the walk of shame to the office.

"You're late," the school secretary said, handing all four of us tardy slips.

"Doreen, we apologize profusely," Dean said, nodding solemnly.

"It was my fault," I said. "Car died."

"The funeral will be after school," Dean added. "It would mean a lot to all of us if you could make it."

"Next time we call your parents," she said, cracking a smile.

I tried to maintain my gutsy image, but inside I was freaking as I took my slip. "I am so, so, so sorry," I said as we exited the office.

"Don't worry about it," Hudson said.

"Shit happens," Vi told me as she waved good-bye and ran up the stairs to the second floor.

Dean put his arm around me. "I said it before and I'll say it again: highlight of my day. It can only be downhill from here."

I laughed. "Thanks for coming to get us."

Hudson rolled his eyes at his brother, then turned to me. "Let me know if you want me to jump-start your car after school," he said.

"Thanks. I might take you up on it."

"Anytime," Hudson said over his shoulder as he hurried down the hall.

Gutsy, huh? I straightened my shoulders and headed to class.

ON THE WAY TO CALCULUS

"So how was night number two?" Marissa asked when we met up after English and walked down the hall to AP Calculus. "Tell me everything."

"Fun. We made spaghetti. We watched TV. Stayed up late chatting."

"Oooo, I'm so jealous," she said with a sigh.

"Well, on the less fabulous side, I didn't bother to start my car on Sunday, and now the battery's dead." I stopped myself before adding the bit about this morning's soap explosion, feeling uncomfortably ashamed at how little I'd managed to do right since moving into Vi's. "But, whatever. What did you do?"

"Finished my Israel application," she said. "Finally."

"Congrats!"

Marissa was applying for a summer program called the Kinneret Israel trip. The association of camps she went to every year sent fifty juniors on an all-expense-paid trip to Israel. Aaron, her summer boyfriend, and Shoshanna and Brittany, her summer best friends, had applied too.

I was jealous.

Marissa's camp friends had her all summer.

"When do you hear?" I asked, following her into our calculus room. A part of me hoped she wouldn't get in. A terrible, selfish, worst-best-friend-ever part.

"Sometime in March," she said.

"Good luck," I said.

A second later, Lucy Michaels, aka the spy who liked to make amateur videos, strolled in and sat down beside us. "How's your car?" she asked me, eyes open wide.

"Um . . ." How did she know about my car? "Fine."

"Yeah? It looked really snowed in this morning."

"Yeah," I said. "It was. How did you see my car?"

"I live two houses down from Vi."

"Oh." That wasn't good.

"So how come you've been staying at Vi's?" Lucy asked. "You've been there since Saturday."

Stalker . . .

"My dad moved to Ohio so I moved in," I said. "With Vi. And her mom." She could not find out that Vi's mom wasn't there. She could *not*.

Lucy gave me a calculated smile. "Very interesting."

Ms. Franklin came in. She was in her early thirties and was one of those young, hot teachers who wore cute outfits. All the guys had a thing for her. "Hope you're all ready," she said, clapping her hands. "I'm going to keep you on your toes this semester."

I snuck a peek at Lucy, fearing Ms. Franklin wasn't the only one.

I SEE YOU

Marissa and I rushed out of class before Lucy could follow. At the door we spotted Noah and Corinne walking out of Mr. Gregory's economics class across the hall. My stomach sank. Now I had two things to worry about during calculus—Lucy hanging all over me, and Corinne hanging all over Noah. I hated that I had no classes with him, and she had at least one. As I watched the two of them share a laugh about who knows what, my shoulders tensed up again. I was probably being paranoid over nothing, but if Corinne happened to get selected for a prestigious high school internship in northern Siberia, I wouldn't be the slightest bit upset. If only she could go on the Israel trip instead of Marissa.

"Hey, Noah," Marissa called.

He looked up and blinked, caught with his pants down. Well, not really, obviously, but he had a guilty air about him that did nothing to reassure me.

"Hey!" he called, abandoning Corinne and crossing the hallway. "What's up?"

He kissed me on the lips, but it did not make me feel better.

Why did he have to talk to her at all? Couldn't they just ignore each other? It was so ridiculous. I tried to relax my shoulders so it looked like I wasn't annoyed. "Hey, babe," I said, resting my hand on his shoulder. I wouldn't let her get to me. He was my boyfriend. And I had my own house. Plus my own car. She was nothing. A fly on my arm. I shook her off and walked with Noah down the stairs. And smack into Hudson.

"Hey," he said. "So do you want me to come over after school to jump-start your car?"

Noah looked from him to me. "What's happening?"

I explained the car issue I'd had that morning. "Would you know how to start it?" I asked Noah.

"Um . . ." He blushed. "I have a Triple A membership."

Hudson nodded. "I can do it. No problem." He turned to me. "Want to meet me at my car after class?"

"I'll take her home," Noah said, putting his arm around me. "Meet us at the house."

"Sure, whatever you say."

Hmm. Maybe we should fix Corinne and Hudson up and call it a day.

A HOP, SKIP, AND A JUMP

"There you go," Hudson said as my car roared to life.

"Thank you! You're the best!" I cheered.

Noah, who was standing beside me, flinched. Whoops. I took his hand.

Hudson started removing the cables. "Let it run for about thirty minutes to recharge the battery and then you should be good."

"Thanks again," I said. "I really appreciate it."

"Yeah. Thanks," Noah said.

"No problem at all."

We all stood around for a second, and then Hudson said, "Okay, well, I'll see you kids around," then hopped in his car.

"Did he just call us 'kids'?" Noah asked after he drove away.

"I do believe so." I pulled Noah back toward the house. "Wanna go downstairs, kid?" I asked.

"I thought you were going grocery shopping."

"Not till five," I told him. "And I mean, *do you want to go downstairs?*" I leaned in and kissed him so he'd know what I meant. I wanted him to know that Hudson coming to my rescue with the jumper cables didn't mean a thing.

He looked at his watch.

"Half an hour," I said. "Plenty of time." I gave him what I hoped was a sly, sexy grin.

"It's just, I got stuff I gotta take care of before dinner," he said.

What?

I was suggesting we both lose our virginity right that very minute on my brand-new futon in total privacy, and he was worried about stuff he had to take care of?

Was there something seriously wrong?

Was he upset about Hudson coming over?

"Just come down for fifteen minutes, then," I told him, tracing my hand up his forearm. "I really missed you over break."

"I gotta motor, April," he said. "I already spent too long over here."

"Oh," I said.

"Yeah." He pulled his car keys out of his pocket. "So I'll see you tomorrow, okay, cutie?"

"Okay. Fine."

"Good." He smiled at me. I loved those dimples.

I did my French homework alone until Vi finally showed a half an hour later. I bounded up the stairs and called, "Hi, honey, you're home! Let's go shopping! I'll drive."

"Wow, are you always this perky après school? Let's move. And I can drive."

FRANKLY, VI, I DON'T GIVE A . . . WAIT, WHAT?

The first ten minutes of grocery shopping were fun. Vi tossed various things in our cart while I watched in awe (French bread! Taco shells! Strawberry cream cheese!). The next ten minutes were less fun. (It was like a maze in there.) The ten minutes after that were painful.

"Grocery shopping is much more annoying than I thought it would be," I said, while struggling to maneuver the cart around a sharp corner in the freezer department.

"You make it sound like you've never been grocery shopping before."

"I haven't. Well, not recently. Penny did all the shopping. And my mom hardly ever brought us along."

Vi looked at me like I was from another planet. "I've done the shopping since I was about ten. But speaking of stuff you *haven't done* . . . why haven't you and Noah had sex yet? Haven't you been together for over two years? If you have to be in a relationship, you may as well be getting sex out of it."

"We're working on it," I said. Any day now.

"It's hardly work, darling," Vi laughed. "It's leisure."

"We could never get any privacy when I lived at my dad's. I didn't want to do it in the back of a car."

Vi nodded knowingly. "So now it'll be any day, yeah?"

You'd think. Wouldn't you? But now I wasn't so sure.

"Are you on the pill?" Vi asked.

"No."

"Do you want to be?"

"Maybe?" I said.

She opened the freezer door and checked out the various sorbets. "I'm going on it."

"Yeah? How come?"

"So I can have sex and not get pregnant. Hello?"

"What did you use the last time you did it? With Frank?"

She picked lemon, dropped it in the cart, and then looked at me. Then back at the cart. Then back at me. "I never slept with Frank."

"Oh," I said, confused. "Then what was the guy's name from your mom's play?"

She pushed the cart down the aisle. "His *name* was Frank. I just never slept with him."

"Excuse me?" I asked, catching up to her, even more confused. "Why did you tell me you did?"

"I told everyone I did. I felt like people expected me to have done it. Dean did it and Hudson did it and Joanna did it—this was before she realized she was gay—so I said I did it too."

I wasn't sure how to process this information. Vi had lied to everyone. Vi—strong, confident Vi—had felt the need to pretend to be something she wasn't. Why did she care so much what other people thought? I guess if all her friends had done it, she hadn't wanted to be the only one.

"So . . . that means . . . you're a virgin?"

"You don't have to announce it over the loudspeaker or anything. But yes. And it's time to change that. So I'm going to have sex." She moved us into the cheese section.

I smiled. "Who are you gonna have it with, though? Dean?"

"No way," she said with a flick of her wrist.

"Why not? I've always wondered why you guys haven't gotten together."

"I am not interested in a boyfriend, thank you very much. And anyway, I know way too much about Dean's sexual escapades. He's constantly hitting on everyone. He hit on Doreen this morning for God's sake."

I laughed. "He wasn't actually hitting on the school secretary!"

"You never know. In a different setting, if we hadn't been there . . ."

"Ha ha," I said. "Why are you so convinced that you don't want a boyfriend?"

"I'm too busy as it is. And I don't want anything keeping me trapped here. I am out of this place come graduation. Hells yeah!" Vi had applied to all the top undergraduate business and economics programs in the country. She was going to go to wherever gave her the best financial aid package. "I just want to have the experience. I want to know what it's all about."

"So who are you going to sleep with?"

"Liam Packinson."

I scrunched my nose. "The redhead? Ew."

"I love redheaded guys! They're hot."

"Redheads are evil."

"Oh, get over it. You can't blame Corinne for what Noah did."

I pretended to be absorbed in the cheese section. "Do you like goat cheese?"

"No. Let's get cheddar," she said, grabbing two wedges and dumping them in the basket. "Nice way to change the subject."

"Back to Liam. If you like him, why didn't you invite him last night?"

"Because Jodi Dillon snatched him up on the first day of school in September. But I just heard this morning that they're splitsville. And I'm up next. Operation Sleep with Liam begins tomorrow." She patted down her hair and squared her shoulders.

"Sleep with Liam? Not date? Just sleep?"

"I told you, I'm not wasting time on a boyfriend. I have too many other things to do than be a *girlfriend*. But it's time for me to have sex."

"But why now?"

"First, because I cannot go to college a virgin. That would be pathetic." She turned down the cereal aisle and tossed a box of Cheerios into our cart. "Second, it's for research. For *The Issue*. I think it's important that I actually do it before I write about it. So I'm going to Planned Parenthood to get the pill first."

"Can't you just use a condom?" That had been my plan.

"I'll be using a condom plus the pill. Condoms can break

and I am not going to be my mother." She pursed her lips. "Accidents happen."

"Fair enough," I said as we turned into the cleaning supplies aisle. I wondered what it was like to know you were an accident. My parents had tried for two years before having me.

"If you want to start the pill too, I'll get both of us appointments."

"Maybe." I rolled the thought around in my mind. Starting the pill sounded responsible. Sexy. Grown-up. "Yes. I would like to go on the pill." One more thing to keep from my dad. Which reminded me . . . "Oh! Oh! Lucy lives on your street? With her parents?"

"It would be a crazy coincidence if she lived without parents on the same street as we live without parents, don't you think?"

"You know what I mean! Why didn't you mention that to me? Isn't that dangerous?"

She shrugged. "She hasn't set the block on fire yet."

"Ha. Ha, ha, ha."

"Don't worry so much."

After half an hour in the cleaning products aisle (apparently we needed garbage bags and recycling bags and laundry detergent and liquid dish soap that did not look like the dishwasher detergent and Swiffer refills and a Miele filter . . . and thank you, parents, for shielding me from all this as long as you did), we finally reached the cash register.

The Miele filter was sixty dollars.

"I don't even know what a Miele is," I said.

"An expensive vacuum cleaner. It was a gift from my grandma."

"Where is your grandma these days?"

"A home. I visit her after school once a week."

"You're a very good granddaughter." I had no grandparents left. Besides Penny's parents. But I didn't count them. Even if I did, I wouldn't expect them to give me a vacuum cleaner as a present.

They did send me fifty dollars for the holidays, come to think of it. Um, come to think of it, I really needed to write them a thank-you note.

The bill came to three hundred and twenty-two dollars. Ouch. "I got it," I said, handing over my debit card. "Consider it rent."

THE FIRST TIME NOAH AND I ALMOST HAD SEX

It was four months earlier, the beginning of junior year. Noah's parents were out of town, his sister was at a movie, and his brother was listening to music in his room. I'd told my parents I was at Marissa's.

We had stuffed ourselves on Chinese food. Noah had over-ordered, as usual. He had big eyes. We would definitely have leftovers. We were in sweats watching a crazy sex scene from *Vampire Nights* in his basement. Noah was fidgeting. He always got antsy whenever he watched anything longer than a half hour.

Vampire Nights was hot. "Maybe we should do it," I said, not sure if I meant it or not.

And he said, "Now?"

And I blushed and said, "Yeah!"

"Okay!" he hollered, and jumped off the couch like it was a trampoline. "Do you have anything?" he'd asked.

I shook my head.

"Me neither. Let's go to the store." Before I could blink he already had an umbrella in hand, his shoes yanked on, and the garage door opened.

The idea of getting all dressed up and facing the rain made me reconsider. "Oh, never mind. It's too wet out."

"What? No!" His face deflated. "I'll go by myself!" he continued, already out the door. "You don't have to do anything!"

"Okay," I'd said, sinking back into the couch.

I'm guessing the entire block heard the squeal of the tires.

We had been together for almost two years. We had decided to wait until at least junior year—having sex as a sophomore seemed too young to me, but junior year seemed acceptable. And now it was junior year. I knew he'd been waiting for me to bring it up. And I had been planning on bringing it up . . . as soon as I felt ready.

Maybe spontaneity was a mistake. First-time sex should

be planned. Considered. You couldn't just cannonball in, like it was a pool.

By the time Noah got back I had a nervous, pounding headache. Was I really ready? Or was it just *Vampire Nights*? The show also made me want to be a vampire, but that didn't mean it was a good idea. Would everyone know? And did my breath smell like General Tso's chicken?

"Don't hate me," I said.

He looked at me. Not in a mad way, but definitely disappointed. He dropped a Walgreens plastic bag on the wooden floor and kicked off his boots. "Hey, that's okay. Whatever you want."

"I don't feel great." The next thing I knew the room was spinning. I sat down on the carpet and bent my head into my knees. "I think I might pass out."

He sat down beside me and put his arm under my neck. "Aw," he'd murmured. "Is it the MSG? Maybe we should have ordered Bertucci's instead."

He ended up taking me home. As we left the basement, I glanced into the Walgreens bag and saw that he had bought five packs of condoms, all different types: lubricated, non-lubricated, non-latex, ribbed (for her pleasure), glow in the dark. Two per pack. Ten total.

"Big eyes," I teased him.

He laughed. "I'm planning on using them all. Whenever you're ready."

FROM THE REAL SUZANNE TO THE FAKE JAKE

From: Suzanne Caldwell <Primadonna@mindjump.com>
Date: Tues, 13 Jan, 2 a.m.
To: Jake Berman <Jake.Berman@pmail.com>
Subject: Settling In

Hi, Jake!
The girls are really enjoying themselves! I just called and they had a whole bunch of people over. I heard singing in the background and everything! I'm so glad they're settling in well. Also, I met a man last night named Jake German! How funny is that! I asked him if he knew you, but he didn't. ☺ I hope things are going well in Cincinnati!
All the very best,
Suzanne

————————

From: Jake Berman <Jake.Berman@pmail.com>
Date: Tues, 13 Jan, 6 a.m.
To: Suzanne Caldwell <Primadonna@mindjump.com>
Subject: RE: Settling In

Suzanne,
I'm thrilled the girls are settling in well. I knew they would. And Jake German?

Sounds like he might be my evil twin. Maybe you should steer clear of him. Just a suggestion. Things in Cleveland (you were close enough) are great.

Best,

Jake

AND GOOD MORNING TO YOU

"Today's the day!" Vi said, throwing open my door. We'd been living together for two weeks, and though I'd learned to change a lightbulb and run the dishwasher without causing a flood, Vi had yet to learn that I wasn't an early riser. She, on the other hand, did a HardCore3000 exercise DVD every morning. There were five—abs; legs and glutes; arms and chest; cardio; and stretch. Yesterday, I'd caught the last two minutes and discovered it involved a gym mat and ten-pound weights. I'd spotted them in the front closet, but hadn't realized they were in active use.

I yawned, glancing at my alarm. "I have ten minutes of sleep left. I don't know why we didn't kick everyone out earlier last night."

"Because we were having fun! And too bad. Our appointments are this morning. I'm eight and you're eight fifteen. And the clinic is in Darien so it's at least a half-hour drive."

I sat up. "Seriously?"

"Yup."

"Why do we have appointments? We didn't make appointments . . . did we?"

"We did." She pulled open my blinds with a flourish.

"But . . . you didn't tell me."

"I did not," she agreed.

"Don't we have school today?"

"Yes, school *is* going on today. But do we have school? No, we do not. We have appointments."

"I can't skip school!" If I got caught skipping, what would happen? Ohio would happen.

"You are not skipping," she said. "You're home with the flu. Your dad already emailed the school."

"He did?"

"He did. Well, Jake.Berman@pmail.com did."

"Oh," I said. How very thoughtful of him.

THE SPY

I moved my car onto the street, and then waited for Vi to pull out of the garage.

"Shit," she muttered as I opened the passenger door. "Get in fast."

"What?" I asked, closing my door. "Why?"

"Too late," she grumbled. She zapped down my window and a gust of cold air blew against the side of my face. I turned to see . . .

. . . Lucy Michaels and her unblinking alien eyes.

Crap.

"Hi, guys," she said, looking from me to Vi and then back to Vi. "Can I get a lift?" Crap, crap, crap.

"We're sick," Vi said smoothly. "Really sick. Contagious. I wouldn't get too close if I were you."

"You don't look sick. And if you are sick, then where are you going?"

"The doctor," I said. Which wasn't a lie. So there.

"Together?"

"Yup," we both answered.

"Where's your mom?" she asked Vi.

"At work," Vi said. "Where's yours?"

"Inside. She drives me to school, but I'd rather go with you two."

"Another time," Vi said. She simultaneously rolled up my window and reversed onto the street.

Lucy stared. I gave an awkward wave.

"Oh crap," I said under my breath as we took off. I peeked in the rearview mirror. She was still standing in our drive- way. "This is bad. Maybe we should go to school."

"We already told her we were sick. And sent emails."

"Yeah. But. What if she tells her mom?"

"What's the worst thing that can happen?" Vi asked.

"We get suspended for skipping? And my dad freaks out? And makes me move to Ohio?" I fidgeted with my seat belt.

"You worry too much," she said.

True. If Lucy realized what was going on, then Lucy realized what was going on. Freaking out wasn't going to help anyone. It certainly wasn't helping me.

THE NIGHT AFTER THE FIRST TIME NOAH AND I ALMOST HAD SEX

"I'm sorry I freaked out last night," I said to Noah. I was huddled under the covers and whispering so my dad and Penny wouldn't know I was on the phone at one A.M. We always spoke before we went to sleep.

"Oh please. Don't be sorry. Couldn't you tell I was nervous, too?"

"No."

"I bought five kinds of condoms 'cause I was worried I wouldn't have the right kind."

"You thought glow in the dark could be the right kind?"

"It was nighttime!"

I giggled, then said, "I just want to feel a hundred percent ready. Do you feel a hundred percent ready?"

"Yup."

"Are guys always a hundred percent ready?"

"If the girl is you and the guy is me, then . . . yup."

"I'm, like, ninety-nine percent ready."

"And how do we get you to a hundred percent? No pressure. I'm just wondering. Hypothetically."

"Uh-huh. I think to get to the hundred, I'll need to plan it. Count down. Know it's coming."

"Get your palate ready."

"Exactly."

"Then plan away."

"How about over Christmas break?"

"Deal," he said.

"Deal," I repeated. But then I worried. Physically I was ready. When we were together, I *wanted to* have sex. But what would doing it mean? Would I love him more? Would it hurt even more when we—if we—ever broke up? Would sex change us?

It had to.

But was I ready for change?

PLANNED NON-PARENTHOOD

I had been expecting something white. And sterile. Maybe like an Apple Store but less funky. I also thought it would be filled with nervous teens and their mothers. But it was just a regular doctor's office with beige carpeting, felty chairs, old magazines, and paintings of Connecticut beaches on the walls. We had the choice to use our insurance or to pay cash. There was no way I was using my dad's insurance for this. Thanks, but no thanks. Cash it was. No paper trail. At least payment was a sliding scale. I calculated how much I "earned" a year and qualified for a smaller fee.

"Have you ever been to a Planned Parenthood before?" Vi asked me. We were sitting side by side in the waiting room. I had just handed in my form but had kept the pen to give my fingers something to do.

"No, you?"

"Once."

"How come?"

"A friend's condom broke. Not her condom. But the guy she was with. So we came here to get the morning-after pill. It made her feel like ass, though. The whole thing freaked her out. At least she realized the condom had broken. What if she hadn't noticed and then gotten pregnant?"

"Would she have had an abortion?"

"I don't know. Probably."

I looked around the room. There was one girl there with her mom; the girl looked slightly older than us, and I wondered if that's what she was here for. Would she come with her mom if it was? "Would you do it? If you got pregnant now?"

"Yes," she said. "Definitely."

I tried not to show my surprise, but I must not have done a very good job.

"My mom was twenty-three," Vi said. "Not seventeen. And my mother had my grandmother to help her. Who would help me?" She paused. "What would you do?"

I felt sad just thinking about it. "I don't know," I said. And I really didn't.

"If you have a kid, I'm totally evicting you. I don't do babies."

I shook off my melancholy. "Hello, I'm not planning on getting pregnant. That's why I'm here."

"Me too. That's why I'm going on the pill *and* using condoms. Liam is not going to be my baby daddy."

"Neither is Noah," I said. Despite all the mental preparation I'd been doing about sex, I hadn't really thought about what I would do if I actually got pregnant. In my mind, losing my virginity and pregnancy had nothing to do with each other. A 3.9 GPA might get me into a good college, but it did not make me a genius.

What would I really do? Have the child? Drop out of school? Would Noah and I get married? Sure, Noah and I joked about it, but I wasn't ready to get married. If I decided to have my hypothetical baby, would I have to go live with my dad and Penny? Or maybe I'd have the baby in France. France was better than Ohio. At least my brother was in France. He could babysit while I unsuccessfully tried to find a husband. What seventeen-year-old guy wanted to date a girl with a baby? I sank into my seat. I didn't want to move anywhere. I wanted to stay here, have sex with Noah, and not have any consequences, ever. I would definitely be using the pill *plus* condoms. If condoms were the goalie, the pill was a defensive line.

"April Berman?" a nurse called.

My stomach leapt.

"I thought I was first," Vi said. "Well, have fun."

I raised an eyebrow and followed the nurse down the hall.

GIDDYUP

It was called a HOPE visit. Hormones with optional pelvic exam. I opted out of the pelvic part. Vi opted in. "Might as well find out what's going on in there," she said. "Plus more details for the article."

First I waited in the little room the nurse put me in. Then a woman with long, flowing blonde hair and a big smile opened the door.

"Hello there!" she cheered, her eyes crinkling. "I'm Dr. Rosini. How are you doing today?"

For some inexplicable reason I loved her immediately and wondered if I could adopt her to be my mother.

She weighed me and took my blood pressure. Then she sat down across from me and started asking questions about my medical history (no problems, regular periods), about my sex life (none yet, but HOPE for future), who my intended partner was (long-term boyfriend; yes, he was my age), did I have someone at home to discuss my sexual relationship with? (Er, yes, Vi was at home.) She asked lots and lots of questions and I gave her lots and lots of answers.

Then we got down to business.

"There are a number of birth control options," she said.

"There's the NuvaRing, there's the Depo-Provera shot, there's condom use, there's the pill."

"I'll take that one," I said.

She laughed. "We can give you a prescription. But remember that while the pill does protect against unintended pregnancy, it does not protect against HIV or STDs."

"Got it," I said. Since I would be Noah's first and he would be mine, we didn't have to worry about that part.

She gave me three months' worth of pills, talked about reactions and side effects, and told me to come back for a prescription when they ran out.

"Take a pink pill every day for twenty-one days, then a white one for seven. Take them at the same time every day."

"Sounds like a plan," I said.

OUT AND ABOUT

Instead of going straight home, since we were playing hooky anyway, we decided to go to the Norwalk mall. "It's time to put another dent in your allowance," Vi said, pulling out of the Planned Parenthood parking lot.

"But what if we need the money?"

"For what?"

"A rainy day?"

She pointed to the gray sky. "Looks like it's about to snow."

"Not sure if that counts."

"You're too good," she said. "You need to live a little."

"Hello! I am skipping school! I went to get birth control! Now I'm shopping when I should be in calculus! I am living a lot!"

"True. But you'd live better in new lingerie."

VICTORIA'S SECRET

After two hours in the mall, I had two new pairs of jeans, a new pair of boots, and three new sweaters. Now I was at Victoria's Secret wearing a black, lacy baby doll in one of the changing rooms in the back of the store.

"How do you look?" Vi called from the changing room next to mine.

Oh. My. God. My boobs were popping over the top, and the lace below showed everything. "Like a porn star," I yelled back, giggling.

"Let me see!"

"Half my butt is hanging out!"

She jumped out of her room and then pulled open the curtain to mine. She was wearing a red silk teddy that tied in the front. "Hells yeah! You do look like a porn star!"

I posed like a pinup girl and slapped my own butt, which looked ridiculous as it was encased in the black baby doll and my own bright pink cotton panties. "I've never actually seen a porn movie."

Vi gave me a wide-eyed look, as if to say, "You sweet, innocent girl, you." Then actually said, "They're demeaning.

But somewhat instructional."

"Look at *you*," I said, indicating her red silkiness.

"It's horrible. I feel like a Christmas gift. I want lingerie that screams power, not please untie me."

I thought of my mother and snort-laughed. "My mother always pronounced it lin-*jer*-y. She is not good with accents."

"Good thing she moved to France."

"She also calls condoms, con-*domes*."

"Ha."

I closed the curtain, slipped off the baby doll, and put my jeans and shirt back on, and then stood in front of her room. "You know, I once made a trip to this very store . . . with my mother."

"You did not!"

"I did. She told me to wait outside with my brother but . . . we got bored."

Vi pulled open her curtain. "Tell me she was buying flannel pajamas."

"Au contraire." I lifted up a package of black thigh-high stockings that the store had conveniently put in a display by the rooms. "She took these on a trip to Cancun."

"Ugh. Did she wear them?"

"Why yes, she did, actually," I said, putting the stockings back.

"It's sick that you know that. It's also sick that I could tell you the symptoms of my mother's UTI infections."

I shook my shoulders as a sign of being creeped out.

"Gross. I'm going to pay for this and check in with Noah."

"Check in? Language like that is why I don't want a boyfriend."

"Call him. You know what I mean. He's probably wondering where I am."

"He must be thrilled you're going on the pill."

I hadn't actually told him yet. I wanted to wait until it was all set. I was thinking I would tell him this weekend when we were casually hanging out in my basement. Finally. He still hadn't been down there with me. Every day after school he had practice or a game or homework, or some family thing he had to do. We'd hung out with other people, I'd cheered at his home games, but we hadn't had a moment alone.

"Oh, by the way," I would say, when we were finally lying next to each other on my futon. "I started taking the pill. In one month it will be working." I'd mention it kind of flippantly, acting all casual and then he'd smile. The joy would radiate across his face. He'd feel loved, I'd feel loved, he'd pull me to him, we'd kiss. In my head it was all very PG. He'd hug me close and tell me he couldn't wait for the month to be up. Maybe we'd even add a fun countdown application to our phones. We'd be super-adorable about it.

But the way things were going . . . he might not make it to my basement for the next month. Maybe I should just tell him.

"Guess where I am?" I said when I reached him.

"I have no idea. Your locker?"

I paused for a sec. "Seriously? You didn't realize I wasn't in school?"

"You're not in school?"

"No, we called in sick."

"What's wrong?"

"Nothing." I suddenly wanted his full attention. "But I did go to the doctor."

"So you are sick?"

"Actually, we went to Planned Parenthood."

Silence. "Really?"

"Yup. And I got the pill."

Another pause. "Oh," he said finally. "Cool."

I had expected something more than "cool." A yippee, or a hooray maybe. He knew what that meant right? "The birth control pill," I said in case it wasn't obvious.

"Yeah, I got that."

Oh. Well. Um. "You sound super-excited."

I heard him cough.

The annoyance bubbled up. "Right. Sorry to bother you."

"April, I'm excited. It's just . . . we never talked about that. I thought we'd just use . . . you know. Other stuff."

Other stuff? If we were old enough to use them I would think we were old enough to say the words. Unless he didn't want anyone to hear him say it out loud. I wondered where he was. In the hallway? He didn't want to use the word condom in the hallway? That I could understand.

"I think we should use both," I said. "Just in case. As backup.

The doc said people usually wait a month for the pill to work."

"So we're going to wait another month?" he asked. Was it my imagination, or did he sound relieved?

"Yeah. Or, we don't have to. We could just use condoms now."

"What's one more month?" he asked. "Better to be safe. One month then."

"Yup. One month."

"Sounds good."

"Yup."

This conversation was definitely less fun than it had been in my head. Maybe I should have waited. Waited until we were together to tell him the news. Not wait for sex.

Sex I was ready for. I already had the outfit.

Noah was the one who didn't sound ready. Maybe he realized what a big step it was. Maybe all the talk about birth control had freaked him out about the actual possibility of getting me pregnant.

I'd have to distract him with my new outfit. I needed to get him in the mood. Maybe I should go back in and get the thigh highs.

My mom's face flashed before my mind.

On second thought . . . I needed to be in the mood, too.

AND THEN THERE WERE THREE

I grabbed our packages then slammed the trunk closed while Vi shut the electronic garage door. Vi opened the

105

door to the house. It was after six—once we were at the mall, we decided to see a movie.

"That's weird," she said. "Do you hear that? Did you leave the music on again?"

"No," I said. Last week I'd left the music on. And the lights. Twice. Vi wasn't thrilled. Turns out you have to pay for electricity—like, every month. Who knew?

"The lights are on too. I definitely turned those off. Maybe it's Zelda."

I stepped back. The murder scenes from *Vampire Nights* and every other horror show replayed in my head. Stupid people walked into their houses and got slaughtered. "Do you think we should call the police?" I asked, but she was already inside. The house wasn't the most burglarproof. And it was next door to the public part of the sound. In low tide anyone could stroll in from the road, down the beach, and climb right onto our deck.

"A burglar doesn't blast the music," she said, her voice trailing off as she went farther down the hall. Then I heard, "Holy shit!"

"What? Vi?" I ran in after her and took the stairs two at a time. What if it really was a killer? What if it was crazy Lucy? And she was going to murder us?

Vi was sitting crossed-legged on the carpet holding a tiny orange-sherbet-colored kitten.

"Is this not the cutest thing you've ever seen?" she asked. "Who's the cutest? You are, you are," she cooed.

Aw! A kitten! "Hello there." I crouched beside them. I missed Libby.

"Meow."

"Aw. Did the adorable kitten turn on the music?" I asked, kicking off my boots.

"Dean did," she said, motioning to a bag and shoes by the door. "That's his. He's such a slob."

"Dean's here?" I asked, looking around. "Where?"

"I'm guessing in the bathroom."

We heard a flush and then Dean appeared. "Your mommies are home, kitty!"

"Ex-squeeze me?" Vi asked, raising an eyebrow.

"A mommy is someone who's supposed to take care of you," I explained. "I know it's a strange concept, but it happens all over the world." Except of course, when she's in France.

Vi snorted.

"A friend of Hudson's has a cat who had kittens," Dean said. "She's looking for homes. Hudson thought April might want her . . . after losing her cat. I told him I'd ask."

That was sweet of him to think of me. "Why didn't Hudson come by?" I asked, disappointed. Hudson made me feel . . . gutsy. Even if he was maybe a drug dealer. No one's perfect.

"He had to work," Dean said, looking down.

"Where does he work again?" Vi asked.

"You know. At a job," Dean said with a laugh.

"What is the big secret?" I asked. "I don't get it. Unless he really is doing something illegal."

Dean shrugged. "I don't know what you're talking about."

"You're so annoying," Vi snapped.

"Ask him yourself. He's coming to get me in two minutes. So nice of you two to finally come home. I've been waiting for hours. Where were you today?"

Vi ignored him and looked over to me. "Should we keep her?"

I twined my fingers around her tail. "Do you want to live with us, cutie?"

She reached over and petted my hand with her paw. Double aw.

"How did you get in?" I asked him.

"I used the key in the birdhouse."

I scratched behind the kitten's ears. She purred. "There's a key in the birdhouse?" I asked. "Good to know."

"So, what do you think?" Dean asked. "Vi's house, party of three?"

The kitten opened her big green eyes and licked her right paw.

"I'm in if you are," I said, already madly in love.

"All right," Vi said. She pointed at the kitten. "You can hang out with us. But you're going to have to behave. No skipping school."

I made kissy faces.

"What should we name her?" Vi asked.

"'We could call her Tiger,'" I sang. "'But there's no bite

in her. Tiger! Kittens would frighten her. . . .'"

Vi rubbed her temples. "Please. No show tunes. And she *is* a kitten. Let's call her Zelda."

"Creepy," I said.

"What about Donut?" Dean asked.

Vi snorted. "Where did that come from?"

"I like donuts."

"You like the food or the name?" I asked.

"Both."

"Me too," I said.

Vi lifted her up and carried her to the kitchen. "Come with Mommy, Donut. Welcome to chateau Vi."

"We promise not to take you lingerie shopping," I said.

"Or discuss our urinary tract infections."

"TMI," Dean groaned.

"Not mine, dumbass. My mother's. Anyway. Donut, we promise not to make you pay bills."

"Or leave you alone," I added. "Ever."

Vi filled a bowl with water. "Although you will have to be alone when we're at school."

"Right," I said, laughing. One day away and I'd forgotten it existed.

The doorbell rang. "Hudson!" I ran to the hallway and called, throwing open the door, "You are the best! Thank you!"

He stayed on the porch, smiling at me. "Does that mean you're keeping her?"

"Of course. How could we not? She had me at meow.

Come in. Donut wants to say hi."

"Donut?"

"Your brother's idea."

"Don't you know by now never to listen to my brother?"

"I heard that!" Dean yelled.

"We gotta go!" Hudson yelled back.

"You're not staying?" I asked, disappointed.

He shrugged. "Can't. Another time."

"Oh, okay. Thanks again," I said. I kind of wanted to give him a hug, but then I thought it might be weird. I didn't want him to think I was throwing myself at him. I'm sure he had enough girls who actually were throwing themselves at him.

Screw it. He just brought me a kitten; I was giving him a hug. "Thank you," I said into his collar. I felt his arms tighten around me. He smelled like new leather. I pulled away. "New jacket?" I asked.

He blinked. "Yeah."

"Looks expensive," I said, putting my hand on my hip. "Coming from work?"

He smiled again.

Dean appeared beside me. "Wouldn't you like to know."

"Whatever," Vi said. She was cradling Donut in her arms.

Hudson reached out and tickled under Donut's chin. "Hey, Donut, you've got a new home now. Be a good girl." Then he tickled under Vi's chin. "You too, Vi."

Vi fake purred.

Dean headed out the door. "All right, ladies, we'd love to

sit and purr with you all night, but . . . actually we wouldn't."

"See you at school," Hudson said before following Dean to the car.

"Ach, that place," I said. "I guess we'll have to go tomorrow."

Vi linked her free arm through mine as I waved good-bye to the boys. "I'm sure Jake.Berman@pmail.com would be happy to email again if you want to skip."

"My dad," I said, "what a giver."

number four:
bought a hot tub

MY REAL DAD'S SCARY EMAIL (FROM HIS NEW REAL
ADDRESS) TO FAKE SUZANNE

From: Jake Berman <Jake.Berman@kljco.com>
Date: Sun, 25 Jan, 7:03 a.m.
To: Suzanne Caldwell <Suzanne_Caldwell@pmail.com>
Subject: Checking In

Suzanne,
Hope all is well. Spoke to April last night and she seems happy. She praised your
cooking, too—thanks for taking such good care of my princess. I wasn't thrilled
with this plan, but it seems to be working out. Am in Chicago for the next week, but
always reachable via email or cell.
Best, Jake

Sent From BlackBerry

NERVOUS NELLY

"Should I be concerned that my father is going to run into your mother on a street corner in Chicago?" I asked.

"Your father's email was sent at 7:03 A.M. I am confident that when my mother is on street corners, your father is fast asleep."

"So that's a no." I scratched Donut behind the ears.

"Meow."

"Stop worrying."

"Right. Grip. Getting one."

LONELY IN CLEVELAND

The cell rang. Private number.

"Hello?" I said uncertainly.

"Hi, April! It's Penny!"

"Oh. Penny. Hey." I had just spilled Donut's food all over the floor, and was in the process of sweeping it up. "Is everything okay? My dad's in Chicago, right?"

"Yes, he's fine. Everything's great! I was just thinking of you. Thought I'd call and see how you're doing."

Weird. Penny doesn't generally call me to see how I'm doing. Or ever. "I'm fine. Thanks. Just . . . cleaning."

"That's great. Good for you." Silence, of the awkward variety. "So. How's school?"

"Same as usual."

"And Vi?"

"Good too."

"And the car?"

"Car's great. Thanks again."

"My pleasure. I told your dad you needed a car. It wasn't safe for you to be without one."

"He told me." I realized it would be wise for me to go on and talk to her for a while so that she'd give a good report to my dad. I also realized—double weird—that she sounded lonely. So I said, "What are you up to?"

"I'm trying to settle in. The house is a mess, of course. And it's freezing here. Colder than Connecticut even. Strange to be back. And I've been trying to do some painting, but it's hard to focus with all the unpacking I still need to do. . . ."

As she kept talking, I tried to balance the phone against my shoulder with the broom, but ended up spilling more cat food on the floor. At one point she told me she missed me (what she actually said was, "I kind of miss cleaning up after you," but I went ahead and read between the lines). If she missed me so much, then she shouldn't have moved to Cleveland and dragged my dad with her.

PENNY

After my dad and Penny got engaged, my dad bought another place in Westport. Sorry, my dad *and Penny* bought another place in Westport. Since we were there every second week-end, Matthew and I each got our own rooms. I took the one next to my dad's because it was the bigger one. I would have taken Matthew's, which was on the other side of the stairs, if I'd known that, unlike Matthew, I was going to move in full-time. But anyway.

Penny bought me a bed with a canopy. She'd always wanted one as a girl, and always wanted to have a girl with a canopy bed. So there you go.

Penny couldn't have kids. I knew this because one day in the car, I'd asked them if they were going to have a baby. Penny got all teary. Later, my father explained that Penny had fibroid tumors. She and her ex-husband tried for seven years, but they never got pregnant. They even tried in vitro a few times but it didn't work.

You'd think she would have been happier about inheriting a stepdaughter.

She was probably excited about the idea of me—less so with the reality.

A fifteen-year-old who you can share makeup with and see every two weeks sounds adorable.

A fifteen-year-old who gets bombed with her friends two weeks after moving in with you full-time? Less so.

PASS THE GUAC

"We need to coordinate," Vi said during taco prep. "When's your big night? We have to make sure that it's not the same as mine. That would be weird."

I grated some cheese. "It would?"

"Hells yeah. We need to each have the house to ourselves."

I hardly ever had the house to myself. Vi was home a lot. As was I. We spent *a lot* of time together. I've never actually spent this much time with anyone . . . besides my family. Not even Noah.

"Definitely," I said. "So I was kind of thinking . . . Valentine's Day."

"Really?" she asked with a raise of the eyebrow while seasoning the pot of beef.

"What's wrong with Valentine's Day? Too cheesy?" I popped some cheddar in my mouth.

"Yes," she said.

"You say cheesy, I say romantic. And practical. I started taking the pill the third week of January. We wanted to wait a month. That Saturday is Valentine's Day. It makes sense to do it for the first time on a Saturday night."

"Will you cover your duvet in rose petals too?"

"Oh, shut up," I said, privately storing the idea away. Rose petals on the duvet could be really cute.

"Can you make the guac?" Vi asked.

"Um . . . we make guac? Don't you just open it?"

"No, darling. Get an avocado, an onion, and a tomato."

I did as I was told. And accidentally dropped a piece of cheese on the floor. Donut gobbled it up. Whoops.

"Now cut the avocado in half, scoop it, smush it, and add in a diced onion and tomato."

Blink. Blink, blink.

She laughed. "What did you eat before you met me? McDonald's?"

"My mom was a fan of the drive-through. Penny cooked, though. Lots of fish. Donut would have loved it."

Donut was now standing in front of the oven. *"Meow?"*

"You just never helped."

"Not so much."

She nodded. "No wonder they kicked you out."

Ouch. That kind of hurt actually. To hide it, I stuck out my tongue and said, "Not exactly. So when is your big night gonna be?"

"I'm thinking . . . the night *before* Valentine's Day."

"Isn't that just as cheesy?"

"No. That way when I get to tell the story of how I lost my virginity, I get to say it was on Friday the thirteenth."

My phone rang. "Hey, Noah," I said, laughing. "How was practice?"

"Tiring," he said over the static of his cell.

"I think we made too much," Vi said. "Tell Noah to come over for dinner."

"Vi wants you to come over for dinner. Where are you?"

"Driving home. Thanks. I'm really tired, though. And my parents are expecting me."

"So tell them you're coming here instead."

"Wish I could," he said.

I hadn't realized I'd wanted to see him until he said he

couldn't come. "Can we talk later? We're just cooking."

"Yup."

"Love you," I said.

"You too."

I clicked off the phone and dropped it on the counter.

"Do you say 'I love you' every time you talk on the phone?"

"Most of the time," I said.

"Does it mean good-bye? Or does it mean *I love you*?" she asked.

"Both," I said. Which was true. Most of the time. Although lately I was always the one saying the "I love you," and he was the one saying the "you too." What was up with that?

"Maybe I should invite Dean and Hud over," she said, stirring the pot.

"Sure," I said, still thinking about Noah. "The more the merrier."

THE FIRST TIME WE SAID I LOVE YOU

"What should I do?" I asked Marissa. It was right before sophomore year, the day after I'd come home from France, the day after I'd found out about Corinne and Noah. I was in her room and I couldn't stop crying.

"It sucks," she said. "If I'd been around this summer and seen the two of them together, I would have kicked their asses."

"Thanks." I sighed.

"But you did tell him he could see other people."

"Yeah."

"I don't know." She shook her head and rubbed my arm. "I think you have to do what feels right. You either have to get over it, or end it."

"Break up?" The idea made me feel weak. Empty. Terrified. "What do you think I should do?"

She bit her lip. "I think it would make me very sad if you broke up. You guys are an amazing couple—the best couple. You've been so much happier since you got together."

I knew what she meant—in the last nine months, since Noah and I had gotten together, I'd felt afloat. Even when my mom decided to move to Paris, I'd kept the black hole at bay. Noah was my lifesaver, I guess. Noah and Marissa. "So you think I should forgive him? Pretend nothing happened?"

"Can you?" she asked.

"I don't know."

My cell rang. "It's Noah."

"Answer," she urged.

"Hi," I said, picking up.

"Hi," he said. "How are you?"

I rolled into a ball and cradled the phone against my ear. "I've been better."

"Do you hate me?"

I laughed. "A little."

"Meet me at the park across from my house?"

"When?"

"Now?"

I looked up at Marissa. She nodded. "Go."

I ran. It was more of a garden than a park. He was waiting for me on the green bench.

"Hello, cutie."

"Don't 'cutie' me," I said. "I'm still mad at you."

"But your cuteness needs to be expressed. Especially now. Have you decided to forgive me yet? Pretty please?"

"No. How do I know you're not going to break up with me to start seeing her?" I asked, sitting beside him.

"Because it's over."

"But how do I know it's over?" I wanted tangible proof. A signed document they'd gotten notarized that I could hold in my hand and refer to.

"Because it is," he said. "I don't love her."

Everything froze. "And——?" I waited.

"I love you."

You imagine hearing the words from someone not related to you, someone not your best friend, but when someone you love, someone you dream about, actually says them, it makes your body melt and your breath get caught in your chest.

"You love me?" I asked, leaning toward him.

He nodded.

"Say it again," I said. I let my knee bump against his.

"I love you," he repeated.

Yes, he had hooked up with someone else. One of my classmates. But did it matter? I'd told him he could. And what was I supposed to do now? Break up with him?

I'd decided to stay in Westport. I'd let my mother and brother move to the other side of the world. If we broke up now, what was I here for?

"I love you too," I said, the words soft and smooth in my mouth. I did love him, I realized.

And we were back together.

STICKY FINGERS

"So where did you apply?" I asked Hudson. The four of us were sitting at the dining room table, enjoying Mexican night. We were on our third taco each.

"Brown," he said.

"Wow. When do you hear?"

"He already heard," Dean said. "Early decision. Jackass. Trying to make me look bad."

"Congrats," I said. "That's amazing." Maybe he wasn't a drug dealer. Maybe he was some kind of junior executive or entrepreneurial genius. "What about you, Dean?"

"I applied everywhere. But I'm hoping for UCLA. Or USC. Or anyplace on the West Coast that takes me. Bring me some of them California girls."

"Do you know how ridiculous you sound?" Vi asked.

"They write songs about California girls for a reason," he

countered. Then he blew her a kiss.

"April, can you pass the guac?" Hudson said. "This is good guac. And I know guac."

"Thank you," I said. "I made it. Plucked the avocados and everything."

"Is it me," Dean said, "or does this feel like a double date?"

I blushed. It kind of felt like that to me too. Not cool.

"You wish," Vi said.

"*You* wish," Dean repeated.

"I have my sights on someone," Vi said, helping herself to another taco. "And it *isn't* you."

Dean put a hand to his heart. "Who?"

"Liam."

Dean narrowed his eyes. "He's a bozo. A lucky bozo."

"Are you guys friends?" Hudson asked.

"No," Vi said. "But I've been trying to get his attention."

"So that's why you've been wearing all those low-cut tops!" Dean exclaimed.

Vi lowered her head and sighed. "At least someone's noticing."

I took another bite of my taco. "Maybe he's playing hard to get."

"He's not playing hard to get. He *is* hard to get. I've been following him for weeks and nothing!"

"Maybe . . . that's the problem?" Hudson offered. "Some guys don't like being chased."

"Please, Sloane chased you all the way through the school and parking lot," Vi said, smirking.

"I didn't say *I* didn't like being chased," Hudson said. He cocked his head and smiled.

"What happened with you and Sloane?" I asked. "Did you break up because of the long distance? What school did she go to?"

"Northwestern," he said. "But no. We just weren't right for each other."

"Hudson knew she wasn't the one," Dean said in a slightly mocking tone.

"She was only the first," Vi added slyly.

Now Hudson blushed. "I realized I didn't feel the way about her that I was supposed to. I didn't think it was fair to stay together."

"She certainly still feels that way about you," Dean said. "She tried to molest him over Christmas break."

"Dean, come on," Hudson said.

"Well, she did. She kept stopping by our house in inappropriate-for-the-weather outfits. But my brother kept turning her down."

"Guys do that?" Vi asked. She pulled out a notebook and a pen from who knows where. "The stereotype is that guys will have sex with anyone. False?"

"True," Dean said. "Usually."

"So why didn't you?" Vi asked Hudson.

Hudson looked uncomfortable. "I didn't want her to

think it meant something that it didn't. And you are not allowed to quote me."

"You'll be anonymous, don't worry. So you would have had sex if there had been no repercussions."

"You mean, would I have had sex if I thought she wouldn't regret it the next day?"

"Exactly. If she was also over you but thought one last night together would be fun."

He considered. "Then I probably would not have asked her to leave, no."

"So it's not a matter of being in love?" I asked, disappointed.

"Not yet," he said, looking at me. "But I hope that next time it will be."

"It's always about love for me," Dean said.

"You must fall in love a lot," I said, laughing.

"I do," he said. "I really do. I could fall in love with both of you tonight if you'd like me to."

"Pass," Vi and I said simultaneously.

"Probably for the best." Dean waved his taco in the air. "You ladies used enough onions in here to kill a vampire."

I laughed and took a long sip of my water. "Vampires are allergic to garlic, not onions," I explained. "Don't you watch *Vampire Nights*?"

"No," Hudson said. "Should we?"

"*Helloo!*" I squealed. "We may have to watch it right now. I have the DVD of season one. And two. And three."

"Marathon! Marathon! Marathon!" Dean cheered,

thumping his fists on the table.

Hudson nodded. "Let's do it."

We each made ourselves another taco, migrated over to the couch, and settled in with our plates on our laps. Donut jumped onto the couch and sat between me and Hudson.

"You," Vi said, pointing to Dean. "Do not touch anything. I don't want salsa stains on every couch cushion."

We all chomped happily while the first episode played. Donut nibbled on my leftover cheese.

"I'm making myself another taco," Vi said before we started the second episode. "Anyone?"

"I'll take one," Hudson said. "Do you want help?" Donut had cuddled into a ball on his lap.

"You look kind of trapped," Vi told him. "I got it. Three tacos coming up. Dean, I'm assuming you want one too."

Halfway through episode two, my cell rang. Noah. "Hey," I whispered. "What's up?"

"Why are you whispering? Did you move back to your dad's?"

"Yeah, right. Hold on." I hoisted myself up and wandered toward Vi's bathroom, away from the TV. "Hi," I said, louder.

"Are you in bed?" he asked. The clock read 12:06. I hadn't realized it had gotten so late.

"No, we're watching *Vampire Nights*."

"You and Vi?"

"Yeah," I said. Guilt flicked through me like a static shot. "And Dean and his brother."

125

"Hudson."

"Yeah."

"Okay," he snipped. "So you're not going to bed?"

"Um . . . not this second. Maybe in fifteen?" I didn't want to call it a night yet. I was having fun. But I couldn't exactly tell my boyfriend I preferred to stay up watching TV with two other guys.

As I hung up, Vi walked passed me, looking a bit pale.

"You okay?" I asked.

"Not feeling great," she said. "I overdid it on the tacos. Boys!" she called. "It's time for you to go home."

Noah would be happy.

"We only got through two episodes," Dean complained. "You two are the worst marathoners ever."

"Next time," I promised. I looked up to see Hudson watching me.

"Next time," Hudson repeated.

Vi attacked the mess in the kitchen. "I'll load, you clean off the table," she instructed.

Guess I wasn't calling Noah back just yet.

GOOD-NIGHT KISSES

Twenty minutes later I was in bed, my cell pressed against my ear. Noah's phone was ringing. And ringing. And ringing. Donut curled into my stomach.

"Hello?" he finally answered, voice hoarse.

"Hi," I said. "Still up?"

"Mmm–hmmm," he said, clearly not.

"Go back to bed," I said.

"'Kay. Love you," he mumbled.

The words warmed my whole body, even though I'd heard them a hundred times. I just hadn't heard them recently. Not from him first. "You too," I said. "Good night."

I hung up the phone and pulled Donut on top of me. "Don't worry, Donut, I love you too."

"Meow," she responded, clearly reciprocating the emotion.

Thump. Thump. Thump. Thump.

What the hell? I stared up at the ceiling.

Thump. Thump. Thump. Thump.

I climbed out of bed and up the stairs, carrying Donut with me. A man's voice was booming on the other side of the door. The voice sounded familiar.

"Vi?" I asked, peeking into the living room.

Vi was on her yoga mat, in her workout gear, doing stomach crunches. Her workout DVD was glowing from the TV.

"Hey," she said. "Is it too loud? I was trying not to wake you."

"It's okay, I was just wondering what was going on."

"I wanted to do a quick workout."

Okay . . . weird. "In the middle of the night?"

Donut meowed, clearly agreeing with me.

"I'm almost done," she said, looking ahead.

"Good night," I said. I closed the door behind me and went back to bed.

MEOW

"You're getting so big!" I told my brother a few days later when we were Skyping. He seemed older somehow. . . . His shoulders seemed wider. I felt pangs of pride and sadness. He was growing up without me. "You're not shaving yet, are you?"

He stuck out his tongue. "Let me get Mom. She wants to Skype with you."

"But I called to talk to you," I told my brother.

"Talk to her for two secs, and then I'll be back."

"'Kay. Really come back, though."

"Hi," my mom chirped. "You look great! I can't believe you got a new cat!"

"You look good too," I said. "Very . . . blond. Why can't you believe I got a cat?"

"Cats are a lot of work!"

"They're not that much work," I said. Donut was sitting on my stomach at that very moment. "And I'm very responsible. Say hi, Donut."

"*Meow.*"

"We'll see," she said.

"You're one to talk," I said. "You gave Libby away."

"I couldn't take her with me!" She shook her head. Then shook her head again.

"You could have," I said. "You just chose not to."

"April—"

"What? It's true." I scratched Donut under the chin. "Where's Matthew? I really wanted to talk to him."

"Oh. Okay. Have you thought about when you want to visit this summer?"

"Not yet," I said.

"When you have a chance . . ."

"Will do." Donut yawned, stretched her paws, then put her head back down on my stomach. I would never leave my cat behind. I would never leave anyone behind.

MY MOM WENT TO CANCUN AND ALL I GOT WAS A FRENCH STEPFATHER

It was not a family trip to Cancun. It was a Divorcées Gone Wild trip to Cancun. My mother went with her older sister, Linda (also recently divorced), and Linda's friend Pamela. They went for a week. My mom wore the thigh highs. She had a wild fling with the Frenchman Daniel. Then she returned to Westport and he returned to Paris and we thought that was it, au revoir.

"You're never going to see him again?" I'd asked. I was in the front seat and fourth-grade Matthew was behind me, kicking my seat. It was February of my freshman year.

"Nope," she said. It had been three weeks since she'd been back, and her tan—as well as her fling—seemed to be long gone. "What would be the point? It's not like I'm going to pick up and move to Paris."

"Why not?" I'd said. "France would be so awesome." I had romantic notions of espressos at street-corner cafés and cinched, lavender trench coats.

"You want to move to Paris?" she'd asked, turning into the elementary school's circular driveway.

"Not right this second," I'd said. "I can't just leave my life. I can't just leave my friends." And Noah. We'd been together for three months. "I'll finish high school in America and then come for college. It'll be *très* glamorous."

It did sound glamorous. But I only encouraged it because I didn't think it could happen. That a mom—my mom—could just pick up and move to Paris.

A week later Daniel emailed. And then my mom emailed back. And then as fast as you could say "bon voyage" my mom was picking up and moving to Paris. And taking Matthew with her. Apparently I was old enough to make my own decisions.

"I'd like you to come too," she said to me.

"Not happening," I said flippantly. "I'm living with Dad," I'd told her. Partially to hurt her.

"For now," my mom responded.

"We'll see," I'd said. Her face scrunched up, giving her forehead extra wrinkles but I didn't care. She deserved it.

It was a clean break. Mom took Matthew. Mom paid for all things Matthew. Dad took me. Dad paid for all things me.

If you peeked into their bank accounts, you'd know I got the better end of the deal.

My dad had been shocked. Even though he'd gotten remarried so quickly, I guess he hadn't expected my mom to do the same. Plus move to France. Plus take Matthew. And leave me. I probably shouldn't have been the one to unload the new plan on him, but I guess my mother didn't want to. I'd always been closer with my mother, and Matthew had been closer with my dad, so once I told him Mom was getting remarried and moving, he assumed Matthew would want to stay and I'd want to go.

Except my mom hadn't given Matthew a choice, and it felt like I didn't have one either.

THE COUGAR IN THE HOOD

I hadn't told my mom the entire truth about Donut.

Taking care of a pet was harder than I'd expected.

When I was little I thought I'd make a great parent. I taught Matthew how to tie his shoelaces, I helped him with his math homework, and I read to him at night. I also had many dolls. Thirty-five. Anytime there was a reason to get a present I begged for a doll. Birthdays, Hanukkah, Valentine's Day, anything. I knew all their names and changed their outfits when I could and pretended to feed them and diaper them, and put them to bed. But dolls (and brothers) didn't push your door closed and then meow when they couldn't reopen it. They didn't dart outside every time someone came in or left the house. Or create a foul smell that wafted from the little alcove we had declared Donut's in the kitchen. Or coil themselves around your calves and try to eat you.

Sure, Donut also snuggled. And licked my fingers. And slept on my stomach. But she also took up a lot of my time. She needed things. Litter boxes. Kitty chow. Fresh water. Shots. More shots. Since Vi was usually busy with *The Issue* stuff after school, I took Donut to the vet. Now, I turned off Grand Road and took a shortcut through Kantor Street. Wait. Was that—?

Hudson. Ringing someone's doorbell.

I hit the brakes so I wouldn't drive past him. "Check it out, Donut!" I said.

"Meow."

Maybe I could finally find out what Hudson's secret was. Not that I thought he was a drug dealer. Would he really be dealing at five P.M. in the suburbs?

The door opened and I craned my neck to see inside. Was it someone from school?

Holy crap.

It was Ms. Franklin. My calculus teacher.

"What the . . . ?"

I called Vi's cell but she didn't answer.

I tried Marissa instead. After explaining the situation, I said, "Why would Hudson be going into Ms. Franklin's house?" As I said the words, I felt a pang of . . . of something.

She laughed. "He wouldn't."

"He just did."

"She doesn't teach senior math," Marissa told me. "Although maybe what they say is true."

"What?"

"That he's an escort."

I snort laughed. "Please."

"You've never heard that? He is hot."

"What guy from Westport is an escort? I bet he models, and that's how he could afford his Jeep."

"Why the big secret if he models?" she asks. "Maybe he's having an affair with Ms. Franklin. She's hot too."

I pushed any weird feelings away and said, "Maybe she's his sugar mommy."

"Can you be a sugar mommy on a teacher's salary?"

"You should see her house," I said, before hanging up. I eyed the multiple floors and BMW in the driveway. Ms. Franklin could afford a young sexy thing if she wanted one.

I took my foot off the brake and kept going. "Donut," I said, "calculus has just gotten a lot more interesting."

A SNAG IN THE PLAN

Vi banged the back of her head against my locker. "Disaster," she said.

"What's wrong?" I said. My thoughts flew immediately to our living arrangements—omigod, had we been caught?—and my pulse quickened.

"I'll show you what's wrong." She grabbed my hand and pulled me down the hall to the cafeteria. "That. Is. Very. Wrong."

Jodi Dillon and Liam Packinson were making out in the back of the cafeteria.

I sighed in relief. Then I refocused, devoting my attention to Vi. "Uh-oh."

"You were right," she said.

"That you shouldn't sleep with someone you barely know?"

"No. That redheads are the devil."

HIT THE ROAD

"There's nothing wrong with waiting," Marissa said from the backseat of my car, on our way home from school that afternoon. "Aaron and I are waiting until this summer. Until we're ready."

"Aaron and you are waiting because you live in Westport and he lives in Boston. Not the same thing," I said. I tapped my fingers on the steering wheel. This morning, Vi had wanted to review her notes before an American history test, so I had been allowed to drive. She'd skipped her *Issue* meeting to come home with us.

"We could have done it last summer, but we didn't. You don't just decide to have sex because you feel like having sex. You decide to have sex once you realize you're in love with someone and want to express that love physically. Are you sure you're ready, April? You don't have to do it. Even though you're on the pill, you can wait until you're sure."

"Oh, blah," Vi said, rolling her eyes at me. "Where did you find her? She's a bigger cheeseball than you are."

"Noah and I are ready," I said, and turned right at the corner. "I'm sure."

"How do you know?" Marissa asked.

Since I didn't know the answer to that, I said, "You just know." We'd been together for over two years, we'd been saying "I love you" for a year and a half . . . we'd done everything else. And I did want things to change. I wanted to change things between us. I wanted to make things . . . better. Stronger. And sex would do that. I could tell that my new life was causing some sort of disconnect between us, and I wanted us to get back that intimate feeling. And sex was nothing if not intimate.

"Vi, how did you know you were ready?" Marissa asked.

I held my breath.

Vi laughed. "Since you're part of the family now, I'll fill you in on my secret. I've never done it."

Marissa gasped. "You lied during I Never?"

"I did."

"Why?"

"Because I . . . I don't know. It was stupid. But it's not like I was under oath. Anyway, I'm sick of being a virgin. I'm doing it on February thirteenth."

I looked over at her. "Um . . . Jodi and Liam are back together. What are you going to do—lure him with candy?"

"No," Vi said. "I'm going to sleep with Dean."

"What?" I shrieked.

Vi's cheeks turned red. "It's a better plan. It would be too messy with Liam anyway."

"Messy . . . how?" I asked. "Physically?"

"Messy *emotionally*. If I slept with Liam, I would have to worry—does he like me? Did I do it right? What is he going to think of me? I don't want to deal with any of that. I want my first experience to be only about the sex. I trust Dean. He taught me how to drive. He can teach me how to have sex, too."

I almost missed a stop sign and slammed on the brakes. "Driving, sex, same thing."

Marissa laughed.

"Have you informed him yet?" I asked.

"Not yet. I want to get ready first."

"Get ready . . . emotionally?" I asked.

"No. Physically. I still don't have the right outfit. Or a plan."

Marissa poked her head between our seats. "How about, 'Come over, Dean, I'd like to have sex'? That might work."

"And then he'll respond, 'yes, yes, yes,'" I told her. "Easy peasy." I made a right onto Marissa's street.

"I think I want it to feel more spontaneous," she said. "That's why I need a really good plan. I need a way to set the stage. Something hot. Something sexy. Something—" She gasped. "Look at that. That is what we need. That is the plan. Look!"

I saw where she was pointing. On Marissa's neighbor's

upstairs deck was a glorious, bubbling hot tub.

"Oh, Vi," I said. "Yes, yes, yes."

PARTY ON, DUDE

"This is insane," I told her. We'd dropped Marissa off, and Vi and I were standing inside the glass walls of Party On!, the hot-tub store. Dance music was blasting, even though it was four o'clock on a Wednesday afternoon.

"This is brilliant," Vi said. Her expression was rapturous as she took in the wood spas, small spas, green spas. All filled with bubbling water.

"We should have brought our bathing suits."

"Maybe they'll let us go in our birthday suits."

"This isn't Cancun," I told her.

A guy in his twenties with a goatee, ripped jeans, and a Party On! navy shirt slunk up behind us. "Hey there, girls, I'm Stan. Are you looking for a party?"

"Um . . ." I giggled.

"We are looking to rent a hot tub," Vi said.

He nodded emphatically. "A party in a tub, that's what I'm talking about."

"Party on then. We'd like some information about renting one?"

"For parties, graduations, bachelor parties . . . whatever." He gave us a big smile and scratched his goatee. "What school do you go to?"

"Hillsdale."

"Yeah? I went to Johnson. Graduated two years ago."

"Congratulations," Vi said.

I adjusted my purse. "How much do the hot tubs cost?"

"They start at a hundred and ninety-nine dollars for a Thursday to Monday rental. Or you can do a Monday to Friday rental. That includes delivery and setup. And your party is ready to rock!"

"Excuse me?" I asked.

"The water is delivered heated. You'll be good to go."

"We'd like to rent one for Valentine's Day weekend," Vi said.

He nodded. "I'll tell you what. I'm getting new inventory in on Monday. For a thousand dollars you can have the Hula."

"Have the Hula . . . to keep?" Vi asked. "You mean buy it?"

"What's a Hula?" I asked.

"The pink spa. Over there." He pointed to a plastic, pink hot tub on the other side of the room. "It seats six. It's winterized. What do you think? Interested?"

"We don't have a thousand dollars," Vi said.

A hot tub in our yard? For the rest of the year . . . and beyond? Yes, yes, yes. "What if we pay you in installments?" I asked.

He scratched the tip of his goatee again. If it was so itchy maybe he should shave it off. "I like you girls, so I'll tell you what. Give me a two-hundred-dollar deposit today. You can give me the rest this weekend when I deliver it."

"I can't afford it," Vi said.

"But I can," I told her. I wanted to do this for Vi. I wanted to make her happy. To thank her for taking me in. "How about two hundred today, another two hundred when you deliver it, and then another four hundred on March first?" I asked.

"And what about the last two hundred?"

"Are you sure?" Vi asked me.

I nodded. "And I think eight hundred is a fair price. All cash."

He laughed. "So, on March first you'll pay the final four hundred?"

I nodded again. The day my dad filled my bank account.

"You girls got yourself a deal."

Vi threw her arms around me. "You're the best."

I felt proud and warm all over. Almost like . . . I was already in the Hula.

CLICK THOSE HEELS TOGETHER

We were two minutes away from my old house on Oakbrook. The house I'd grown up in. The house I'd lived in with my mom and dad and Matthew. The whole happy family. All I'd have to do is turn left at the light and then take a right and then another right.

"I can't believe the score we just got," Vi exclaimed, her feet up on the dashboard.

"He liked us." When I stopped at the light on Morgan Street I could feel the old pull to turn left. Turn left! Turn left!

"He liked imagining us in his hot tubs," Vi said.

I turned left.

Vi squinted out the window. "Are we going to your old house?"

"You remember?"

"Of course I remember."

"Do you mind?"

"Not at all."

I could taste the nervous anticipation as we got closer. Left on Woodward Way. Would it look different? Right on West Columbia. Was I different? Right again, and there we were on Oakbrook Road. My street, on my block, in front of my house.

My *old* house. I pulled up to the curb and put the Honda in PARK. My shoulders relaxed.

"Wow, it looks exactly the same," Vi said. It did. But didn't. The door, which used to be reddish brown, was now painted crisp and white. Same with the windowsills. The pine trees my dad and I had planted at the side of the house by the garage were taller now and came right up to my window, which was on the second floor. I loved that room. My cherry wallpaper. My white-and-pink carpet. My amazing bed. I loved that bed. It was a wooden platform bed, the pine stained pale pink. The mattress had just the right softness and was always the right temperature. My comforter matched the platform. Best bed in the history of beds.

I shook my head to clear it. Romanticizing? Me?

Remembering details about the new owners, I expected to see a mom playing with her toddler in the family room, where my parents used to play with me. But the room was empty. The window shades were a quarter up, and the lights were off. And—oh!—a FOR SALE sign was in the yard.

"They're selling already," Vi said. "Didn't they just move in?"

"A year and a half ago."

"Fast."

A year and a half seemed like a lifetime ago for me. Two years earlier I lived behind those blinds with my mother and brother. Double that and my father lived there too.

"We should go inside," Vi said.

"No one's home."

"I bet there's a window open or something."

"You want to break into my old house?" I said. I thought about the back door and how we used to keep an extra key under the mat. I wondered if it was still there. I almost told Vi, but I knew she'd want to go for it, and I wasn't sure I did. I wasn't sure if it would make me feel better or worse. Looking at my house made me feel rooted. It should have made me feel the opposite, but it didn't. Once upon a time, my whole family had lived here together. And yeah, maybe everyone else had left, but my street was still here. My house was still here. I was still here.

Last woman standing.

"Let's go home," Vi said, startling me.

Home. Where was home? What was home?

I swallowed and put the car into DRIVE. My chest tightened as we pulled away.

LET THE PARTY BEGIN

Stan and two other Party On! employees arrived on Sunday to set up our hot tub. Our beautiful, glorious, flamingo-pink hot tub, with preheated water and cup holders. Squee!

"We probably didn't really *need* a hot tub," Vi said.

"Of course we don't *need* a hot tub. Nobody *needs* a hot tub. We *want* a hot tub. We are two hot girls living on our own. Why shouldn't we have a hot tub?" I said.

"Good point."

We watched them through the glass doors.

"But it's twenty degrees outside," I said. "Do you think we might lose body parts if we try it tonight?" The backyard was covered in snow. Even the sound was frozen over.

"We might," she said. "On the other hand . . ."

"How could we not?"

When they were done, Stan knocked and waved. "All set! Wanna test this baby out?" he called through the glass.

"You know he just wants to see us in our bathing suits," I muttered to Vi.

"Tell me about it," Vi said. "I think he's kind of cute, though."

"Lose-your-virginity cute?"

"Not that cute," she said, sliding open the door. She called out, "I think we'll wait for the weather to warm up a bit."

"But there's nothing like hot water on a freezing day," he said.

I paid Stan installment number two and told him I'd come by the store with the rest of the money on March 1.

"Don't forget to test the pH levels and add chlorine every few days," he told us as he left.

Maybe next month. This month we couldn't afford it.

ROOM FOR THREE

On the other side of the glass door, the hot tub bubbled.

"Should we do it?" I asked.

"We should."

"But—"

"No buts. I'll count. One. Two. Three!" She slid the door open and we ran. We dropped our robes (Cold legs! Cold feet! Really cold boobs!), scrambled over the plastic rim, and jumped in.

Ow, ow, ow! "It hurts! It hurts!" I cried. And then . . . ahhhhhhh. I closed my eyes and let my body melt. Heaven.

"This is amazing," I said. "Hula, you're amazing."

Vi murmured in agreement and then we soaked in silence.

"I feel bad that you paid for it," Vi said eventually.

I opened my eyes and saw her watching me, biting her lip. "Oh, don't worry about it," I said. "I don't mind."

"You should take it with you next year," she suggested.

I tilted my head back and looked up at the stars. The sky was huge and dark and sparkly. "Take it . . . where exactly?"

She laughed. "Well, you'll have to go somewhere! Or you can always stay here with my mom. If she ever comes back."

"I thought she was coming home for a weekend at some point."

Vi shrugged. "Yeah. I'm kidding. She will. Of course she's coming back."

"Do you miss her?" I asked.

"I miss having her here," Vi said slowly. "But I don't miss taking care of her."

"Do you want to live in a dorm next year?" I cupped water in my hand and poured it over my shoulders.

"Can't wait. Not having to buy groceries. Pay bills. Be responsible." She laughed. "And nothing says 'responsible' like buying a hot tub."

"It's our responsibility to relax once in a while. We're stressed enough as it is."

I saw a shadow race across the deck. "Oh crap. Was that Donut?"

"No, the door is closed."

I saw another shadow. A taller shadow. "Hello?" I said into the darkness.

Creak.

"Did you hear that?" Vi asked.

My heart pounded. "Yes. It was from behind the stairs. Are you expecting anyone?"

"No."

Creak.

"Zelda? Is that you?" Vi asked, her voice higher than usual.

Lucy stepped into the porch light.

"Hi, guys," she said, her eyes glowing. She was wearing a black winter coat that came down to her ankles and gray boots. I sank back into the water, pressing my hand to my chest.

"Jesus, Lucy, you scared us half to death," Vi said. "What are you doing here?"

"I saw the Party On! guys earlier and I thought I'd come by and see what's up."

"We have a doorbell," Vi said.

"I rang. No one answered so I've been hanging out back here with you."

Vi and I looked at each other.

"For how long exactly?" I asked.

She smiled. "Oh, long enough."

Creepy. For several moments, none of us spoke. Finally I said, "Um . . . can we help you with something?"

She crossed her arms in front of her chest. "I want in."

"Into . . . the hot tub?" I asked.

"No. Yes. But also into your little group."

"What are you talking about?" I asked.

"Come on. I know about your parents. Or more accurately, your lack thereof. I know it's just the two of you living here. I've been listening. And following. And I know about your soirées and your taco dinners and your trips to Planned Parenthood. I know everything." She stepped closer, and once again she smiled. It was creepy and disturbing and wrong in so many ways. "So unless you want me to tell my mother everything I know, I want in."

Holy crap. I grabbed Vi's wrist under the water and squeezed. Psycho. Then I started to laugh at the ridiculousness of the situation.

Vi started to laugh too.

"I'm glad you find me so amusing," Lucy huffed.

"If you want in that badly . . ." I started.

Vi shrugged. "Then get in. But you better keep your mouth shut."

Her eyes lit up. "Really?"

"Do we have a choice?" I asked.

Lucy kicked off her boots and unzipped her coat, revealing a purple one-piece and a . . . holy crap, a kick-ass body. She slipped into the tub. Vi and I exchanged glances. Who knew?

"Oh, that's hot!" she cried, lifting herself partially back out. *"Ahhh,"* she said eventually, sliding back in.

"You know," Vi commented, "I've never been blackmailed before."

"Me neither," I said.

"I always thought that it would happen eventually," Vi said, "but I assumed it would be for having an illicit affair."

"You're having an illicit affair?" Lucy asked.

Vi put her hand in front of Lucy's mouth. "I said you could get in. I did not say you could talk."

"Vi! Be nice," I said. If all Creepy Lucy wanted was to hang out with us, we could make that happen. At least she wouldn't rat us out.

"Fine," Vi said. "But can we all just be quiet and appreciate the hot tub?"

I dipped my head back, looked up at the sky, and for the first time in months, felt myself truly relax.

number five:
lost our virginity

I BET KOBE KNEW WHAT DAY IT WAS

The Monday before the big V-Day weekend—and yes, when I said V-Day, I meant V-Day—I hinted at my plan. We were standing by Noah's locker, and he was fiddling with his combination.

"So," I said. "You know what this weekend is, don't you?"

"The NBA All-Star Game?" he asked.

"Ha, ha, ha."

"Sunday at four. Why?"

He was kidding. He had to be. I stepped closer, twined my fingers through his, and said, "Okay . . . but do you have something planned for Saturday?"

"All-Star Saturday Night."

"Huh?"

"The slam dunk contest."

I stared at him, willing him to tell me he was joking.

Did he really not remember? I'd been planning and waiting and working on the details for the last three weeks (Pills every night! Sex playlist! Exfoliating!), and he didn't have a clue? "It's Valentine's Day," I said pointedly.

"I knew that," he said, nodding. "I mean, I knew it was coming up but I didn't realize it was . . . well, this Saturday."

"February fourteenth," I said. "Every year." He was acting like a weirdo, and it was making my stomach clench. "It's also been a month."

"A month from what?"

He was definitely kidding me. Here I was planning sex and he . . . barely remembered?

"A month since my trip to the doctor." A month since my boobs, hips, and tummy had begun expanding from the ingested hormones.

He blinked. "So . . . Saturday's the big night?"

"If you want to." I crossed my arms. He was ruining it. I didn't want to help him by growing pouty, but I was having a hard time fighting it.

"Of course I want to. Why wouldn't I want to?" He looked at me all wide-eyed.

Why wouldn't he want to? Of course he wanted to. Breathe, April. Breathe.

"So you'll come over? And tell your parents you're sleeping at RJ's?"

"I don't know if I can do that on Valentine's Day. They'd

get suspicious. They already think it's weird that . . ." He trailed off.

"That what?"

"That you live with someone else's family."

My stomach felt queasy. I thought it was weird that I lived with another family too. But that didn't mean I wanted Noah's parents thinking about it.

"Hey, come here," he said, pulling me into him. "So this weekend, huh?"

"This weekend," I said.

"I can't wait."

I closed my eyes and let my cheek rest against his shirt.

THE REAL JAKE BERMAN REMEMBERED

From: Jake Berman <Jake.Berman@kljco.com>
Date: Tues, 10 Feb, 6:31 a.m.
To: Suzanne Caldwell <Suzanne_Caldwell@pmail.com>
Subject: Valentine's Day

Suzanne,
Wondering if you could do me a favor . . . when April was a little girl I always used to leave a chocolate heart under her pillow for Valentine's Day. Do you think you could do that for me? Much appreciated.
Best, Jake

Sent From BlackBerry

From: Suzanne Caldwell <Suzanne_Caldwell@pmail.com>
Date: Wed, 11 Feb, 4:40 p.m.
To: Jake Berman <Jake.Berman@kljco.com>
Subject: RE: Valentine's Day

Dear Jake,
Consider it done. ☺
All the very best,
Suzanne

DON'T GET TOO COMFY

"What are you guys doing tonight?" Lucy asked, accosting me before calculus on Thursday morning.

"Homework," I told her. "I have an English paper to write."

She looked at me suspiciously.

"She does," Marissa said. I'd told her about Lucy's midnight stalker episode, so she knew Lucy was now, um, part of the family. "Swear. We're in the same class."

"So when can I come over again?" Lucy asked.

"The next time we have a party," I told her. I really did have an English paper due. But anyway, Vi and I had decided that Lucy could come to all our soirées, but that we didn't want her hanging around all the time. There was something off about her. "You will one hundred percent be invited, promise."

"When's the next party?" she asked, crossing her arms. "This weekend?"

"Not this weekend," I told her. "Definitely not this weekend. We're kind of spontaneous. But whenever it is, you will be invited. I'll text you."

"You don't have to text me," she said. "I'll know."

"Remind me to check the cactus for a camera," I mumbled to Marissa.

THE LEOPARD'S SPOTS

"So you're absolutely positive you want to do this on a Friday the thirteenth?" I asked.

"Too late now," Vi said, blow-drying. "He's on his way over."

"It's not too late until the fat lady . . ." I put my hand on my hip. "Why would the fat lady sing?"

She flipped her hair and shrugged. "It's from the opera."

I sat on her bed and stretched out. The water moved beneath my body. "You don't think Friday the thirteenth is a bad omen?"

"No. I think it's funny."

"If we were in a horror movie you would get hacked to death right after you have sex."

"Oh, hush. Are you sure you're not just trying to stop me because you want to go first?"

I pulled her duvet over my legs. "Why would I care that you're going first?"

"You've been with Noah for a long time. It seems like you should go first."

"You're older. You should go first. You do everything first."

She considered. "True."

Vi had kissed a boy first. Vi had gotten her period first. Vi had gotten drunk first. Vi lived with one parent first. Vi was the trailblazer. Vi was gutsy. No matter what Hudson said, I was the follower.

"So you're not nervous?" I asked.

"No. I'm excited."

"But Dean is your best friend. What if sex . . . changes that?"

She shook her head. "It won't. It's not going to change anything for me. I'll still think of him as a best friend. And what's the worst that it does to him? Make him want to have sex with me all the time? He already wants to have sex with me all the time."

"But it could change the dynamic of the friendship."

"Not if I don't let it. You *can* control these things."

"You can't control everything," I said.

She smiled. "I can try."

"And you're sure you don't want to wait to be in love? Wait for the lightning?"

"The what?"

"You know—the lightning. The omigod, I'm in love."

"No. I don't. Cheeseball." She rolled her eyes. "So what are you doing tonight? Going out with Noah?"

"No, he has a game in Ridgefield. Marissa and I are going to see a movie about a girl who loses her virginity on Friday the thirteenth and then gets hacked to death."

"Have fun. We should be done by the time you get back."

"Do you think he'll stay over?"

She rolled her eyes. "Of course not! It's not about cuddling. It's about doing it."

"What if Dean *wants* to stay over?" Unlike Noah. No, that wasn't fair. Noah wanted to. He just couldn't.

"He can sleep on the couch. Or in my mom's room."

"What if he wants to sleep in your bed with you and whisper sweet nothings in your ear?"

She purposefully ignored me.

"So he has no idea what's about to happen?" I asked.

"I told him we needed to work on our economics project tonight."

"On a Friday night?"

She waved her hands in the air. "He has no clue. I always tell him what he has to be working on. Honestly, I run his life. If he wasn't in my homeroom he would fail out of school."

"So he thinks he's coming over to work on a project and instead . . ."

"Instead we're going to have sex."

"But . . . what if he doesn't want to have sex?" I asked.

She snorted. "Of course he does. He's a guy."

I left her to prepare for her night, trying not to think about the fact that Noah seemed almost uninterested in sex. Was he no longer into me? Was he into someone else?

When the doorbell rang twenty minutes later, I waited for Vi to get it but she was blow-drying and couldn't hear.

"Hey, Dean, what's up?" I wasn't sure if I should look at him or not. Kind of bizarro that I knew what was about to happen and he didn't.

"Hey," he said. He was carrying his schoolbag. "Hope you're up to something more fun than we are tonight."

Doubtful. "Just going to see a movie with Marissa. Leaving now actually. Let me go tell Vi you're here."

I knocked on Vi's door and then stuck my head in. Vi was wearing a plunging brown-and-black leopard leotard that tied up the front.

"That is not from Victoria's Secret," I said. "That's from Victoria's Sluts."

"It's actually from the drugstore. It was right next to the condoms. What, I don't look hot? You wouldn't sleep with me?"

"Shush, he's here," I said, motioning with my head. "You look very hot. But I thought sleeping with your friend meant you wouldn't have to try so hard."

"This isn't trying," she said. "This is me having fun. I'm not giving up the opportunity to wear leopard spots."

"Nice setup," I said, looking around. The music was playing and she was clearly ready to rock. Or at least crawl on the floor and hunt gazelles. "Should I send him into the leopard's den? Or are you gonna Hula first?"

"Send him in," she said, dimming the lights. "I'm ready."

I closed the door behind me and then waved at Dean, who was on the couch. "She's all yours." I laughed to myself. "Good luck." I stepped into my shoes and grabbed my coat, and watched as he lazily walked away from me and toward her room. I wished I could see the reaction on his face when he opened the door. I stood on my tiptoes trying to watch. Door was opening . . . opening . . . opening. . . .

"Holy shit," I heard.

I left the house, giggling. I hoped she wouldn't eat him alive.

THE LIGHTNING

When I was ten, I'd asked my dad how he'd known my mom was the one for him. He'd proposed after five dates— they'd only known each other a month.

"Lightning only strikes once," my dad said. "And when it hits, you know."

"So are you sure you want to do it?" Marissa asked. We were sitting in the theater sharing popcorn, waiting for the previews. We really *were* at a horror movie, but it was about werewolves, not girls losing their virginity.

"I like scary movies," I said.

"Not about the movie, silly. About tomorrow night."

How many times did we have to have the same conversation? I popped a kernel into my mouth. "Yeah."

"But what if it's a mistake?"

I turned to her. "Why would it be a mistake?"

She shook her head. "I don't know."

"I guess I won't know till after," I said, and laughed.

"Once you do it, it's too late to go back," she said seriously.

"I get it," I told her. "Why are you being weird?"

"I'm not," she said quickly. "I just want to make sure you're sure."

"I'm sure," I said again. "I'll call you afterward. Let you know if I'm still sure."

"What, from under the covers?"

"No, when he *leaves*. Or the next morning."

The lights in the theater dimmed. "Okay," she said. "I'm here for you. No matter what."

"Thanks, Marissa. Truly. I'll give you the full report."

"Promise?" she asked.

I thought of my mom. "Promise."

WHY I THOUGHT OF MY MOM

I promised my mother that I would tell her before I had sex. This was before Noah, before she moved to France, before the divorce even. We were in her bed, under the covers watching something on TV. I don't remember what, but it was something that had to do with teenagers and sex, which is how the subject came up.

"It's very important," she said, playing with my hair. "When you're thinking about it, I want you to call me."

"Mo-ooom." I knew I was bright red.

"You pick up the phone and call me. Promise me, April."

The idea of me having sex—or sex at all—had been foreign at the time. Like Europe or getting my license.

"I promise," I said.

VI GETS HACKED TO DEATH. KIDDING.

I turned the key in the lock and opened the door extra loudly. Just in case they were in the living room doing something that might scar my retinas.

"Hello?" I asked carefully.

The TV was on and Vi and Dean were sprawled across the couch. Vi was wearing a tank top and her yoga pants. They were both laughing at something on the screen. "Hey!" Vi called to me. "How was the movie?"

"Scary," I said, leaving my boots in a pile by the door.

"How was . . . your night?"

"Pretty good," Dean said. "I think we'll get an A."

Vi laughed hysterically and kicked his foot.

His hand was on her shoulder. "That was the best economics project I've ever worked on."

I wasn't sure what I should say and what I shouldn't.

"He knows you know," Vi said, still staring at the TV.

"Ah."

"I told him about our plan. About *my* plan," she clarified.

"Best plan *ever*," Dean added.

"We're going to hit Hula," Vi said. "Wanna come?"

I did not want to get in their way. Also, I did not want to get in a hot tub with two people who had just had sex. And anyway, if I was awake, then I'd have to think about tomorrow and I didn't want to think about tomorrow. "Nah, I'm going to sleep." Donut followed me to the basement and I closed my door behind us.

NO LAUGHING MATTER

The next morning I heard footsteps upstairs. Then the door close. A few minutes later a car pulled out of the driveway. "Vi, get your butt down here!" I sang at the top of my lungs.

Ten seconds later Vi opened the basement door. Donut shot out.

Vi crawled under my covers. "Good morning," I greeted

her. "Do not come too close, I have not brushed my teeth. But details please!"

She gave me a lazy smile. "What do you want to know?"

"Um, everything! Was he surprised?"

She laughed. "Honestly, I thought he was going to pass out when he saw me. His face looked like this." She did an impression of Dean with his mouth open and his eyebrows raised that resembled what one might look like post-electrocution. "Then he said, 'Is this for the assignment?'"

"Ha, ha, ha. So what did you say?"

"I told him he had a new assignment. Operation Lose Virginity."

"You told him you were a virgin?" I shrieked. Donut scurried back inside at my exclamation.

"I had to. I didn't want him thinking I was suddenly attracted to him. And I assumed he'd figure it out during . . ."

"Was he shocked?"

"No! He said he'd always wondered if I'd made up the Frank story. Do you believe it?"

I wondered why I hadn't wondered the same thing. I shook my head.

"Then he started laughing. And I told him he better stop laughing and that I had decided that it was time for me to have sex and that he was always offering his services, so did he have the balls to go through with it or not?"

"And?"

She nodded. "He stopped laughing."

My breath caught. "And then?"

"His face got all serious and then he walked right up to me. He was an inch away. So I kissed him."

"Omigod!"

"And then I took off his shirt."

"Wait, wait, wait. The kiss! How was the kiss? That was the first time you kissed him, wasn't it?"

She blushed. "I guess. Whatever. He was kind of frozen in shock at first, until I started with the removal of clothing. And then it was *on*."

"Omigod. I can't believe it. So . . . did it hurt?" At the word *hurt*, Donut nipped at my fingers. "No, Donut. No biting, remember?"

"A little," Vi said. "The first time."

"Wait—how many times did you do it?"

"Three."

"Shut up!"

She smiled. "Honestly, the first time was about four and a half seconds."

I covered my mouth with the palm of my hand.

"I know. I thought he was going to cry. But then he was ready for round two four and a half seconds later, so we did it again."

"And how long did that last?"

"A while." She scratched behind Donut's ears. "Like forty minutes."

"That long?!"

"I know, huh?"

"But what did you guys do for that long?"

"Like every position. I needed to test them out for my article. It was research."

"You're very methodical. You didn't . . . take notes or anything, right?"

"I didn't need to. I have the whole thing on videotape."

"Oh God."

She laughed. "Kidding."

"And he just left now? Where did he sleep?"

She studied her hands. "With me. He didn't feel like driving home, and I was going to kick him out of my room, but we did it again after you went to sleep and then we both passed out."

I raised an eyebrow. "So there was cuddling."

"There was no cuddling!" She sighed. "Fine. There was limited cuddling. But it was more like spooning. And it doesn't count because it was right after sex."

"That's the important kind." Not that I'd know.

"Whatever."

"So what happens now?"

"Nothing. It was one night."

"You think you can go from cuddling back to normal?"

"Of course we can," she said, shaking her head. "Sex doesn't have to change everything."

I hoped she was wrong. I wanted things with Noah to

change. Even though I saw him every day, I missed him. Something was different. I was losing him somehow. And I wanted him back.

MY TURN

The plan: I was going to make dinner.

Vi would be out. She promised to walk over to Joanna's and stay there until at least two.

"You don't want to see Dean?" I asked.

"No!" she scoffed, then changed the subject. "Do you even know how to make dinner? You've been living here a month and a half and I've never seen you cook anything."

"I guess it's time to learn," I said. "What do you recommend? Something easy."

"Maybe ravioli?"

"I like ravioli! And so does Noah. Perfect. And maybe I can start with a salad and then do a side of garlic bread!"

She waved her hand in front of her mouth. "Skip the garlic bread. Fresh French bread."

"Good point."

After returning to the dreaded grocery store on Saturday afternoon, I prepared the salad, and set out the pots in their proper position.

"This is how you use your stove, right?" I asked Vi, turning the knob on and off. I did not want a repeat of the flood.

"You're not going to burn down my house, are you?"

"Hopefully not. But it's possible. What should I wear?"

"The new outfit?"

"Not during dinner!"

"Do you want to borrow my red dress?"

I nodded. I hung it up downstairs, then stepped into my shower. My last shower as a virgin. I blow-dried my hair (my last blow-dry as a virgin!), did my makeup (my last makeup application as a virgin!), and got dressed (my last . . . okay, I'll stop).

I made my bed, set out the candles, and cued the music. Then I started to pace.

"I think you need a drink," Vi said. We were upstairs. She was going to leave the moment Noah pulled up.

A drink was probably not the best idea. But it would give me something to do. "Okay."

"What would you like?" Vi asked.

"Sex in the basement," I said.

She laughed. "Did you mean Sex on the Beach?"

"I think I did. Oh God. I'm too nervous. I don't think I should have a drink. I think it would make me puke."

"There's nothing to be nervous about. You're about to have sex! With your boyfriend, who you *love*! Be excited! This is huge!"

It was huge. One of the biggest moments in my life. I thought back to Marissa's questioning.

Was I sure? Yes. I was sure.

Vi poured me a mix of vodka and orange juice. We had

no cranberry. I took a long gulp and let it burn as it went down. Now I was even more sure.

My cell phone rang. *WEEEooooWEEEooooWEEEoooo!* The police siren. My dad. I did not want to answer. But since I also did not want the actual police to appear and crash my sex party, I picked up.

"Hi," I said, trying not to sound nervous.

"Hi, hon. Happy Valentine's Day!"

"Thanks, Dad, you too. Oh! Thanks for the chocolate heart." Vi had read his email too and somehow managed to slip one under my pillow last night. Cute, huh?

"You're welcome! What are you up to tonight?"

You do not want to know. "Noah and a bunch of us are going to a party."

"That's nice. Be back by curfew."

"What about you? You and Penny doing something special?"

"We're having her parents over for dinner."

"Oh. Okay." Not exactly romantic.

"Love you, Princess."

"You too," I said, a feeling of sadness overwhelming me. I took another sip and tried not to think about it.

THE BACHELOR PAD

After my parents separated and my dad moved into his bachelor pad—aka his two-bedroom rental apartment in

Stamford—we stayed there for a weekend every two weeks.

At night, Matthew would toss and turn and sigh and sleep with his eyes half open. Sometimes I'd watch him sleep. He was so sweet. I would have watched him more often if I'd known we would hardly get to see each other a year later.

On Saturday mornings, my dad made us the best omelets. Stuffed with cheese and mushrooms that he picked up at the market after he came to get us. After we helped him with the dishes, we liked to look at old photo albums of family. My grandmother had stick-straight hair and was always holding my grandfather's hand. He was always holding a cigarette.

"My mom used to iron her hair straight," he told us.

"With an actual iron?" I asked, incredulous.

They had both died when my dad was in college. My grandmother from breast cancer, and my grandfather from a heart attack. Wham, bam, good-bye.

When we looked at pictures, my dad always kept his arm around me, keeping me close.

Matthew would go to sleep early and my dad and I would stay awake watching *Letterman* or *Saturday Night Live*. The TV would cast a kaleidoscope-like glow over his white walls.

I felt closer to him than I ever had.

My dad met Penny eight months after he and my mom separated, around the same time Noah and I finally got together. She was the first woman he introduced us to.

In the previous three months, he had gone out with fifteen women. I knew he was a hot commodity. I hadn't realized fifteen-in-three-months hot.

I knew this not because he told me—he was the parent who didn't overshare about his love life—but because one Sunday I used his computer when mine was acting slow and I'd found an open Excel document on his screen. The page listed all the women he'd gone out with, the dates he'd gone out with them, along with their numerical values. He graded them on looks, personality, character.

"Dad! I can't believe you rank the girls you date," I said. "That's so gross!"

He looked offended. "Why is it gross? I'm trying to be scientific. It's practical."

"People aren't numbers, Dad. You can't just objectify them."

"Did you see the notes section?"

"But what about the lightning?" I asked.

"There's more to life than lightning," he answered, looking away.

And maybe there was. He married Penny a year after my mom left him.

Penny got an 8, 8, 9.

ENOUGH WITH THE PARENTS

My mom called next. "Isn't it the middle of the night there?" I asked her.

"It is. I couldn't sleep. I had a dream about you. Is everything okay?" My mom fancied herself psychic. She claims to have dreamt about her own grandfather's death the night before he died. I've yet to see this psychic ability play out. Although it was weird that she was calling me an hour before I was going to lose my virginity.

"I'm good, Mom," I said. I took another sip of my drink.

"You sound funny. Where are you?"

"At home. At Vi's."

"Are you alone?"

"Vi's here."

"No Noah?"

"He's on his way."

Pause. "Is tonight the night?"

"Mom!" How did she know?

"You promised you'd tell me! Is it?"

Oh God. "Mom, I don't want to talk about this."

"I'm your mother. I have a right to know these things."

"No, you don't." This was too much.

"Please? I just want to know what's going on with you."

I took another sip. "Yes."

"I knew it! I told you I was psychic. But . . ." She choked up. "I wish I were there. It's one of the biggest moments in your life."

"I probably wouldn't be doing it if you were *here*."

"I don't mean there-there, I just . . . It's a big step. Are you sure you're ready?"

I sighed. "Don't be annoying about this, 'kay?"

"I won't, I won't! But you're going to be careful, right? Are you using a con-dome?"

"Yes. And I'm on the pill."

"You are? Since when?"

"Since . . . a while. Since the summer." I don't know why I lied. Did I want her to feel left out?

"Oh." She sighed.

The doorbell rang. I hadn't heard him pull up to the house.

"Mom, I have to go. He's here."

"Oh. Right. So. Be careful. You're sure you're good?"

"Mom, I'm good." Have to go, have to go, have to go. I should brush my teeth again.

"And can you call me later?"

Was she still talking? "Um . . . how about tomorrow?"

"Not tonight?"

"No, Mom."

"Okay. Tomorrow. I love you."

"You too," I said. I hung up, wondering if it was weird that my mom and I just discussed my impending loss of virginity. I opened my mouth to ask Vi, then shut it. Was it better to have a mom who discussed your impending loss of virginity, or a mom who didn't?

"I'm leaving," Vi said. "Do you want me to let Noah in on my way out?"

"No, I've got it." It really should be me to open the door to my soon-to-be . . . lover. *Eeeek*. I took a deep breath. "How do I look?"

"Gorge."

"Thanks."

I opened the door.

Unblinking navy eyes stared back at me.

"You've got to be kidding," I said.

Lucy stepped into the house. "Hi, guys! What are we doing tonight? I brought a DVD. And some popcorn?"

I turned to Vi. "Vi? Help? Please?"

Vi put on her coat and grabbed Lucy by the arm. "You're coming with me."

"Where are we going?"

"Away from here before April hits you." Vi waved at me. "Have fun. Have another drink."

The door slammed behind them.

"I'm good," I said to the closed door.

MY TURN, TAKE TWO

The doorbell rang.

He was here.

Not creeper-sneaker Lucy, but sweet, adorable Noah.

Here.

Now.

He was freshly shaven and wearing the cologne that we had bought together in the mall.

"Hi," I said.

"Hi," he said, looking at my dress. "You look . . . amazing. And this is . . . wow."

My heart was thumping out of my chest. This was it.

What to do now? Dinner. We needed to have dinner. Or maybe we'd skip dinner entirely. Yes! He'd kiss me and we'd start making out right here in the entranceway and we would just do it and then we could have dinner afterward and relax. "Happy Valentine's Day."

"You too," he said, and handed me a bottle of wine. "For you. Us."

"Thank you. Let me take your coat," I said super-formally. I wondered if he'd "borrowed" the wine from his parents.

"Thanks." He slipped it off and I hung it in the closet. He stood in the living room staring out the window.

"Should we open the bottle?" I asked. My voice sounded squeaky.

He turned to look at me. "Okay."

In the kitchen, I took out the wine opener. Hmm. "Do you know how to do this?"

"I guess," he said. "I can try." I handed him the opener and stood beside him. My shoulder brushed against his arm.

He started twisting the corkscrew in, our sides pressing against each other.

We were going to do it. We were really going to do it.

"I don't think . . . I don't know if I did this right," he said finally.

We stared at the bottle uncertainly. Half the cork was stuck in the bottle. Oh God, was this a bad omen?

"Can you get it out?" I asked. I giggled, thinking we sounded like a sitcom. Like one of those scenes where someone can't see the characters and only hears what they're saying and gets the totally wrong idea. Noah laughed too, and I felt giddy with relief.

He dug his fingers into the bottle. "I don't know. Maybe if I . . ." He pushed the remainder of the cork into the bottle. "Whoops."

"At least it will pour," I said. I took down two wine-glasses and poured. A fair amount of cork poured out as well. I pretended it didn't. "Here you go!"

I lifted my glass. He lifted his. "Cheers," I said, and we clinked.

THE END

For a minute there, with the wine bottle and the cork, things felt fun. Fun and . . . right. But the night went back to being weird over dinner. It was like I was having a meal with an estranged uncle. The conversation ranged from:

"It's cold out there, isn't it?"

To:

"And how was your day?"

And then we were done.

"Do you want to watch a movie?" he asked.

"Um . . ." I had been thinking we'd just go downstairs. But maybe that was too obvious. Maybe we were supposed to be chill about it. I'd put in a movie. And then as soon as the movie began we'd start kissing. And then during our kiss he'd say, "Let's go downstairs," and away we'd go.

I put in a movie. We sat down. I pressed PLAY.

We did not start making out.

He was watching the movie. Why wasn't he doing anything? I had told him this was the night. It was Valentine's Day. He used to always want to do it. He had run out in the middle of a thunderstorm! But now he was watching the movie? He hated movies! He thought they were too long! He got restless halfway through.

He was nervous. He had to be. Guys got nervous too. They worry about getting it up, about not going too fast, about hurting us, about whether or not we're enjoying it, about getting the condom on . . . they worry about a lot. Right?

Did I smell? Discreetly, I sniffed my underarms. I did not think I smelled. Had there been hidden garlic in the pasta sauce?

The movie played on. And on. I drank my cork. Noah drank his cork. He laughed too loud at the funny parts. Something was wrong. Really wrong.

I was a pathetic girl in a red dress. I was drinking cork. And then I realized.

Noah didn't want to be with me anymore. He was going to break up with me.

My body felt numb. I thought of what Hudson had said. About not wanting sex to give the wrong impression. It was so obvious now. How could I have missed the signs? Any other guy would have been all over this situation. It was Valentine's Day! We were alone! We were drinking wine! I was on the pill! I was throwing myself at him, and he didn't want to take advantage because he was planning on breaking up with me. Today.

No, he wouldn't do that. He didn't love me anymore, but he wasn't a jackass. He was going to wait until after Valentine's Day to tell me. Like my parents waited until the day after my birthday. He was going to pass up sleeping with me and then he was going to wait until tomorrow, the day after Valentine's Day, and then he was going to break up with me.

I had stayed in Westport to be with him and he was going to break up with me.

I looked over at him and watched him transfixed by the screen, glued to it. As though missing even a second would be the end of the world. I was standing in the middle of a canyon and the dam had broken and the water was about to come crashing down.

THE CHANGING OF THE TIDE

How was I supposed to sit through the rest of the movie pretending that everything was fine, that I wasn't about to drown? I couldn't do it. I reached for the remote and pressed STOP.

He turned to me. "Snack?"

He thought I was hungry? I scooted closer to him so

that our faces were only a few inches apart. "Is everything okay?"

He blinked. "Yeah."

"You're not . . . mad at me about anything, are you?"

He shook his head. "No. Not at all."

"And do you . . . still love me?"

He nodded quickly and decisively. "Yes. I do. I love you."

"Then why are you acting like you want to break up with me?"

"What? I don't. That's the last thing I want."

I paused, waiting for him to tell me what was wrong.

He said nothing.

I waited.

"So nothing's wrong?"

"No," he said, looking up and pulling me toward him. He kissed me.

I kissed him back. Maybe I'd been right. He was just freaked out about the sex thing too. I pulled back an inch. "It's overwhelming, huh?"

He nodded. I could smell the wine on his breath. I could taste it. My whole body started to tingle.

"We don't have to do it," I said, moving closer, whispering. "Not if you don't want to."

"I want to," he said, his voice husky. He put his hand on the back of my neck and pulled me against him. I forgot about everything else except him, his body, his mouth, his hands. Then he pulled me up and said the words I'd been waiting to hear all night: "Let's go downstairs."

AFTER THE END

We did it. It was done.

It was perfect.

It really was.

We'd both been a little nervous, giggling when we shouldn't have, kissing, whatever. He'd taken at least two minutes to put the condom on, but then there it was, on, and yes, it hurt, but it also felt good to have him so close. We cuddled up against each other under the duvet. His skin was damp and it pressed against mine and stuck to it, in a good way.

"I love you," he said.

I kissed him. "I love you too. So much."

LATER

We both woke up at three.

"Shit," he said, and laughed. "This bed is ridiculously comfortable."

"I know, huh? You wouldn't think so, but it is."

"It's bigger than an ordinary single."

"It's like a bed and a half."

"Why didn't you take your old bed?"

"Penny said it would make more sense for me to have a bed that was easily transportable. I think she wanted to take the canopy bed with her to Cleveland."

He laughed.

"I like being so close to the floor," I said. "Easier for Donut to climb on and off."

"Hurts less if you fall off too," he said, holding on to me.

"It could be my new favorite bed," I told him.

"How many have you had?"

"Four. The one on Oakbrook, the hard one at my dad's apartment, the canopy bed, and this one."

"This one is definitely my favorite," he said. He kissed me lightly. "I have to go."

"I know. It's late. Are your parents going to hate me?" I asked.

He smiled. "Never." He looked around for his clothes while I stayed warm under the covers. Donut sat on my stomach and purred.

Once he was dressed I stood up and wrapped my duvet around my shoulders (much to Donut's dismay), and followed him up the stairs.

The lights were off, and Vi's door was closed. We hadn't even heard her come in.

We kissed at the door. "Drive safe," I whispered. "Call me when you get home?"

"Will do."

I waved him out and then slunk back down to my basement. I picked the silver chocolate heart my dad and Vi had left me off my night table, unwrapped it, and let it melt in my mouth. I lay on the pillow that Noah had been on and breathed him in. I found the warm spot of my futon where we had cuddled. I felt loved. Completely and totally loved. I dozed off feeling full.

My cell rang.

"Hi," he whispered. "I'm home."

"Were your parents up?"

"Fast asleep."

"Lucky," I said.

"Good night," he said. "April, I . . ."

"Yeah?"

His voice deepened. "I really love you."

"I really love you, too," I repeated, and hung up. I fell asleep with Donut curled against my stomach and the phone still in my hand and stayed that way until the next morning.

number six:
spent three thousand dollars on a donut

KEEPING IN TOUCH

> Noah: hi, cutie
> Me: hi, babe
> Noah: thinking about you
> Me: thinking about you too. Where r u?
> Noah: math
> Me: r u coming over after school
> Noah: yes please

THE HOT DAYS OF FEBRUARY

Noah spent the next few weeks at our place. Now that basketball had ended, he had lots of free time. We didn't have sex every day. But we did most days. We were working our way through the many condom packs Noah had bought during the thunderstorm.

It was nice. Not just the sex part, but the after-sex part. My favorite moment was when we cuddled and his chest was pressed against mine and I could feel his heart beating.

Life was good. Noah and I were better than ever.

Vi was hooking up with Dean.

I had money in my bank account.

I had a hot tub.

I had a car. Not that I used it too often—Vi preferred to take hers.

I traced the letters I.L.O.V.E.Y.O.U. on his back.

"You too," Noah murmured.

BUDGET FOR DAD

What I Spent in February
Rent	$200.00
Groceries	$200.00
Cosmetics	$50.00
Clothes	$50.00
~~Cat Food & Care~~ Entertainment	$100.00
~~Hot Tub Semiprivate Swimming Lessons~~	
Miscellaneous	$400.00
Total	$1,000.00

Vi's *Issue* came out on March 4.

"I don't get it," I asked her. "How come your article isn't in here?" I stood by my locker and flipped through the pages. I saw an article about safe sex. An article about abstinence. An article about teen pregnancy. An article about STDs. A playlist of songs to make out to. But where was Vi's "It Happened to Me"?

"I made an editorial decision to leave it out," she said nonchalantly.

"But . . . after everything you did? You were so excited about writing it!"

Her mouth opened to say something but then her face fell. "I couldn't."

Huh? "Why not?"

"I don't know! I tried. And tried. But nothing came out." She slammed her fist against my locker. "What's wrong with me?"

I laughed. "You *like* him."

"I do not!" She sighed. "This isn't good. I can't like him."

"Why not?"

"It made me mushy! I couldn't write about him. I can't do something that's going to make me weak."

"Liking someone doesn't make you weak," I said.

"It makes you lose yourself," she said. "I'm proof. No. I have to put an end to this *thing* with Dean. Immediately."

"Vi," I said, wanting to tell her that she was *not* proof of any sort of weakness and that it made my heart hurt to hear her say that.

She scanned the hallway. "Aha. Pinky."

"What are you doing, Vi?"

"Getting my mojo back," she said, and hurried down the hall.

THE FIRST TIME I MET PINKY

"Why is her name Pinky?" I'd asked Vi back at the beginning of my sophomore year. Pinky was only a freshman then but had signed up to work on the paper.

"Unclear."

"Is it for the color? Did she like pink as a kid?"

"I don't know. I haven't noticed her wearing an abundance of pink."

"Maybe it's after the finger? Perhaps she has a very versatile pinkie?"

"What, like it can lift a hundred pounds or something?" Vi asked, laughing.

"She's barely a hundred pounds herself." I didn't want to dislike Pinky on sight but . . .

She was Miss Teen Westport.

Literally. Right before starting high school she had secured the crown. And she was a gazelle. Tall, long limbed, blonde, and stunning. Everyone stared. Guys. Girls. Me. Noah. Not that I thought Noah was going to hit on her or anything, but you couldn't look at her and not be jealous.

"Don't be that person," Vi said, wagging her finger.

"What person?"

"The person who tries to bring Pinky down because she's so gorgeous. It's antifeminist. She's cool. Young. But cool. And smart too. I see her as my protégé. Yes, entering the Miss Teen Westport pageant was misguided, but since she was fourteen at the time, I blame her parents. Obviously she needs a solid role model."

"You're right, you're right," I admitted. "I won't hate her for no reason."

But if she even *looked* at Noah, she was a dead girl.

AND THEN EVERYTHING WENT WRONG

Noah was over, but he left around six, just after Vi got home. I noticed he did that a lot, but I didn't want to make it an issue.

When Noah left, I did some calculus homework and Vi paid some bills. Then we started cooking. We ate. Then we took our nightly Hula soak, while hoping to avoid pneumonia.

Vi called Joanna, but there was no answer. "She's seeing someone new," Vi said.

"Good for her," I said.

"But bad for me. She's been totally MIA."

Vi's cell rang, and she checked the caller ID. Then she let it ring again.

I dunked all the way down until my chin floated on top of the water. "Aren't you going to get that?"

"It's just Dean," she said.

"What, wham, bam, thank you, monsieur? You won't answer his calls now?"

"Not if he keeps calling. Again and again. We are *not* in a relationship."

"I knew this would happen," I said. "You can't just have sex with someone and expect everything to stay the same."

"Yes, I can. I did. And he should too. Is your relationship so different now that you've had sex?"

"Not different," I said. "Just . . . better." More intimate. "What would be so wrong with having a relationship with Dean?" I wanted her to have what I had. To be as happy as I was.

"If we're in a relationship then I have to look out for him. Be responsible for him. I don't want to be tied down like that. I want to go to college free and clear." She looked away. "I told Pinky she should go for him."

I couldn't believe she was being so dumb. She was so smart about so many things, but not about this. I hugged my knees. "You're going to keep in touch with me, aren't you?"

"Wanna come with me? You can transfer schools."

"I wish."

"What are you going to do anyway? I don't mind if you stay here but . . ."

I did not want to think about next year. Maybe I *could* just stay here. I'd just tell my dad Vi was going to school in Connecticut. It's not like my dad would know the difference.

"We'll see," I said.

My cell rang. Noah.

I picked up. "Hey, can I call you back?"

"Hello to you too," he said, and laughed.

"Sorry, we're just in the tub."

"Of course you are. You guys are going to turn into prunes."

"Come over and join us."

"I can't. Would you do me a favor? Can you just check if I left my cell at your place? I can't find it anywhere."

"If I find it will you come get it?" I asked flirtatiously.

"Maybe."

"Fun. Then let me look."

Vi made a whipping motion with her hand. I stuck out my tongue. I would not let her fear of relationships rub off on me. I threw my towel over my shoulders and got out of the hot tub. Even though it was already March it was still cold. There was still snow on the ground although not on the deck. "Be back in two minutes," I said, and then, barefoot, hurried inside and down the stairs.

"Call it and we'll see if it's here," I told Noah.

Two seconds after disconnecting, his phone rang from behind my futon.

"Find it, Donut, find it!"

Donut scurried toward the sound and dug it out of a twisted sheet.

"Good work, Donut!"

She batted it with her paws. *"Meow!"*

I untangled the sheet and answered. "Donut to the rescue," I said.

"Meow!" Donut bolted out of the room and up the stairs.

"Way to go," Noah cheered.

"So now you're coming over to get it, right?"

"I should. But the 'rents have been giving me serious guilt about never being here and I promised I'd watch some TV with them. Can you just bring it to school tomorrow?"

"Booo. But, yeah. Can do."

"Cool. I'll call you later, though, 'kay?"

"Yup. Love you."

"You too."

I studied his phone. Thin. Black. It would be wrong to read his texts, right? It would be wrong to see who he last called. Only crazy girls did that. Girls who weren't in love. Noah and I were amazing.

I tossed the phone on my bed. If there was something he didn't want me to see he wouldn't leave the phone here overnight, would he? I think not. I laid down on my futon, soaking the duvet with my wet bathing suit. My heart raced. Just in case . . . I clicked open his texts. One from me. Another from RJ. From RJ. From . . . whose number was that? Was that Corinne's?

What time you coming?

Coming where????

Oh. I knew that number. It was his brother. I exhaled.

I kept scrolling and scrolling, scrolling back a week, two weeks, three . . . since before we slept together . . . and there were no sketchy texts. Nothing. Nothing weird at all. I hugged my towel to me and headed back up the stairs.

The house was freezing. I stepped onto the deck.

"You forgot to close the door," Vi said, head back, eyes closed.

I shut it firmly behind me and ran back to the hot tub. "Sorry." My limbs sank into the delicious warmth. *Ahhhhh.*

"Everything okay?"

"No," I told her. "I'm crazy."

She nodded. "We're all crazy. What's your specific form of crazy?"

"Noah left his phone here and I read through all his texts."

"Uh-huh. Why?"

"To make sure he wasn't cheating on me with Corinne."

She nodded again. "Do you think he's cheating on you with Corinne?"

"No. Things are amazing with us. That's why my craziness makes no sense."

"Not no sense. It's not like you've never encountered cheating *before*."

"You mean Noah?"

"Nooooo."

"Oh," I said, getting it. "You mean my mom."

"Yup."

"So I think Noah is my mom?" I asked.

She nodded. "Or you think you're your dad."

"Maybe," I said. I looked over at her. "And you're afraid that if you fall for Dean you're going to end up like your mom."

"I would never let that happen," she said adamantly. "When my so-called father left my mom, she had to give up *everything*. Guys suck."

"Why do you think people cheat?" I asked.

"Because they're bored? Because they can? Because they're selfish and think they're entitled to anything they want? Because they don't think they'll get caught?"

I closed my eyes. Poor Vi. Poor me. I opened them when I heard a screech of tires from the road in front of our house. "What was that?"

"Bad driving."

The car continued on, zooming down the rest of the street and over the bridge. Without headlights.

"What is wrong with people?" I asked, shaking my head. "Who drives without headlights?" Who leaves his pregnant girlfriend in another country? Who abandons her child?

"Crazy people," Vi said, with a sigh. "So what did you find in Noah's phone? Anything suspicious?"

"No," I said. "Nothing at all."

"Good. Then stop worrying."

I tried to let my shoulders relax, but they were not cooperating. Something was nagging at me, but I wasn't sure what.

ANOTHER TIME I KNEW SOMETHING WAS WRONG

I was in fifth grade and my father had come home with a dozen roses.

"Are those for me?" I'd asked. Roses were the prettiest flowers I'd ever seen. Sleeping Beauty had roses.

"They're for your mother," he'd said, giving me a kiss on the forehead. I'd been disappointed, but the gesture made me happy. Someday I would have someone who brought me roses. I wasn't sure why my dad had brought flowers but I guessed they were having a fight. My parents' door had been closed a lot lately, and not at night, in the good way.

"Mom! Mom!" I screamed. "Daddy brought you flowers! Come see! Come see!"

My mother stayed in the kitchen.

"Mom," I'd said. "Come see!"

"I'm doing something, sweetie," my mother said. I didn't understand what could be more important than roses.

Eventually my dad took off his shoes and his coat and carried the flowers into the kitchen. They were wrapped in thin pink wrapping paper, the tops peeking out.

"For you," he'd said to her.

My mom looked up. "Thanks. I guess I should put those in water."

"I can do it."

She sighed. "I got it. Dinner in five."

He nodded and then went upstairs.

"Don't you love roses, Mom?" I asked. "Are they your favorite flower?"

She sighed again. "No, orchids," she said, and then ripped off the paper and cut the bottoms under running water.

"Mine are tulips," I said. My dad trooped back in and I turned to him. "Dad, Mom's favorite flowers are orchids! And mine are tulips. Next time, can you get those instead?"

His face fell.

"Roses are my second favorite," I said.

Something in my stomach felt funny, like the beginnings of the flu.

STILL CONCERNED

The nagging thought that something was wrong continued through my post-Hula shower. And then when I was doing more homework. And during my nighttime call to Noah. And then when I was trying to fall asleep. Something wasn't right. But what? Was it guilt? Possibly. The right thing to do was to tell Noah I searched through his phone, but I was confident that wasn't going to happen. Was it my feelings of suspicion? Possibly. Had my mom screwed up my ability to trust for life? Also possible. It was so quiet. I stared at the ceiling. I flipped on my back. I flipped on my stomach. I sat up in bed. That was it.

It was *too* quiet. Where was Donut?

"Donut?" I called. I padded up the stairs. "Donut?" I asked again.

Donut spent her nights in the basement. Ever since Valentine's Day she had taken to falling asleep on my bed with me. Maybe she fell asleep upstairs?

"Donut? Here Donut, Donut. Where are you?"

The stairs creaked as I climbed them. When I got to the landing I opened the door and peered around the living room. No Donut. I checked under the couch. Around the kitchen. Maybe Vi knew. "Vi?" I asked softly. "Are you still up?"

"Yeah," she answered. "What's up?"

"Have you seen Donut?" I asked.

"Doesn't she sleep downstairs with you?"

"Usually," I said. "But I can't find her. I haven't seen her since . . ."

When was the last time I saw her? When she had found Noah's phone. Then she ran upstairs.

Where I had left the back door open.

The back of my neck felt cold. "Do you think she got outside?" I whispered.

"I didn't let her out," Vi said.

"I left the door open. Remember?"

"Shit."

I ran to the back door and pulled it open. A blast of cold air attacked my face. Vi flipped on the outdoor lights. "Donut?"

No Donut.

I looked out at the Sound feeling sick. The water looked cold, dark, and menacing.

"Do you think she could have . . ." Her voice trailed off.

"Oh God, I hope not. Can't cats swim? I think cats can swim."

"Not if the water's freezing."

I ran outside toward the shore.

"April! You're not wearing any shoes! Or a coat! Plus, your hair is wet—"

I ignored her and hurried down the stairs of the deck. I was cold. But Donut! If she was in the water, then she was definitely colder than I was. I couldn't believe I'd left the door open. How dumb was that? How irresponsible! What was wrong with me?

Once I reached the ground, and the snow, I stopped in my tracks. Yeah, running through the snow in my bare feet was not a brilliant strategy. Frostbite would not help my search. Luckily Vi was behind me with my Uggs and a coat. I stuffed my feet inside, pulled on the sleeves, and scurried down to the rocky sand.

The lights from across the way illuminated the water.

"You're not going to jump in are you?" Vi asked. "Hula's one thing, but this—this would be crazy."

"I guess not," I said, looking out. A weight pressed against my chest. "Do you think she's in there?"

"I don't know," she said, her voice wavering.

"Donut!" I called. "Come here, Donut!" I ran down to the floating dock and looked out, calling her name all the while.

"I bet she's not in the water," Vi said. "She's not an idiot. She figured out how to work the remote, didn't she?"

"True." I looked back at the Sound. The tide was low. "Do you think she could have gotten around the fence and made it to the road?"

"What, you think she ran away? She's too good for us?" Vi laughed a squeaky, un-Vi-like laugh.

"Maybe she was exploring and got lost."

"She might not even have left the house," Vi said. "She could be hiding under my bed as we speak. Or maybe she figured out how to get in the oven. She loves that oven."

"You check inside," I said. "I'll look around in front."

"'Kay."

The door to the fence was open. Not wide, but wide enough that something Donut's size could squeeze through. Uh-oh. I pushed through and ended up to the left of the driveway.

"April?" I heard. Lucy was standing on her porch. "Is everything okay?"

"No," I said. "Donut's missing." I passed my car and looked at the street.

"Donut?" I called. "Are you there? *Dooooonut!* Do—"

I saw her.

In a ball on the road, near the sidewalk. "Donut!" I called. She didn't move.

I hurried over to her and crouched in the middle of the street. She looked up at me and blinked. Her eyes looked terrified. She shivered.

"Get Vi," I called to Lucy.

I stroked the back of Donut's head. Poor, poor, Donut.

I'm sorry, Donut. My eyes prickled with tears. A few seconds later Vi and Lucy were both beside me.

"Someone hit her," I said, my voice shaking with tears.

"Omigod. Is she . . ."

I scooped her up. "She needs to go to the vet."

BAD THINGS ALWAYS HAPPEN IN THE MIDDLE OF THE NIGHT

It happened at around one A.M.

My dad was on a business trip to LA. My brother was in bed. I was in bed. My mom was in bed. I couldn't sleep. I had a math test the next morning. Seventh-grade math was not my specialty. I heard my mom's voice. I assumed she was on the phone with my dad. I picked up.

I don't know why they didn't hear a click. But they didn't. I was going to say hello but they seemed to be in the middle of a conversation. So I waited. And listened.

"Tell me what you want to do to me," my mom said.

"I'll tell you," a voice said. "I want to take my lips and kiss all the way down your body."

My first thought was—gross. My second was . . . that voice is not my father's. *That voice is not my father's.*

They kept talking. It was dirty. It was awful. It was my *mother*, saying dirty awful things to a dirty awful person *who wasn't my dad.*

My face was hot but I was too frozen to hang up. Waves of emotions crashed over me as I sat under my covers, gripping the phone. Nausea. Fear. Betrayal. Hatred. How could she do that? To my dad? To us? I held on to the phone, not saying a word. Not making a sound. Maybe I was dreaming. But the words kept coming. Until I couldn't listen anymore. I didn't want to hang up in case they would hear it and then they would know I knew. So instead I unplugged the phone.

There. It was dead. I felt dead. I hid under my covers. My brain buzzed. I wanted to cry but I couldn't. My body started to shake.

I huddled under my covers and shook until morning.

BUMPY RIDE

Vi drove while I held Donut and purred, "Donut, Donut, you're okay, aren't you?"

I called our vet but the message referred us to an emergency vet open on nights and weekends. Lucy directed Vi to their office while I continued to pet Donut. She was not moving. Her eyes fluttered open every few minutes and then closed again.

"I can't believe we killed our cat," Vi said.

I blinked back tears. "Vi! We didn't kill Donut. She's going to be fine. We have to be positive. Right, Donut?"

"This is so awful. Is she still breathing?"

"Yes!" Not just breathing. My leg felt warm. Pinkish cat urine had soaked through my pajama bottoms.

When we arrived at the vet we were the only ones

there. With rounded shoulders I held Donut out in front of me very, very carefully. She lifted her head. I burst into tears. "She got run over. It's my fault, I didn't close the door. Is she going to be okay?"

A technician in a white coat came right over to us. "Hello, little friend," she cooed. "You don't look so good, but we're going to take care of you. Why don't we all go into the exam room?"

Vi and I followed her while Lucy waited in the reception area. "Good luck," she called to us as we walked down the hall.

The exam itself was a blur. Donut tried to sit up but started gasping. The doctor felt her abdomen and listened with a stethoscope. Donut was crying in pain.

I think I was too.

"We need to take some X-rays," the vet said.

I nodded and she wheeled Donut away.

A COMPLICATED SITUATION

"I'm concerned that there are many things going on," the vet said when she returned. I leapt to my feet. She held out a printout in front of her. "One, she has a pelvic fracture."

"Okay," I said. "What needs to be done for that?"

"Usually a pelvic fracture just requires cage rest and pain medication. But Donut also has a bilateral fracture in her hind leg. We might need a specialist for that . . . but the real concern is the diaphragmatic hernia. Basically it's a division between her chest and abdomen. Bowel loops and intestines can get inside the chest. She'll need surgery for that. Immediately."

"Then do it," I choked out.

The vet hesitated. "It's risky. She could die on the table. We'd be opening up the chest."

"Is she going to die if we don't do it?"

The vet nodded.

"Then we don't have an option," I said, my arms fluttering by my side.

Vi stepped up beside me. "How much is the surgery?"

"With the X-rays and IV and tracheal tube . . . and then the fractures . . . about three thousand dollars."

Shit. I must have turned white because the vet smiled sadly and said, "If you can't afford to do that, putting her to sleep is the kindest option. Otherwise, she'd be in a lot of pain."

"Oh my God," I said. I was going to be sick. "We can't kill her. I'll find the money. Can we pay in installments?" *Installments* was my new favorite word.

She hesitated. "Not if you're under eighteen. Can one of your parents come and sign for you?"

My shoulders sagged. "No. I don't think so. But maybe they'll give us the money."

Vi grabbed my shoulders. "Can we talk about this for a second?"

"I'll be right back," the doctor said, excusing herself.

"April, it's a lot of money. Three thousand dollars? That's insane." She leaned against the examination table.

"We can't just let her die!" I wailed. I sat down in the corner chair.

"It's three thousand dollars! I don't have three thousand dollars! You don't have three thousand dollars!"

"My dad gave me my allowance a few days ago," I said stubbornly. "I have six hundred left."

"But you need that money. For food. Stuff. And you just paid off Hula."

"So we can pay off our cat!"

"I just . . ." She shook her head. "I don't have that kind of money. I have maybe five hundred in my savings account. We can use that."

"Let me talk to my dad," I said, pulling out my phone. "I'll ask him for the money."

"Hello?" he answered sleepily.

"Daddy?"

"April? What time is it?"

I glanced at the clock above the examining table. "One thirty. I'm at the hospital," I began.

"Are you okay?" he asked, sounding panicked. "Which hospital? I'm getting on a plane."

"No, Dad, I'm fine. I'm at the pet hospital. It's Donut."

"You're eating a donut?"

"No. Dad. My cat's name is Donut."

"Didn't your mom give away your cat because she couldn't take it to France?"

"No, it's my new cat!" I hadn't told him about Donut in case he objected. "I got a cat. When I moved into Vi's. But

I left the back door open when"—I definitely never mentioned buying Hula—"I came inside. And she got run over by a car. And she needs to have surgery or she's going to die. And it's expensive."

He sighed. "How much?"

"Three thousand dollars."

Pause.

"April, you can't spend three thousand dollars on a cat."

"It's not a cat," I said, feeling panicked. "It's *my* cat. And Dad, I have to! It's my fault she needs the surgery! I can't let her die."

"I'm sorry, Princess, but that's just crazy. You've only had the cat for, what, a few months? You never even mentioned you had a cat. I'm not giving you three thousand dollars to pay for cat surgery. You're not being rational. Why don't you sleep on it? In the morning I'm sure you'll realize that I'm right."

I couldn't decide if he was being heartless or if I was being ridiculous. But I couldn't let Donut die. I wasn't just going to abandon her. "Maybe I'll sell the car."

"You are absolutely not allowed to sell your car," he said. "That is not your car to sell. It's in Penny's name."

Great. "Dad, I gotta go."

"I'm sorry, Princess. I'm really sorry about your cat."

Tears welled up in my eyes. Not sorry enough to save her. "Bye," I said before hanging up.

"No go?" Vi asked.

"No go," I said.

I called my mom next. At least it was morning there. I led with: "Any chance you want to give me three thousand dollars so I can save Donut?"

She responded with, "I wish I had three thousand dollars. What happened to Donut?"

I spilled the story in a rush.

"Did you ask your father?"

"He won't help."

"Typical."

I shut my eyes. "Mom—not now."

"Call me when you get home?" she said.

"Yeah. I have to go."

"I'd give you the money if I had it," she added.

"This coming from the woman who left her cat in another country," I mumbled.

"What, hon?"

"Nothing. Bye." I hung up. "Do you want to try your mother?" I asked Vi.

"My mother does not have an extra three thousand dollars."

"Anyone else we can ask?"

"Noah?"

I didn't know if he had access to that kind of money but I could try. I dialed his cell and listened to the voice mail. "Oh right, his cell is at our place."

"Can you call his house line?"

"At one thirty in the morning?"

"It's an emergency," Vi said.

My heart pounded as I dialed the number. I hoped he answered. "Hello?" his mother squeaked.

Aw, man. I should've hung up. No. Caller ID. They knew it was me. That'd be worse. "Hi, Mrs. Friedman," I said, cringing. "I'm so, so sorry to be calling so late. Is Noah there?" Obviously he was there. It was the middle of the night.

"April?"

"Yes."

"He's fast asleep. Can I tell him you called in the morning?"

"Oh." Now what? Insist that she wake him up so I can borrow money?

There was a rumble and then we heard a "Hello?" Noah.

"Hi," I said. "It's me."

"I got it, Mom," he said.

"It's late, Noah."

"Sorry, Mrs. Friedman," I said. "It's an emergency."

"All right. Good night. Noah, I'm here if you need me." Finally, she hung up.

"What's wrong?" he asked.

"Donut got hit by a car," I said, sniffing.

"Oh shit. Is . . . did . . ."

"She's still alive. We're at the vet. She needs surgery. Three thousand dollars' worth. And I don't have the money. I asked my dad and my mom and Vi doesn't have it either. We probably have eleven hundred, nine if we want to eat. So I was wondering . . . do you have it? I would pay you back. In installments. I could pay you at least five hundred a month until I paid it off. What do you think?"

He paused. "That's a lot of money. My parents would kill me."

"So . . ." I held my breath.

"I can't."

He can't. He can't or he won't? I knew he had money in his bank account. Bar mitzvah money. "Never mind."

"Where's the vet?"

"It's Norwalk Emergency."

"Do you know who ran it over?"

"Ran *her* over. Not it."

"Her."

"No. I don't know who did it." What kind of a jerk runs over a kitten and doesn't even stop, anyway?

"Oh, April, don't cry."

"I have to go." I hung up. "Well, that was a bust." My face burnt from the humiliation. "What now?"

"Marissa?"

"She has zero money. Joanna?"

"Same."

"Lucy?"

I shook my head. "Last resort. What about Dean?"

"Dean's always broke. But you can ask Hudson."

"Me?"

"Yes! Hudson gave her to you."

"But that's even worse. He gave me a present and I killed her."

"You didn't kill her. We're going to save her. You should

ask Hudson." She looked up at me. "He has extra cash. Plus, he likes you."

I flushed. "He does not."

"Trust me. He does. He thinks you're the hottest girl in Westport. Call him. He's up. He's always up."

The hottest girl in Westport? Was that a joke? It wasn't that I thought I was ugly. But there were many girls more attractive than I was. Like Pinky.

Wait. Stop. Donut.

"I don't even know his number," I said.

She reeled it off to me from her cell's contact list. I dialed. What choice did I have?

He answered after two rings. "Hello," he said, all calm as though he normally got calls at two in the morning. Which he probably did. Teacher calls. Sex calls. Drug calls even. Maybe he dealt to Ms. Franklin. No. Maybe?

"Hey, Hudson? Sorry to bother you—this is April. I was wondering if I could ask you for a favor."

"What's up?"

I couldn't keep the tears out of my voice. "I . . . we're at the vet. Donut had an accident. They won't do the surgery unless we pay them up front and we're short twenty-one hundred dollars. You seem to always have extra cash on you and I wondered if I could borrow some. I swear I'll pay you back. I get money from my dad once a month, so I can give it to you in installments and—"

He didn't hesitate. "Where are you? I'll be there in ten."

Hudson met us in the waiting room in fifteen. Not that I was complaining. "This is the second time you came to my rescue," I said, looking up at him. He thought I was the hottest girl in Westport? Insane. Especially coming from the guy who *could* be the hottest guy in Westport. Those cheekbones. Those blue eyes.

He blushed. "Don't worry about it." He handed a credit card over to the receptionist.

He motioned to Vi and Lucy, both asleep on the couch. "Dean is doing a Starbucks run. There's a twenty-four-hour one down the street. He's getting Frappuccinos for everyone unless I call and tell him otherwise."

"That sounds great," I gushed. "Thank you, guys. So much. And I'll pay you back as soon as I can. Starting next week."

"Don't worry. It's not a big deal," Hudson said.

The receptionist ran the card through and then handed it back. "The doctor will start the procedure in about twenty minutes. You guys can go home or you can have a seat. It'll probably be a few hours until we can see how she's doing."

"Thank you," I said to her. "I think we're going to stay." I looked over at Hudson. "You guys don't have to stay, though. Obviously."

"We'll keep you company. We have nothing else to do."

"Psht," I said, waving my hand. "Who needs sleep?" I was giddy with relief. Donut might not make it, but at least she had a chance. "Seriously, Hudson, it is a big deal. I swear I'll pay you back."

He nodded. "I trust you. If you think it's worth it, then it's worth it."

I stared at him. Noah hadn't trusted my judgment. My dad hadn't either. "But why? You barely know me."

He smiled. "There's something about you. . . . You don't screw around."

I swallowed. Our eyes locked. What did that even mean? I wasn't sure what to say to that, so instead I asked, "How do you happen to have so much extra money?"

He smiled and took a step closer to me. "Does it matter?"

I thought about it. "No. I'm just curious."

"You think I'm a dealer?"

"No," I said, embarrassed. "Maybe."

"So you'd take my money even if it was drug money?"

"Oh, now you're testing my ethics."

He nodded. "Yup."

"No, I wouldn't take it."

He shrugged. "Then I guess I can't help you."

"Seriously?"

He cracked another smile. "No. I can still help you."

I motioned to the empty row of seats across from the sleeping Lucy and Vi and we sat down. "But, Hudson— where, or who, is the money from?"

205

He put his feet up on the table. "If I told you I'd have to kill you."

I put my feet up beside him and kicked the side of his shoe. "Lines like that make people think you're up to no good."

He continued smiling. "I like a little mystery. What else do these people say?"

"I've heard a few career ideas tossed around."

"Such as?"

"Gigolo," I said. "Boy toy." Then felt my cheeks burn up.

He laughed out loud. "Seriously? That's awesome."

"You've been spotted entering single women's houses at odd hours."

He laughed. "Like who?"

"Like Ms. Franklin's."

His eyes widened and he laughed even harder. "You think Ms. Franklin is hiring me for sex?"

"I didn't say that. You asked what people are saying."

"What do *you* think I do?"

"Model maybe?" I blushed again as soon as I said it. Now he knew I thought he was hot. He thought I was flirting with him. Was I flirting with him? It was easy to flirt with a guy who you knew thought you were pretty.

He laughed. "I have been told I have a nice ear."

"And what would an ear-model model exactly?"

"Earmuffs? Earphones? Q-tips? My ear could get a lot of work."

"Can I see this glamorous ear?"

He bent his head closer to me. "Not bad, huh?"

"Nice size. Not too big, not too small. Flat. Not too much lobe. Excellent ear. How's the other one?"

"Not as good. It has a weird Spock-like bump on the top." He turned to show me. "Feel."

I giggled. What was I doing giggling at Norwalk Emergency? "You want me to feel your ear?"

"It sounds weird when you say it like *that*. Just touch the edge."

I reached up and rubbed my finger against the top. His skin was cold and smooth and soft. His hair tickled the tips of my fingers. Warmth spread through my hand, and up my arm and down my spine.

"Hey," Hudson said, looking toward the doorway.

I followed Hudson's gaze and dropped my hand. Noah. "Hey!" I said. "What are you doing here?"

He shuffled from side to side. "I thought you might want company," he said. "But it seems like you already have some."

"I . . ." My heart raced. I jumped out of my seat. "Hudson lent me—lent us—the money."

Noah eyed Hudson warily. "Wow, man, that was big of you."

"No problem," he said, returning Noah's look.

Dean showed up then carrying a cardboard tray of coffees. "Who knew the most happening place to be at two A.M. on a Tuesday was the Norwalk Vet Emergency? Frappuccinos?"

"Actually, I think I'm going to go," Hudson said, standing.

"You don't have to," I added quickly, touching his jacket sleeve. Then I dropped my hand. "I mean, go home if you want to. Obviously you don't want to hang out *here*."

He zipped up his coat. "Good luck."

"But I just got here," Dean said. "And I already drank half my Frap. I can't go to sleep *now*."

"I can drop you off later," Noah said. "If your brother wants to take off."

"Cool. Thanks, man."

Hudson waved and headed to the door.

"Thank you," I called after him.

He winked and let the door swing behind him.

Dean placed the tray down on the table. "I brought six. Would you like one, Marcy?" he asked the receptionist, reading her nameplate.

"Sure," she said. "Don't mind if I do."

Vi stretched her arms over her head and opened one eye. "What's going on here?"

"Good morning, sleepyhead," Dean said, sitting on her lap. "I came to rescue you."

"Your brother came to rescue us. What do you have to offer?"

"My body?"

Vi shook her head. "Not interested. Anything else?"

A hurt expression crossed Dean's face, but he quickly washed it away. "Would you be interested in an icy, dessert-y

208

coffee drink?" he asked with a flourish of his hand.

"Oh, that I'll take." She looked up at Noah. "Hey. You're not Hudson."

Did she want to torpedo my relationship as well as her own? "Noah came by," I said. "To keep us company. Hudson just left."

"But he gave you the money?"

Not helping, Vi. "Yup. All good."

Noah looked at me quizzically. "So. Hudson gave you three thousand dollars."

"Actually, I only needed twenty-one hundred. And he didn't give it to me. It's a loan."

"Why?"

"Because I needed it?"

"But why would he lend it to you?"

I crossed my arms. "Because he trusts me to pay him back? Because he doesn't want Donut to die?"

Vi smirked. "Noah, are you jealous that Hudson saved the day instead of you?"

Noah ignored her and turned to me. "Can you come outside with me for a sec?" He marched out the door. I followed. The air bit my skin. I didn't remember where my coat was but it wasn't on me.

"April," he said, "a guy doesn't lend a girl two thousand dollars. Unless he wants you."

"We're just friends," I said.

"Then why were you touching him?"

"I was feeling his"—this was going to sound weird—"ear."

He narrowed his eyes. "Is something going on with you two?"

"No! Of course not!" I laughed. "You don't really think I'd do something like that, do you?" Did he think I was . . . my mother?

He shook his head. "I'm sorry. I know you wouldn't. I just don't like some other guy hitting on my girlfriend."

I nodded. "I'll pay him back. As soon as I can."

"I bet this was all Vi's idea," he grumbled. "She's such a bitch."

"She is not! Noah!"

"She wants to hook you up with Hudson so you guys can be a little foursome."

"You're acting crazy." What was his problem? "First you're jealous of Hudson. Now you're jealous of Vi?"

"I'm not jealous," he said. "I don't like when you get bossed around. And Vi is always bossing you around."

"She is not." What was happening? Things had been amazing—the best they'd been in months—and suddenly the ground we stood on was covered in cracks. One misstep and we'd fall through.

"She is. I know you think she's God's gift to—"

"Noah—not now, okay?" I couldn't deal with this here. I just couldn't.

He looked at me. He must have seen the pained expression

on my face because he pulled me into his arms. "Sorry."

"Can we go back in?"

He held open the door.

Inside, Dean was scowling. "If you don't want me to be here, I'll go home."

"You don't have to be here," Vi said.

Dean sighed. "I know I don't have to. I don't *have* to do anything."

They looked up at us and then back at each other.

"You know what?" Dean said. "I think I'm going to call a cab."

"I can take you home," Noah said. "And then I'll come back."

"You don't have to come back," I said quickly. Maybe it would be better if I was just here with Vi and still-sleeping Lucy.

"I know," he said, kissing me on the forehead. "But I want to."

I hesitated, then put my arms around him. "Thank you."

"I love you."

"You too," I said.

After they took off, I turned to Vi. "What was that about?"

She waved her hand in the air. "He was being way too boyfriendy. Clingy. Not cool."

"But he came to keep you company." I drained the last of my coffee.

"Did I ask him to do that? No, I did not."

Lucy groaned in her chair. "Did I hear something about coffee?"

I handed her a Frappuccino, then leaned the back of my head against the wall. "I'm tired."

"Me too," Vi said. "It's almost three."

"Lucy, do your parents know where you are?" I asked.

"Nah. My mother took two sleeping pills before bed. She's out cold."

"What about your dad?"

She looked up at me. "He died."

"Oh." I lost my breath. "I didn't know."

"Cancer," she said.

"That sucks," Vi said.

My eyes stung, but I blinked them away. Here I was worrying about my cat, when she had lost her *father*. "When did it happen?"

"Four years ago."

"I'm really sorry," I told her.

"Yeah, well . . . shitty things happen." She motioned to the waiting room. "Did you see the car that hit Donut?"

"No," I said. I wanted to know more about her dad, but I didn't want to push her if she didn't want to talk about it.

I sat back up. "But we *heard* it. When we were in the hot tub. Vi, Do you remember?"

"Omigod, I do," Vi said.

"And you know what was weird? The car that did it didn't have its headlights on."

"You're right," she said. "I remember that."

"So why would someone be driving by our house with their headlights off?"

"Maybe the headlights were broken," Lucy said.

"Or maybe they didn't want us to see them," Vi said.

"That's crazy," I said. "Who would do that?"

"I don't know," Vi said, narrowing her eyes. "But I'd give anything to find out."

Maybe my dad was right. Maybe bad things did always happen after ten P.M.

number seven:
harbored a fugitive

LIAR, LIAR, PANTS ON FIRE

WEEEooooWEEEoooWEEEoooo!

On Sunday, Noah and I were downstairs when my dad called. Vi was upstairs with Joanna. We stayed downstairs a lot, whenever Vi was home. These days Vi and Noah were like two dogs, marking their territory. Me.

"Hi, Dad," I said, motioning for Noah to be quiet.

"How are you feeling today?"

"Fine," I sighed.

"I'm sorry about Donut," he said.

"Me too."

"But you did the right thing. He would have suffered a lot."

He thought Donut was dead. I should tell him the truth.

And that Donut was female.

Or I could make him feel bad.

"Yes, well, the end was still hard."

I was pretending that my cat was dead. What was wrong with me? When did I become a person who pretended to have a dead cat? A person who motioned to her boyfriend in bed beside her to be quiet when she spoke to her dad and lied about having a dead cat?

"I'm sorry, honey. Is there anything I can do to cheer you up?"

"No," I said. Unless . . . I could use more cash. How could I say that without sounding crass? "Maybe I just need to get out. Go to the river. Walk down Main Street."

"That's a great idea. Go do it. Take Vi out for lunch. Buy yourself a present. On me. I'll put some extra money in your account."

Score! "Thanks, Dad." I kept my voice sad. When did I become a person who used her fake–dead cat for cash?

"Did you just scam your dad out of more money?" Noah asked after I'd said good-bye.

"Maybe."

"Good. Then you can pay Hudson back faster."

Clearly, Hudson giving me money was still a sore spot. Although not sore enough for Noah to lend me the money. Instead of saying any of this to him, I put my hand under the back of his shirt and pulled him on top of me.

FOLLOW-UP EMAIL FROM MY DAD TO FAKE SUZANNE

From: Jake Berman <Jake.Berman@kljco.com>
Date: Sun, 8 March, 8:10 p.m.
To: Suzanne Caldwell <Suzanne_Caldwell@pmail.com>
Subject: The Cat

Suzanne,
I hope all is well. I wanted to check in with you to see how April is handling the situation with her cat. I didn't even realize she'd gotten a cat. I assume you were okay with it. This seems to have really affected her—she sounded so upset when I last spoke to her. Can you keep an eye on her and let me know how she's handling it? She went through a mild depression a couple years ago—after the divorce—and I want to make sure she keeps her spirits up. If you have any concerns, please call me ASAP. Thank you.
Best, Jake

Sent From BlackBerry

AFTER READING MY DAD'S EMAIL TO "SUZANNE"

Who felt like a jackass? I did, I did!

LOST IN SPACE

My dad took Matthew and me to Disney the summer after the separation, the summer right before I started high school. I was fourteen.

I had a panic attack on Spaceship Earth.

Something about the ride, and the trip through 40,000 years—the Egyptians, the Romans, the future, and I just kept thinking that we were all just small and meaningless and we pretend that our lives matter but really we're irrelevant. Everything ends. Years. Generations. Civilizations. Everyone dies. I looked over the rim of the ride, and all I saw was a bottomless black hole. If my parents could break up, then nothing was forever. Nothing was unbreakable. Everything was doomed. Breathing felt like knives stabbing at my ribs.

Back in the sunlight, it got worse. There were people everywhere, strangers, and I was so insignificant, so pointless, it was all so pointless. I was lost, a deflated balloon sinking downward instead of up into the sky. At night in the hotel, I couldn't stop crying. I tried to muffle my sobs into my pillow so my brother and Dad wouldn't hear.

WELCOME TO THE CRAZY HOUSE

We were never going to find out who ran over Donut. How could we? It wasn't like there were cameras on the street. No one was going to admit to it, or volunteer any information. "Guess what," the criminal would say, "I was driving down your street and I accidentally ran over your cat! Sorry!"

It was the second week of March, after school on a Tuesday, and Vi and I were sprawled across our couch. Donut was on my lap. She had survived the surgery. After three days at the vet she had been back home for a week, and besides the pathetic-looking cast on her back leg, life was back to normal. The doctor warned that she'd probably always have a limp, but at least she was alive.

I scratched the back of her head and she let out a low meow.

"Who has nine lives?" I cooed at her. "Who does, who does?"

She licked my hand.

I was never letting her out of my sight again.

"Do you think it was Lucy?" Vi asked.

"Oh, come on. No. Of course not." I thought about her dad.

"She showed up out front exactly when we did. What was she doing on the street in the middle of the night?"

"She said she heard us," I said. "Not impossible. We were pretty loud."

"But then she got to come with us to the vet."

"What, you think she ran over our cat so she could have an adventure?" I asked. "That's insane. Even for her."

The doorbell rang and I jumped up to get it.

"Probably Lucy. She has a wire in the cactus and she heard us talking about her."

But it was Marissa. Her cheeks were streaked with tears. She had a small, navy duffel bag beside her, the bag she brought to camp. Her name was written on it in black cursive.

"I . . . I . . ." she started sobbing.

"Come in," I said, throwing my arms around her. "What happened?"

"Can I move in?"

AFTER MY MOM'S AFFAIR

"April, are you staying for dinner?" Dana, Marissa's mother, had asked me.

It was Wednesday afternoon, seventh grade, the day after the phone-sex fiasco.

I nodded. I was sitting at the wooden kitchen table, pretending to do my homework. Marissa was pouring us glasses of juice. Her little sister was on the kitchen floor doing an art project. Her older sister was chatting on the phone, and her two younger brothers were wrestling on the front hall carpet.

"How are your parents?" Dana asked me.

I opened my mouth to speak, but sobbed instead.

"Oh, sweetie," she said, sitting down beside me and enveloping me in a hug. "What's wrong? Do you want me to call your mom?"

"No," I said. "I'm just . . . she's just . . ." I started crying again.

Marissa ran up behind me and hugged my back. "Is your mom sick?" Marissa asked.

Yes, I thought. But then I shook my head. "No, not

that . . . it's my mom and dad . . . they're . . . things are bad."

Dana looked surprised, but nodded, and pulled me back into her. She smelled like laundry sheets.

"Mom, can April stay here tonight?" Marissa asked.

Dana pulled away and rubbed my arm. "Do you want to?"

Yes. Yes. Please don't make me go home. Please don't make me talk to her. In the car that morning I hadn't been able to look her in the eye without wanting to reach over and slap her.

"I'll call your mom," Dana said.

I panicked. "But you can't say . . ."

"I won't," she said. "Don't worry. Everything's going to be okay. You two just go relax."

"Let's go watch TV," Marissa said, pulling me up, taking my hand, and not letting go.

MY TURN TO HOUSE MARISSA

After two minutes of incomprehensible crying, Marissa finally explained what went down. "I got on the Israel trip this summer!"

"I don't understand," I said. "That's good news."

"No—my parents won't let me go!"

Part of me—the good part—felt terrible for her. Part of me—the bad part—felt happy for me.

"I don't understand," I said. "It's a free trip."

"I know! But then they discussed it and decided that it's too dangerous! They're convinced I'm going to get blown up by a terrorist."

"That seems unlikely," Vi said. "You're probably just as likely to get blown up in Manhattan."

"I doubt Vi's right," I said, hugging Marissa. "But your parents are being a bit overprotective."

"I know! They're ruining everything! Aaron's going on the trip! All my friends are going on the trip!"

"Thanks," I said.

"My summer friends. You know what I mean." She pulled back and wiped her eyes on the back of her sleeve. "My mom's acting like a total nut job."

"Do you think she'll change her mind?" Vi asked.

"I told her I hated her and that she was ruining my life and that I would never speak to her again *unless* she changed her mind."

"And what did she say?" I asked, a little shocked.

"That she wasn't changing her mind. So I called my dad at work and he said that he wasn't changing his mind either!"

"That sucks, Marissa," I said. I looked at her duffel. "And you packed a bag because . . . ?"

"Because I can't stay there. I'm not talking to either of them."

"How did you even get here?" I asked.

"I walked."

Was she crazy? "It's a half-hour walk. And you had your duffel."

"I was pissed. I needed some air."

"You should have called me!" I said. "I would have picked you up."

"I know but . . . I wasn't thinking. I just packed and left." She hoisted her bag over her arm. "It's not heavy. It was mostly for show."

"Do your parents know you're here?" I wondered.

"Not exactly," Marissa said.

"But they saw you leave," Vi said.

"My sisters did. Mom will find out when she gets back from Target."

This wasn't going to go well. "So, basically, you ran away?"

"Not away," Marissa said. "I ran here."

"Marissa," I said, shaking my head. "Your parents are going to freak out."

"Good," she said, eyes shining. "Let them! At least they'll have a reason to."

Marissa's phone rang and she glanced at the caller ID. "It's them. I'm not answering."

"You have to tell them where you are," I told her. "They're going to think you got abducted or something."

"Whatever."

"They're going to call the police!" I told her. Just what we needed. A massive police hunt, which would end here.

With two minors living illegally in a house.

She considered. "I have *at least* a few hours before they call the police. Don't you have to wait twenty-four hours?" She looked at Vi.

"Not sure," Vi said. "But I agree. I doubt your parents will call the police *yet*. It's only five in the afternoon. They'll give it at least until eight or nine."

I sighed. "So you'll call them after dinner?"

"Maybe. But I'm still not going home unless they change their minds."

"Stay as long as you want," Vi said. "You can move into my mom's room."

"She won't need it?"

"I don't think she has a weekend off for a while." Vi shrugged. I wondered if that was true.

Marissa's cell rang again. "Them."

"They're going to call every two minutes until you answer," I said.

She turned off her phone.

GREAT MOMS THINK ALIKE

Dana called me at seven. I was downstairs changing into sweatpants before dinner. Vi was making stir-fry. Marissa was keeping her company.

"April, is she there? She must be there." Marissa's mom sounded panicked.

223

I wanted Marissa to stay but I didn't want Dana to worry for no reason. Forget Dr. Rosini. If I could adopt a new mom, it would be Dana. "She's fine," I said, my voice soft. "She's here."

"Oh, good," she said. Her tone reminded me of me, when the vet told me Donut was going to be all right. "Can you put her on the phone?"

"She's really upset," I said. I sat down on the corner of the futon.

"I know. But I have to do what's best for her even if it upsets her. I'm her mother. That's my job."

I wondered what my mom thought her job was.

"Did she take a bag with her?" Dana asked.

"Yeah."

She sighed. "I'm coming to pick her up."

"Wait. Maybe you should let her stay over for a night or two. She'll come to her senses and calm down. She'll miss home."

"I don't know. . . . If it's okay with Vi's mom . . ."

"Absolutely," I said.

"Is she home? Let me have a quick chat with her."

"Oh . . . um . . . I'm not sure . . . let me find her and I'll get her to call you right back."

Back upstairs, I handed Vi my phone. "Suzanne, would you mind calling Marissa's mom back and telling her that Marissa can stay here as long as she'd like?"

"Good idea!" Marissa said.

Vi took the phone, and walked into the other room.

224

"Hi there," she began in a low, mom-like voice. "This is Suzanne, Vi's mom. . . . No, it's no problem at all, it's my pleasure. . . . I know, I know. . . . Best for them to blow off steam in a safe environment. . . . Why doesn't she stay tonight and Vi will drive her to school in the morning . . . perfect. No, no, we have plenty for dinner. I was about to make a meat loaf."

I raised an eyebrow.

"Great. We'll touch base tomorrow," Vi said, before hanging up. "Done and done."

"Meat loaf?" I asked.

Vi shrugged. "It sounded mom-like."

"Woohoo!" I cheered. Now that I didn't have to worry about an amber alert, I was free to enjoy the moment. Marissa was staying here! With me and Vi! The three of us living together. Marissa had always been there for me, and now it was my turn to be there for her. "What now?"

Marissa pointed to Hula. "I'm going to have to borrow a bathing suit."

MISS TEEN WESTPORT CLAIMS HER PRIZE

Wednesday and Thursday with Marissa were awesome. We ate breakfast together, went to school together, came home together, Hulaed together. Stayed up late watching movies and eating Oreos out of the box. It was like a permanent sleepover. I even showed her how to do her wash when she ran out of underwear.

"Look at you, Suzy Homemaker!" she exclaimed as I measured out the Tide.

"I'm learning," I told her.

"Should I come over?" Noah asked at school.

"It's kind of a girls' week," I told him. I wasn't sure why, but having Noah here with us would feel odd. I didn't want Marissa to feel like she wasn't wanted. "We'll do something fun on the weekend."

Dana checked in with Vi-as-Suzanne nightly.

Dana also checked in with Marissa nightly.

"I am not coming home until you and Dad change your minds!" Marissa told her.

They did not change their minds. She didn't go home.

"I can't believe my mom hasn't arrived on your doorstep," Marissa said, Thursday night while we were Hulaing.

"Maybe she's enjoying having one less kid to worry about," Vi said.

Marissa leaned her head back against the tub. "You're probably right. We are a lot to keep track of. Last week my brother locked himself in the garage, and no one noticed for three hours."

I couldn't stop smiling. Sure, I felt bad that Marissa was fighting with Dana, but . . . I loved having Marissa here.

My phone beeped. Text from Hudson.

Hudson: What's up?
Me: Chillaxing in the tub.

Hudson: How's Donut?

Me: Doing great.

"Who're you texting?" Marissa asked.

"Hudson," I said while typing.

"Reeeaaaally," Vi said with a smile. "Flirting a little?"

"Why are you so pro-Hudson and so anti-Noah?" I wondered out loud.

"I'm not anti-Noah. I just think Hudson's a great guy. And when he's around, you're . . . different," she went on. "In a good way. Bolder. You're—"

"More like you?" I asked, and splashed her.

"I was going to say fearless, but 'more like me' will do. And Noah is a little stuffy, don't you think? I wonder if you're really still in love with him or if it's a comfort thing."

Ouch. "I'm still in love with him," I told her. "I am."

She raised an eyebrow. "Does *he* think you're the hottest girl in Westport?"

I splashed her again. "He better."

"That's right," Marissa said. "Otherwise you should dump his ass."

I looked over at her in surprise. Marissa used to think Noah and I were the world's best couple. What had happened?

"Invite him over to join us," Vi said.

"Noah?"

227

"Hudson," Vi said.

I shook my head. "Now *that* would be flirting."

"Then I'll invite him over," Vi said with an exaggerated sigh. "I swear, I have to do everything around here." She dialed a number and then said, "Hey, Hudson, what's up?"

I splashed her with my foot.

"Stop splashing," she said to me. "If you get my phone wet I'm going to beat you. Hud? Why don't you and your delinquent brother come over and hang out with us?"

Dean had not been over since their fight at the vet. There had been definite weirdness between Vi and him. Weirdness that probably would not just disappear by inviting him over via his brother.

Vi scowled for a second, but then her face was blank. "Oh. Yeah. Whatever. Don't worry about it. Later." She hung up.

"They can't make it?" Marissa asked.

I felt vaguely disappointed, even though I knew it was for the best. Hudson being in my hot tub would not make Noah happy. Also, if he spent too much time with me, surely he would notice that I was not, in fact, the hottest girl in Westport.

"Dean is at Pinky's," she said, eyes steely.

"Pinky who writes for your paper?" Marissa asked.

"Yes, that Pinky. Do you know any other Pinkys?" Vi's voice was tight. She carved her hands through the water like knives.

"You told her to go for him," I reminded her.

"I know," she snapped.

"I don't understand," Marissa said. "Why would you do that?"

"She's a real go-getter." Vi's voice was snide. "I didn't know he was going to go for it, though."

Marissa shook her head. "You were testing him?"

"No. I was trying to get him to . . ." Vi sighed. "Never mind."

"You okay?" I asked carefully.

Vi rolled her eyes. "Yeah. Why wouldn't I be? I don't care who he hangs out with. We're just friends."

Marissa and I shared a look.

"I'm hungry," Vi said, pulling herself out of the tub. "Do either of you want nachos?"

Marissa shook her head. "No thanks."

Vi let the door slide closed with a bang.

"She likes him, right?" Marissa asked.

"Yup."

"Commitment issues?" Marissa wondered.

"She has this thing about boyfriends tying her down and then deserting her. Parent issues."

She nodded. "Speaking of parent issues, how are you doing here? You seem really good on your own."

"I am," I said, smiling. "I'm getting the hang of it."

"And you're happy?" She looked at me across the water, eyes hopeful.

I considered. "Yes," I said. I *was* happy.

"And Noah?"

"Noah is great," I said. "We're great."

She ran her fingers through the water. "If you're happy, I'm happy."

"I'm happy," I assured her. "But Vi isn't."

"Then let's go eat some nachos and cheer her up."

Once inside, I put my arm around Vi. "Now can I hate her? Or is that antifeminist?"

"Both," she said, and popped a chip in her mouth. "But please. Go right ahead."

AND THEN THERE WERE FOUR

"So," Marissa said on our Friday morning drive to school. She was sitting up front with Vi while I stretched out across the back. "I spoke to Aaron last night and we were wondering something . . ."

"Yeah?"

"Since you have no parents and since I'm very sad that I will not be spending the summer with my boyfriend, can he come visit?"

"Here?" I was glad I wasn't driving because I would have veered into the sidewalk.

"Yeah," she said. "Unless that's not cool. Which I totally understand. But he wants to see me and he could drive in after school if you guys didn't mind. . . ."

"Of course we don't mind!" Vi shrieked.

We didn't? We were kind of enjoying the BFF-bonding time, I thought. Especially me, since I was with both of my BFFs. "No, that's fine. Fun!" I lied.

"Really? You guys are the best! I'm going to call and tell him right now. Hi!" she squealed into the phone. "They said it was cool! Yay! I told you they had a hot tub, right?"

Is it wrong that I wasn't overjoyed to share my house—or my Hula—with a guy I had only met a few times?

"Does he have any cute friends?" Vi asked. "Tell him to bring one along."

Two strange guys. Even better.

ONE MORE MONKEY SLEEPING IN THE BED

They rolled in at eleven. Aaron. Plus Brett.

Aaron ran inside, picked Marissa up and twirled her around. "I missed you," he said.

She kissed him firmly on the mouth.

"Get a room," Vi sang.

Marissa blushed and pulled away. I wondered if she was rethinking her sex plan. She *was* going to wait until this summer, but now . . .

"Hey, April," Aaron said, giving me a hug. Aaron was tall and had dark hair, almost black, and thick eyebrows. He looked a little like Bert from *Sesame Street*, but cute.

"This is for you guys," Brett said. He had long, blond, straight hair and looked like a surfer. He handed Vi a large bouquet of flowers. "Thank you for having us."

"That is so sweet!" Vi said, smelling them and appraising Brett. "Very thoughtful."

"So where should we put our stuff?" he asked.

"Aaron should put his things in my mom's room with Marissa's. That's where he's sleeping. And you leave your things in the living room beside the TV. And if you play your cards right, you may be able to move them into my room."

Oh God.

His eyes widened. "I'm a champ at poker."

Game on.

ALL TOGETHER NOW

Upstairs, all of them were Hulaing, including Lucy.

Aaron had his arm around Marissa, and the two of them were gazing at each other and whispering and giggling adorably.

"Do you find Lucy has a weird stare?" Noah whispered when he got there.

"You get used to it," I whispered back. "Did you bring your bathing suit?"

"No. That thing is a bacteria soup."

I didn't press. He'd been in the hot tub once with me, only

232

when Vi wasn't home. I guessed he was self-conscious about his weight. Not that I thought he was too skinny, but I knew he did. Or maybe he just didn't want to have to talk to Vi.

"Hey, everyone!"

"April!" Vi called. She had her arm around Brett. "We're having such a great time."

"Great," I said.

"You have to come Hula. It's so hot in here. It's the hottest tub in Westport! Noah, do you know who the hottest girl in Westport is? According to—"

"It seems kind of full," I interrupted her.

"Ah, Hula can take it," she said. "Can't you, Hula? But guess who's coming over? Miss Teen Westport and her boyfriend."

"I don't know if that's a good idea."

"Why not?"

"Um . . ." Because you are secretly in love with Dean and you invited him over to make him jealous with your surfer boy. "Are you drunk?"

"No. I've had one beer. I'm going to get Pinky to do her wave." She flickered her fingers.

"What is she talking about?" Noah asked me.

"Her beauty pageant wave!" Lucy shrieked. Her eyes were shining and I guessed she had already had more than one beer. Maybe I should call her mother.

"Can you get more beers?" Vi asked me. "Since you're up. And dry."

I heard the doorbell and dreaded opening it. Dean and

Pinky were bad enough. But was Hudson with them? Noah was already weirded out by the random guys here. It would not help if Hudson showed up too.

It was just Dean and Pinky.

"Hey," I said with a hand flourish. "Welcome."

Noah and Dean nodded to each other.

"There she is," Vi sang from the other side of the glass.

"Let's see a wave!" Lucy hollered.

Oh my. This was not good.

Lucy, Vi, and Brett were now all waving their hands, beauty pageant style.

Pinky waved back, laughing. Dean looked like he wanted to retreat right out the door. "Is she drunk?" he asked me.

"No. Just obnoxious."

"Who's that guy?" he asked.

"Friend of Marissa's boyfriend. They drove in from Boston."

"And they're staying . . . ?"

"Here."

Dean's jaw dropped. "Both of them."

"Yes."

"Where are they sleeping?"

"Aaron is sleeping with Marissa, and Brett will be on the couch," I said. "Definitely the couch." I hoped.

As we watched through the glass, Vi put her arms around Brett and kissed him on the mouth.

Poor Jane! Poor Jilted Jane!

"Vi," Marissa told us an hour earlier, pulling Vi and me into the kitchen. "Brett has a girlfriend named Jane."

I was emptying a bag of tortilla chips into a bowl. "His girlfriend didn't mind him coming over and spending the weekend with us?" I said.

"I don't know," Marissa said, twirling a curl around her finger. "I told Aaron to bring someone else, but Brett has a car and . . . sorry. Seriously. I wanted to warn you."

"He doesn't act like he has a girlfriend," Vi said, shaking her head. "He's been eyeballing me since the bed comments. What is wrong with guys? No one is forcing him to have a girlfriend. He could choose to be single. Yet instead he chooses to have one, and then still flirts with me. I should hook up with him, take a picture, and send it to his girlfriend."

I shook my head and knelt down in front of the fridge to find the salsa.

"That's terrible!" Marissa shrieked. "Why would you do that? Jane would be devastated!"

"Better now than later, don't you think? Doesn't she deserve to know that he's an ass?"

"He might not be an ass! He hasn't even done anything! He just flirted with you! We don't know that he did anything. It's just a rumor!" Marissa said.

"What rumor?" I asked, rummaging through the shelves. Some of these yogurts had expired. We needed to do a sweep back here. Found it! "What are you talking about?" I closed the fridge and put the jar on the counter.

Marissa was red. "Nothing. I'm just saying . . . it's entrapment."

"Jane will appreciate it later," Vi said.

I laughed. "That is a picture I would *never* want to see. Noah with some other girl? No thanks. Trust me. Jane won't appreciate it at all. She'll despise you. You'll be *that* girl. Don't be *that* girl."

Vi put her hand on her hip. "Who'd you rather be, the girl who participates in the cheating or the girl who gets cheated on?"

Marissa throws up her hands. "The girl who gets cheated on isn't doing anything wrong! It's not her fault. The girl who participates in the cheating sucks!"

"I know which one I'd rather be," I said, carrying the bowl into the living room. "Neither."

SOIRÉE CONTINUED

Vi still had her tongue down Brett's throat in the hot tub.

"You know what?" Dean said. "I think we're going to go."

No, no, no! "You just got here! Don't go. She's just . . ."

"Pinky, wanna go to Kernan's?"

Kernan was a senior who was apparently having a competing soirée.

"Already?" Pinky asked. Her voice was deeper than

you'd expect. She sounded kind of like a forty-year-old woman.

"Don't go," I said. "Hold on." I ran back outside, knelt down, and squeezed Vi's shoulder. "Can I talk to you for a second?"

She pulled away from Brett. "What?"

"You're being a jerk," I said. "Dean is here."

"I'm being a jerk? He brought *Pinky*."

"You made him bring Pinky!"

"Hey," Pinky said, suddenly looming over the tub. "Thanks for inviting us."

"Yeah, thanks so much," Dean said. "We're just stopping by to say hi. We're going to Kernan's."

"Oh, you are, are you?" Vi asked.

"We are," Dean said, glaring.

Vi smiled. "Pinky can't leave without giving us her best beauty pageant wave, now can she?"

Pinky laughed, and did her wave. Everyone in the hot tub cheered. When she was done, she put her arm around Dean. "Ready?"

Dean was still looking at Vi. "Yeah," he said slowly. "Sure."

Oh God. Vi very obviously put her hand on Brett's leg. Maybe it was better if Dean and Pinky left. Having the four of them here was encouraging an X-rated game of chicken. "Okay," I said quietly, so Vi wouldn't hear. "Bye. Have a great night."

After locking the door behind Dean and Pinky, I pulled Noah back outside.

"Did he really leave?" Vi asked, standing up. Water dripped down her back.

"Yup."

"I can't believe he left."

"I guess he didn't want to stay and watch you hook up with some random guy," I barked.

"I wasn't . . ." She climbed out of the tub, and wrapped a towel around herself. "Uch. He's so annoying."

"Where are you going?" Brett asked.

"To get something to eat. I want pizza."

"Yes!" Brett cheered. "Pepperoni!"

"I'll order," Noah said taking out his cell. "I know the guys at Bertucci's."

"I can order my own pizza," she snapped.

"Okaaaay," Noah said, passing the phone to her. "Here you go."

Vi barked her order into the phone. "I'm freezing. I'm getting back in the water." She hurried back outside and slid down in the tub.

Brett tried to put his arm around Vi, but she pushed it off. I guessed he would be sleeping on the couch after all.

"Can I invite RJ?" Noah asked me.

"No," I said. "He always brings Corinne."

"Then can we go to your room?" he asked.

I sighed. "Fair enough."

Noah pulled my covers over his head. "Do we have to go back upstairs?" We'd been hiding out in the basement for the last hour.

"I hope not," I said. "But do we want food? There's pizza."

"Hardly. She ordered from Pete's Pie. Yuck. Not worth the trip upstairs." He shook his head. "I don't know how you can stand living with her."

"Noah!"

"What? She's so obnoxious."

"She is not. She's just . . . opinionated."

"I'm glad it's not me. I couldn't take Vi twenty-four seven."

"It's not twenty-four seven," I said. "It's not like she's in any of my classes."

Not that I'd admit it to Noah, but I was glad we were in different grades. It was nice to have some away time. Instead I changed the subject. "I'm hungry."

"You must have some food squirreled away down here."

"No. Nothing."

"Too bad Donut isn't an actual donut."

Donut meowed. Loudly. She batted at her leg cast.

"Don't worry, Donut," I said. "We promise not to eat you."

Noah shook his head. "Don't make promises you can't keep, cutie."

I pushed him back and looked him in the eye. "Donut is cute. I want to be hot."

He patted my head. "Don't make promises you can't keep, hottie."

Not quite what I was going for.

ONE DAY TOO MANY

"Is it Sunday yet?" Vi said, lying across my futon the next morning.

I sat up and laughed. "Not yet."

"A one-night sleepover would have been fine."

"Two nights . . . a bit much?"

"I want my living room back. And they are such slobs. They leave my toilet seat up! And dishes in the sink! You and Donut are lucky to have your own floor."

"Truth. Where is everyone?"

"Marissa and Aaron are locked away in my mom's room."

"Really . . . and what are they doing in there?"

"Hopefully not going through her closets. You do not want to know what she has in there."

"Oh God. What?"

She laughed. "Nothing *you* would want, my friend. Costumes. From every play she's ever been in. She steals them."

"I think I'll pass," I said, flipping my pillow. "And Brett?"

She crawled into bed with me. "Asleep on the couch."

"You decided not to be the other woman?" I asked.

"Not worth it. He's cute but . . . maybe he would have

240

been a good *first*-timer. Better than Dean. At least he would have disappeared to Boston after."

"Speaking of Dean . . ." I raised an eyebrow. "Did you call him?"

She scrunched up her face. "No. Why would I?"

"Come on, Vi." I flicked her shoulder. "First of all, he's your friend. But also, he likes you. And you like him. You must know that."

"If he liked me, why would he be with Pinky?" she huffed.

"Because you basically threw her at him?"

She shrugged. "Whatever. I don't care."

Yeah. Whatever.

We heard stomping overhead. Vi buried her head in my pillow. "Make them go home."

I felt bad. This was her house, and Marissa was my friend. "I'll tell them to leave if you want me to."

"Yes. No." She sighed. She scratched Donut behind the ears. "I'll try to be nice. But Donut, if you happen to bite their ankles, there will be a can of tuna in your future."

BON VOYAGE

There was a teary good-bye. Not for everyone, obviously, but for Marissa and Aaron.

"I'll drive in again soon," Aaron said. "Promise."

We waved good-bye to the boys as they drove off. I wrapped

my arm around Marissa's shoulders. "Did you have fun?"

"So much. Thank you two for letting them stay."

"And so . . . did you do it?" Vi asked, leaning forward.

"I don't kiss and tell," Marissa said haughtily.

Vi swatted her on the arm. "Oh, come on!"

She smiled. "Okay, okay. No. I didn't."

"Really? How come?"

"How come you didn't hook up with Brett?"

"Because I'm not a total skank." She laughed. "Because it didn't feel right."

"Exactly. It wasn't the right time," she said. "Not yet."

I squeezed her shoulder. I was happy to have Marissa all to myself again.

"Can we go back inside now?" Vi said. "Snack?"

"Sure," I said, about to follow.

Marissa pulled me back when Vi walked in. "Wait, I want to talk to you for a sec. I went to the bathroom in the middle of the night and saw Vi doing an exercise video."

I laughed. "Where was Brett?"

"Passed out on the couch."

"Yeah, she's obsessed with those videos. She probably wanted to work off the pizza."

"April, working out at three in the morning is odd behavior. Especially if she does it a lot."

"She does it a lot," I admitted.

"Maybe you need to talk to her mom about it?"

"Omigod, Vi'd kill me. And it's not like her mom would

242

do anything." And Vi and I had a code. We were the abandoned girls. Calling her mom would be throwing our code off the roof of the house and then backing up over it.

"Maybe *you* should talk to her."

"And say what?"

"Tell her that you think she's overdoing it. That you're concerned. That you love her."

I sighed. "I guess." Was it really that big a deal? So she worked out a lot. Sometimes in the middle of the night. There were worse ways to handle stress, right? It wasn't like she was shooting heroin.

"Good." She nodded "And I should go home anyway."

"What?" I took a step back. "You're leaving? Why? You don't have to!"

She shook her head. "I think I've overstayed my welcome."

"No! You haven't at all! This weekend was hectic, yeah, but it'll be calmer tonight."

Marissa looked at the ground. "The truth is I miss my family."

Her words were like a kick to my stomach. "I thought you liked being here."

"I do," she said. "But I've been gone for five nights. That's a long time."

"But I . . ." I didn't know what to say. I didn't want her to leave. "Don't go."

"I can't live with you guys forever. We knew I'd have to go home eventually, right?"

I guess I had. But I hadn't. I knew it was a stupid thing to think, or to hope, that she'd move in with us for good. Ever since she'd come to stay, I'd been so happy. I'd barely thought about my parents at all. I finally felt like I had a family again.

But everyone else got to go home.

Everyone except me.

number eight:
threw a crazy party

From: Jake Berman <Jake.Berman@kljco.com>
Date: Mon, 16 March, 6:10 a.m.
To: April Berman <April.Berman@pmail.com>
Subject: NYC Visit

Hi Princess,
We're coming to NYC for a wedding the weekend of your birthday—staying at the Plaza. Won't have time to make it up to Westport—we're flying into LaGuardia late Saturday morning, wedding's Saturday at five. Sorry we can't make it for your actual birthday (present is on the way), but we're hoping you'll take the train in and join us for the out-of-towners' brunch on Sunday?
Love, Dad

Sent From BlackBerry

"So," Vi said, when she, Lucy, and I were Hulaing. "Is Noah still being a baby about the money you borrowed from Hudson?"

I cringed as Vi called Noah a baby. I was allowed to think he was being a baby. Vi wasn't. Just as I was allowed to think Vi was bossy but Noah wasn't. And no one but me was allowed to think that my parents sucked.

"Noah'd like me to pay the money off as fast as possible," I said. "Which makes sense. No one wants to be in debt to someone else."

"How much do you still owe?" Lucy asked.

"Nineteen hundred. At the beginning of the month I'll have another eight hundred. And hopefully the gift my dad mentioned in his email would be a check."

"We should have a fund-raiser," Vi said, eyes sparkling.

Lucy leaned back. "What kind? Wash cars?"

Vi waved no with her index finger. "I am not standing outside in a bathing suit bending over cars. We'll have a party."

"We always have parties," I said.

"No, I mean a *party*."

"Like the kind they have in teen movies!" Lucy exclaimed. "The ones where the house gets trashed!"

"Exactly," Vi said. "Except without the house-trashing."

"I see how that *costs* us money," I said. "But how does that *make* us money?"

Vi shrugged, as though it were obvious. "We'll charge people five bucks to get in and then overcharge them for drinks and food. And there you go."

"Sure," I said. "Why not?"

"When are you having it?" Lucy asked.

"Next Saturday night," she said. "Obviously. On April's birthday."

"Let's do it on Friday night," I said. "I have to take the train into the city on Sunday morning and can't be all hung over."

I couldn't believe my dad was going to New York and making me take the train to see him instead of coming to see me. Not that I really wanted him anywhere near the house. But still. My birthday weekend, yet I had to make all the effort.

"Friday night then. It'll be your birthday at midnight anyway."

"Woohoo," I fake cheered.

"What do you have against birthdays?" Lucy asked.

Vi laughed. "Here she goes . . ."

BIRTHDAY BLUES

The problem with my birthday was not my actual birthday. No, my actual birthdays were usually pretty fun.

The problem with my birthday was the day afterward.

March 29.

It wasn't just that my parents announced their separation on March 29.

I got food poisoning from bad shrimp on a March 29.

My mother's father had a stroke and died on a March 29.

I got lost in O'Hare on a March 29 and had to find security, and my mom, dad, Matthew, and I missed our connecting flight.

Those last three were unintentional. The separation announcement was not. My parents wanted me to have one last happy birthday before telling me the news. Woohoo. Happy birthday to me.

TEXTS FROM MATTHEW

Matthew: r you coming to visit this summr?

Matthew: hellllllo

Me: hi. Sorry. Not sure.

Matthew: need to know dates. I'm going to Cleveland but I don't want to be there when ur here

Me: I'll figure it out

Matthew: When

Me: soon. xo

WHO WE INVITED TO THE PARTY

Everyone.

Seriously.

Everyone.

It was Wednesday morning, two days before our big bash. I was in the bathroom.

It burned when I peed.

Ouch. Ouch ouch ouch.

I flushed and hurried back up the stairs. Vi was on her mat scissoring her legs. "Vi, remember you told me about your mom's urinary tract infections?"

"Seriously? That's what you want to talk about at"—she scissored, then took a break—"seven in the morning?"

"I don't want to talk about it. I think I have one."

"Oh, that sucks. Does it hurt?"

"A little."

"My mom hated them. They made her pee every five seconds. But you just have to go to the doctor and they'll give you amoxicillin. It's probably from Hula. We have to do a better job managing the pH levels. We're supposed to add chlorine every day. Not every few weeks. You'll be fine, though."

I motioned to the TV with my chin. "Do you think you overdo it on these DVDs?"

"No," she said. Left leg up. Right leg up. Both back down. "I have to work out or I'm going to look like my mom. I'm fighting nature here."

I wasn't sure what to say that to that. When she explained it, it didn't seem so wrong. Speaking of nature . . .

"I have to pee again," I said, running back down the stairs.

It didn't burn for the rest of the day so I pushed the experience to the back of my mind and filed it under Annoying Things That Happen That Then Go Away. Like when you misplace your keys but then find them in your jacket pocket along with a loose piece of Trident.

But it happened again the next afternoon.

I decided to stop in for a quick visit with Dr. Rosini after school. I didn't want to have to deal with a urinary tract infection on my birthday. I was probably going to want to have sex on my birthday, and I wasn't sure if sex and urinary tract infections were compatible.

"How are the birth control pills working for you?" the doctor asked me when I finally saw her.

"Great, thanks," I said. "But that's not why I'm here. I think I have a urinary tract infection."

"Pressure when you pee? Does it burn?"

"Yup. Not crazy pain or anything but . . . a little. It burned a bit yesterday and today. It's my birthday on Saturday so I thought I'd get it taken care of first. . . ."

"We can do a urine test right now," she said, and handed me a cup to pee in.

Peeing in a cup is harder than you'd think. Well, it's not the peeing in the cup that's hard, it's the not peeing on your fingers. Which I did. Anyway. It did not burn when I peed. Maybe I was here for nothing. I returned to the exam room.

The doctor put some sort of litmus test in the cup, left the room, and then came back a few minutes later.

"No, doesn't seem to be a urinary tract infection," she said.

"It's not? Oh good." Relief washed over me. "But then what is it?"

"I wouldn't worry. It's probably just a temporary irritation. Have you had sexual intercourse lately?"

I blushed. "Two nights ago." And three nights ago. We had sex a lot.

"It could just be from that," she said. "But we'll run a few other tests and let you know what turns up."

"Thanks," I said. "It actually didn't hurt just now. So maybe it's gone."

"Could be. So we'll see you next month for your birth control follow-up?"

"Yup."

"Good. And April?"

"Yes?"

She smiled. "Happy birthday."

MY FOURTEENTH BIRTHDAY

We had a party in the basement on Oakbrook Road. On my actual birthday. We had fifty kids. And a DJ. I wore a green velvet dress and my first pair of heels. When my cake arrived (chocolate fudge cake, baked by my mom), I wished for a boyfriend.

If I'd known that my parents were going to announce their separation the next day, I probably would have wished for something else.

HIT AND RUN

On Thursday morning I was in the passenger seat of Vi's car, about a block from school when she suddenly sped up.

Toward Pinky.

"Um . . . Vi? You want to slow down?" It was pouring rain, and accelerating was not a great plan. Never mind toward a person.

"Hmm?" she said, eyeing her prey.

"Vi! Slow down! You're going to run her over."

She hit the brakes in the middle of the street. "What are you talking about?"

"What, you don't see Pinky over there?"

Pinky stood, clearly a few feet away, in all her tall, gazelle glory. She was wearing a fuchsia raincoat cinched at the waist.

"Guess she does wear pink," I said. Pinky hadn't even noticed what had almost happened. She should really look around once in a while. A girl could get killed if she wasn't paying attention.

Vi gripped both hands around the steering wheel. "She thinks she's so fantastic, Miss Teen Westport, la-di-da."

"I thought it wasn't her fault," I said wryly. "That her parents made her do it. That she just needed a good role model."

"We can't blame her parents for everything."

"Why not?" I asked. "I blame my parents for everything."

"Well, Pinky didn't enter the competition at gunpoint. She walked the catwalk. She strutted in her bathing suit and evening gown. She told them she wanted world peace. She participated in the misogynistic ritual. It's ridiculous. How would men feel if they were dehumanized in beauty pageants?"

"They'd probably love it," I said.

She sighed. "They probably would."

"I wouldn't mind seeing it either," I said, giggling. "Can you imagine Noah and Dean—"

"—and Hudson."

"—and Hudson peacocking their stuff onstage?"

"Bathing suit? Evening attire? Answering the 'If you could change one thing in the world what would it be' question?"

"Free beer," I said in a deep voice.

We both laughed.

She drummed her fingers on the steering wheel. "Maybe the next *Issue* should be about beauty pageants," she said.

"You'd have to interview Pinky," I said.

She scrunched up her nose. "Never mind. Racism it is."

GET READY TO RUMBLE. I MEAN PARTY.

"You don't have to have a party just to pay me back," Hudson said later that day. "Honestly, I'm not in a rush for the money."

253

We were standing in the caf, beside the door. I was waiting for Noah to meet me. "I think Vi just wanted an excuse for a giant bash," I admitted.

"Do you know how many people are coming?"

"The entire world?"

"Pretty much everyone who goes to school here at least," he said.

"True. Plus some people who don't go to school here." Aaron was planning on making the drive in again. With Brett. And an additional friend. A single one. We agreed to it on the condition that they only stay one night and that all three had to help us clean the next day, aka, be our slaves.

I'd believe the last part when I saw it.

"Are you sure you want to do it? It could get unruly," Hudson said.

"I think we can handle it. And you'll be there for backup, right?"

He shook his head. "Actually, I already have plans on Friday night."

"Oh," I said, surprised. I had expected him to be there. "But it's my birthday!"

"I thought your birthday was on Saturday."

He knew my actual birthday? Aw. "Still. Who do you have plans with? Who's not coming to our party? I'll kill 'em."

He wiggled his eyebrows. "Wouldn't you like to know."

"I would, actually. What could possibly be more important

than my party? Is it Ms. Franklin?"

He just smiled. "Tell you what. I'll try to stop by afterward. After midnight. For your real birthday. And some cake."

"Oh sure, get your jollies with Ms. Franklin and then swing by for some food. I feel used."

I felt a hand on my shoulder and turned around to see Noah. "Hey," I said, feeling vaguely guilty. "Hudson here has better plans than coming to my party. Is that even possible?"

"We'll have to soldier on without you," Noah said with a tight smile.

"See you later, guys," Hudson said before taking off.

"Why are you always so rude to him?" I asked, squeezing Noah's side.

"Why shouldn't I be? It's not like he's nice to me. Anyway, he's a sketchball."

"He's not."

"I heard he's a dealer."

"He isn't," I said.

He looked at me. "How do you know?"

"I . . . I don't." I still didn't know what Hudson's story was, but I was pretty sure that wasn't it. "Are you excited for the party?"

"I can't wait," he said. "It's going to be crazy fun. I watched *Cocktail* to prepare." Noah was going to be the bartender.

"We're only serving punch," I reminded him. "We can't afford anything else."

"Don't trivialize punch. Especially spiked punch," he

255

said. "My punch will be gourmet."

"Whatever you say, dear."

He put his arms around me. "You doubt my abilities?"

"Never," I told him. He kissed me, and even here, in the middle of the hall, he made me feel warm and safe.

THE FIRST KISS

It was November. Freshman year. It was the Saturday after our lunch with Marissa at the Burger Palace. He'd called me that night and asked me if I wanted to see a movie on Saturday, and I'd agreed.

On Saturday, I was rummaging in my mother's drawers for a shirt to wear with my jeans. Instead I stumbled across the divorce papers.

I ran back to my room, crawled under my covers and called Marissa. "I think I should cancel."

"You're going to stay home and feel sorry for yourself?"

"Yes."

"No. You're going. Go shower."

"I have nothing to wear. I'm not going back to my mom's room."

"I'll bring clothes. Go shower."

I listened, and did my hair and borrowed one of the dresses Marissa had brought over. Noah and his dad picked me up and dropped us off at the theater.

He put his arm around me in the dark. The weight of it

felt good on my shoulders—safe.

Halfway through the movie, I felt him move closer to me. I turned slightly to him, and he turned slightly to me, and our lips were an inch apart. He looked at me, then leaned in. His lips were sweet and buttery from the popcorn and I thought, This feels nice. I thought, I choose this. I thought, Maybe everything's going to be okay, after all.

THE OUTFIT

"You should keep it," Vi said when we were getting ready. I was wearing her red dress to my party. The Valentine's Day red dress.

"What? No."

"Seriously. Consider it your birthday present. It looks better on you than it does on me and it's already been worn for your oh-so-special-moment so . . . it's yours." Vi was wearing tight gray jeans, a plunging, green silk shirt, and big, gold hoop earrings. Her hair was slicked back in a tight ponytail. She looked vaguely gypsyish.

I threw my arms around her. "Omigod, you're the best!"

"Yes. I know," she said, and clucked her tongue.

OTHER PRESENTS

I got a tin of Mittleman Chocolate Company's freshly baked fudge cookies, wrapped in a blue ribbon. It had been waiting by the door when we got home from school. I assumed they were from Noah, but the card said:

> *Love you. Miss you. Wish we were there. Have a sweet birthday. Love, Mom, Daniel, and Matthew*

I kinda wished they were here too. My mom always used to make me her famous chocolate fudge cake, my favorite. Still, under the circumstances I wished she'd sent cash.

"There are, like, a hundred cookies in here," Vi said, pulling one out and eating it. "We can sell them at two bucks a pop."

My dad had sent a check for three hundred dollars. Officially, the most money he'd ever given me for my birthday. Clearly, he was still feeling guilty about making me kill my cat.

When Noah arrived at around five, he gave me a cute card and beautiful dangly silver earrings. I put them right in.

NOAH'S FIRST PRESENT

Noah gave me a digital frame as a fifteenth-birthday present.

He had somehow managed to load it with all the photos from my laptop when I hadn't been paying attention. Images of my friends, my parents, me, him, all popped out at me in random order. Sixth-grade carnival! Mother's Day last year!

Father's Day two years ago! Marissa and me in front of our lockers! My life remixed. My favorite was a photo of Noah and me that Marissa had taken at school the day before he gave it to me. Sitting together. A couple. I loved that he was mine. I had a boyfriend. My birthday wish had come true, albeit eight months later. I wondered if I had unknowingly made a trade. Parents for boyfriend.

And if I'd trade back if I could.

NO TIME FOR MOM

From: Mom <Robin.Frank@pmail.com>
Date: Fri, 27 March, 6:07 p.m.
To: April Berman <April.Berman@pmail.com>
Subject: Happy Birthday!

Happy birthday to you! Happy birthday to you! Happy birthday, dear April . . . Happy birthday to you! I wanted to be the first to wish you a happy birthday . . . I know it's not your birthday yet there but it is here! I just called, but maybe you're celebrating! I left a few messages this week but . . . I guess you're busy. Did you get my present? I got you some other stuff too, but I want to give you them in person. Have you thought about dates for this summer? I'm going to get you a ticket, as soon as you figure out your schedule. I'll call you again tomorrow! Love you lots. Mom

THE PARTY

The doorbell rang.

"Everyone ready?" Vi called.

We nodded. We were all at our posts. Donut was firmly locked away in my bedroom. Lucy and I were at the door waiting to charge people five bucks a head. I had a Ziploc bag ready to be stuffed with money. Noah was at the table/bar. He had taken the large glass bowl that used to sit on the coffee table, removed the fake fruit, filled it with ice, water, fruit punch Kool-Aid, and whatever booze we had found in the cupboards. (Cheap wine. Old vodka. Something brown that smelled like rubbing alcohol.) His plan was to stretch the aforementioned alcohol as much as possible. We had also bought cheap paper cups at the dollar store. We were charging five bucks a glass. Four if you reused your cup. We were banking on the assumption that this crowd would pay anything for booze, even disgusting, sugary, watered-down booze.

I placed Marissa beside Noah, in charge of food. She had stolen leftover desserts from her Friday night dinner and we had a bona fide bake sale on our hands. (There was also a white box in the back of the fridge that held a "Happy Birthday, April!" cake that I had accidentally spotted.)

Now that I had my dad's three-hundred-dollar check, we were hoping to clear sixteen hundred dollars between the booze and the food and the door.

Probably impossible.

Vi was Party Coordinator. She was also in charge of making sure nothing got broken. All vases/televisions/exercise DVDs had been carefully stowed away.

We could not afford to have anything replaced.

IT BEGINS

Marissa opened the door.

It was Aaron and co. "Yay!" Marissa cheered, throwing her arms around her boyfriend. Co. was Brett and his single friend, Zachary. Zachary had short, buzzed hair and was wearing camouflage. Seriously. Army pants and a military jacket.

"Are you shipping out?" Vi asked, eyebrow raised.

He nodded. "When I graduate," he mumbled.

She tilted her head to the side. I could tell she was debating if she found Zachary sexy or not.

Next came RJ and Corinne and Joanna. Then came Pinky and Dean.

I watched as every emotion crossed Vi's face. Happiness that he was there, jealousy that he was with Pinky, lust, annoyance. And this was all in the split second she allowed herself to look at him.

Dean also had beer. Lots and lots of beer. "From me and Hudson," he said as we unloaded it from Hudson's car. "For you to sell."

"We're throwing the party to pay Hudson back," I said.

"Not so he can spend more money!"

By eight thirty, the rest of our school was over. By nine, the rest of Westport. By ten, the rest of Connecticut. Everyone was here. Even Liam Packinson was here. Plus girlfriend. Even Stan the Hula man was here.

Everyone except Hudson. Even his car was here. Where was he anyway?

By ten thirty, we had made a ton of money at the door and Noah was cleaning up at the bar. Half the guests had red-stained lips, including me. Although I drank for free.

I went over to tell Noah that he was doing a great job but he wasn't there. People were helping themselves to the booze. Fantastic. I looked around the room. I could usually spot him anywhere, anytime. His stance, his neck, his chin. Any angle, I could find him. Maybe he was in the bathroom? There he was. Outside in the back.

About a quarter of the party had spilled out of the house and onto the deck. The door was open. I pushed through the crowd of people and found him standing with Corinne.

Really? He had to talk to her at my party? Was that necessary? I had already spotted her lurking by the punch bowl for the first half of the night.

"Hi," I said, adding extra frost to my voice. "You left your post."

"It's a hundred degrees in there," he said. "Decided to get some air."

Air with Corinne. On my birthday.

"Blowout party," she said to me then added a lip lick for effect.

"I know," I said.

"Do you need me to get back there?" Noah asked.

I was about to tell him yes when the lights in the house flickered then turned off.

Birthday cake time! Aw! I waited to see the glow of the candles. Instead the lights turned back on.

Vi stepped up on the coffee table, as though it was a stage. She was waving the Ziploc of money. What was she doing?

"I'd like to make an announcement," she yelled. She teetered on the table. I hoped it was because of her heels and not because she was *that* drunk. "We've raised sixteen hundred and seventy dollars to help Donut!"

Noah put his arm around me and squeezed my shoulder. That was insane. I wouldn't have to use any of next month's allowance.

"Since sixteen hundred was the goal, drinks are free the rest of the night. And we have seventy dollars to play with! Does anyone want to win seventy dollars?" Vi screamed.

Everyone cheered, and a bunch of people raised their hands.

"I thought so. So here's what we're going to do. We're going to have ourselves a little competition. Ladies, you are ineligible. But you won't mind. Because we're going to have ourselves a . . . Mr. Teen Westport contest! Winner gets the seventy dollars!"

Oh no. Vi. Don't.

The crowd whooped and cheered.

"Wait a sec," Brett, Aaron's friend, called. "Why just Mr. Westport? I'm from Boston and you know I'm a serious contender."

Vi considered. "When you're right, you're right. Hells yeah. I changed my mind. We're going to have ourselves a Mr. Teen Universe Contest!" Vi raised her arms in a V.

The crowd cheered even louder.

number nine:
hosted the
mr. teen universe contest

THE CONTEST

We chose four contestants: Aaron. Brett. Zachary. Dean. Aaron, Brett, and Zachary because we felt it was their duty as our slaves. Dean because clearly this whole thing was about him and he knew it. And he wasn't one to walk away from a challenge. Vi wanted to get Noah up there, but he said no way.

"Baby," Vi muttered, her lips fiery red. "He's such a party pooper. It's for your birthday! Can't he do it for you?"

I shook my head. "Don't pretend you're doing this for me. You're doing it to piss off Dean."

"Both," she said. "Dean, unlike Noah, is a good sport." She turned back to the contestants. "To the dock!"

"What?" I asked. "Why?"

"It's the perfect catwalk," she explained. "We even have lights. Everyone can watch from the house or the deck. And the judges can sit on the deck steps."

"Who are the judges?"

"Pinky, *of course*," she drawled. "She is the one with the most beauty pageant *experience*."

I rolled my eyes. "Yes. Pinky."

"And me."

"Aren't you the MC?"

"I can do both. I'm an excellent multitasker."

"Okay then. And?"

"And Lucy," Vi continued. "Because she can stare them down. And because she grew on me. And Marissa. Because I like her. And Joanna because I like her too, even though she's been ridiculously absent lately. And you. Because it's your present!"

"I already have my present," I said, motioning to my dress.

"Your second present," she cheered, and took a gulp of punch. "Because being a judge at a Mr. Teen Universe Contest is the most awesome present in world, and I am the most awesome housemate in the world!"

"Plus, you have cake," I said.

She slapped her hand on her forehead. "Your cake! I forgot about your cake! If only it was bigger so the winner could jump out of it!"

"Next time," I said.

As the crowd behind us cheered, Lucy, Pinky, Marissa, Joanna, and I sat on the steps watching while Vi orchestrated.

We had dived into Vi's mom's costume closet and came up with many, many looks for "Evening Wear." Draping lavender dresses, feather boas, strands of pearls, platform heels . . . and right now, while someone dimmed the lights, all the contestants were tossing off their clothes and dressing up in Suzanne's costumes.

And now here they came. One at a time. Dressed in drag.

The crowd went wild.

Aaron laughed through the entire walk. Brett kept a straight face. I wondered if Zachary was going to choose jumping into the Sound and swimming his way back to shore rather than do it—but chicken he was not. He skipped the heels, though, and went barefoot. Dean was surprisingly adept at heels. Plus, he blew kisses at the crowd.

"He's really good," I said to Pinky.

She nodded, eyes wide. "I know, huh? Better than me, I think."

Vi couldn't take her eyes off Dean either. "We're going to skip the question and answers," she yelled. "No one really cares about what these boys have to say, do they?"

The girls cheered.

"We're going straight to the final round," Vi said, rubbing her hands together. "The 'Swimsuit Round!'"

The girls cheered again.

"Since no one has swimsuits, our boys will be walking the plank—I mean catwalk—in their skivvies!"

Crazy cheering.

Oh my. Were they really going to do this? It was warm for this time of year, but only about sixty degrees.

They turned the lights back off and the guys started undressing, throwing Suzanne's outfits in a heap. Guess they were going through with this.

Marissa grabbed my hand and squeezed. "Omigod, Omigod." Aaron was first.

He was wearing black Calvin Klein boxer briefs, and had a lot of hair on his chest. A lot.

"Woohoo!" Marissa cheered.

"Woohoo!" I echoed. Why *wasn't* my boyfriend up there? I looked around for him and spotted him back in the house with RJ. At least he wasn't with Corinne.

I turned back for Brett. He seemed to be wearing surfer shorts that hung down to his slightly knobby knees.

Next was . . . Wow.

Hello, Zachary.

A hush fell over the crowd. Zachary was hot. Six pack. Arm muscles. Black, fitted Calvins. He had it *all* going on.

Marissa whistled. "Vi should hit *that*."

"No kidding," I agreed. "If only she'd stop staring at Dean."

"What?" Pinky said, stretching her gazelle-like neck. "Vi

has a thing for Dean?"

Uh-oh. "Um. No?"

"Why did you say that then?"

"I . . ."

"Speak of the devil," Marissa said. We watched as Dean worked his way down the dock. In his . . . tighty whities.

"Omigod," I whispered. I closed my eyes immediately.

The crowd was screaming. I opened one eye. Dean was doing a handstand.

"He's very . . . flexible," Marissa said.

Dean had reached the beginning of the dock and had turned around to walk back to the end. I glanced at Pinky to see what her reaction was, then realized she wasn't watching Dean. She was looking at Vi. Who was looking at Dean. Who was looking at Vi.

Uh-oh.

MAY I HAVE THE ENVELOPE PLEASE?

Joanna and I chose Dean. "I'd have to agree," Vi said with a sigh. "The boy has pizzazz. Did you see his pirouette?"

"Boooo," said Marissa. "You're all wrong. Aaron was the best."

"Did you see Zachary's abs?" Lucy asked. "Winner. Clearly."

Instead of responding, Pinky just played with her fingers. "I think I'm going to take off," she said.

"Why?" Vi cried. "You can't leave. You have to congratulate the winner. Don't you want to give him a big kiss?"

"No," she said, giving Vi a hard look. "Don't you?"

Vi stared back but didn't respond. "I need four of us to announce the winner. Who's in?"

AND THE WINNER IS . . .

The eight of us were all on the dock. Marissa stood behind Aaron. Lucy stood behind Zachary. And Vi stood behind Dean. I stood behind Brett. I wished I were standing behind Noah.

Aaron and Brett were perched on the west side of the dock, Zachary and Dean perched on the east. Both were facing the water. Each of us girls were standing behind them, our hands on their shoulders. The boys were all in their skivvies. Brett had goose bumps down his arms.

And Pinky? Pinky was watching from the deck, arms crossed.

"On the count of three," Vi hollered, "The winner will be pushed into the water. Are you ready?"

Hollers from the deck.

A breeze blew through my dress. This was a crazy plan. But for some reason none of the guys had argued. Maybe because whoever got wet also received the cash. Or maybe because they were morons. Or had drunk too much Kool-Aid.

"Repeat after me, everyone!" Vi yelled. "One!"

"One!" everyone repeated.

"Two!" Vi yelled.

"Two!" everyone echoed.

"Three!" Vi screamed.

As everyone yelled back, "Three," Vi pushed Dean over the edge of the dock. Unfortunately for Vi, Dean reached back and grabbed hold of Vi's waist, so both of them went tumbling into and under the water.

Vi resurfaced, shrieking. "This top is silk! You will be paying for my dry cleaning!"

Dean just laughed. "Really? You didn't see that coming?"

Vi swam up toward the dock. "Can someone help me out of here? It's goddamn freezing!"

Dean did an underwater somersault. "I'll share my winnings with anyone who jumps in! Five bucks a head!"

Brett dipped his toe in. "It's not that bad."

"Oh, it's bad," Vi said. She let go of the dock and floated on her back. "But it grows on you. Like Lucy! Come in, Lucy, come in!"

Lucy laughed and then dove in. "Holy shit!" she screamed, when her head came up.

"It's good for the soul," Dean added.

Brett did a shallow dive. "Arghhhh!" He hollered when he popped above the surface. "That's cold."

"Omigod," Marissa said. "They're going to get hypothermia."

Zachary cannonballed in, screaming, "Geronimo!"

Vi howled with laughter.

Aaron, holding on to Marissa, was next.

"No, no, no!" Marissa screamed all the way over the edge.

I was the last one standing. The rest were splashing and frolicking in the freezing water.

"Birthday girl! Get your ass in here!" Vi ordered.

"Not in this dress," I said.

She swallowed a mouthful of water and then coughed, laughing. "Then take it off."

Oh God. Should I? No. Or maybe I should. I was wearing decent, matching black undies and bra. Oh, what the hell. I pulled the dress off my head and jumped in, before I could change my mind.

My friends cheered.

As the freezing water engulfed me the first feeling was shock and numbness. But then. Slowly. I felt good. Alive. Refreshed. Happy. Giggly. I swam over to Vi. Her mascara dripped down her face. I assumed I looked the same. "This is hilarious," I said. "Thank you."

She nodded. "My toes are going to fall off."

"How long are we staying in here?"

"Until someone brings us towels," she said.

"We can just make a run for Hula," I suggested.

"Ooo. Good plan. Everyone ready?" she yelled. "To Hula on three. Repeat after me. One!"

"One!" I hollered. I was the only one. I swam toward the shore.

Vi swam toward Dean and climbed on his back. "I said repeat after me! One!"

"One!" most of us yelled.

"Two!"

"Two!"

"Three!" she squealed and everyone swam toward the shore, and ran up the stairs.

Dean's arms were out in front of him. "Out of our way!"

Within a few seconds we were all in the tub. About twenty seconds later, more people had joined us.

Ahhhhh. Despite the fact that the tub was ridiculously packed, the water had never felt so good. I leaned my head back and let the heat soak through my body, melting my limbs.

"That was incredible," Vi said. She had stripped off her jeans and top before getting into the tub.

"I think I'm in heaven," Marissa said.

"Me too," I said, closing my eyes.

I felt a hand on my shoulder. "April?"

I tilted my head back to see Noah kneeling down beside me. "Hey," I said. "Get in here."

"Um . . . not tonight. I brought you guys towels. You looked cold out there. In your . . . underwear."

My cheeks flushed. He sounded so . . . disapproving.

"Noah, I don't think I've ever seen you Hula," Vi said.

"Why is that?"

"Not my thing," he snapped.

"How can a hot tub not be your thing?" she asked. "Aren't they everyone's thing? Like presents?"

"I'm going back inside," he told me.

"And cake! Like presents and cake! Noah! We should do the cake!"

"I got you a cake," he said. "It was supposed to be a surprise."

Aw. "Thank you," I said.

"April, act surprised, 'kay?" Vi hoisted herself out of the tub.

I grabbed a towel and wrapped it around myself. "I think I'd like to be wearing clothes for my cake."

She winked. "Party pooper."

"Gimme two secs." I picked up my dress from the dock and then ran back inside. I did not feel like putting the dress back on, so instead I pulled on jeans and a long-sleeved shirt. I removed the makeup that had pooled under my eyes, and brushed my hair. It was exactly twelve oh one. My birthday. Happy birthday to me! When I returned upstairs. The lights were off, and Noah was holding a cake lit up by eighteen candles. Seventeen and one for good luck.

"Happy birthday to you. Happy birthday to you . . ."

I couldn't keep the smile off my face. I was surrounded by over a hundred people, all singing me 'Happy Birthday.'

Maybe I didn't have a family to celebrate with. Big deal. I had a hundred friends to celebrate with. That was good enough.

After the song was done and the cake was cut, I still couldn't wipe the smile off my face. I squeezed Noah's hand. He didn't squeeze back.

"What's wrong?"

"Nothing."

I pulled him toward me. "Thanks for the cake. And for the earrings. I love them." I lifted my hands to touch them and felt . . . one. Not two. Crap.

I hoped he hadn't noticed.

He noticed. "You lost one already?"

"I'm sure it's somewhere," I said quickly.

"Yeah. Somewhere in the Long Island Sound."

I opened my mouth but nothing came out. "I'll find it. It's probably in my room."

He looked down at the floor. "Whatever."

"It's time for birthday shots!" Vi said, grabbing a bottle of schnapps, a handful of shot glasses, and squeezing between us.

"I'll pass," Noah said, then turned and walked away.

"Noah, wait—" I said, but he had already gone outside to the deck.

"What's his problem?" Vi grumbled. "Why does he always have such a poker up his ass?"

"Vi!"

"He does."

"Where's the aluminum foil?" Lucy asked popping up. Then saw our glasses. "Me too!"

"Top drawer to the left of the stove," Vi said. "Why?"

"I think Zachary deserves a tiara. Did you see that stomach? Whoa."

"First we do shots. Marissa! Birthday shots!"

Marissa joined us, and Vi passed out the glasses. "To the birthday girl!"

"To the birthday girl!" they cheered.

"Thanks, guys," I said, feeling teary. I loved my friends. Loved loved loved.

We drank.

"Again!" Vi ordered.

THREE SHOTS LATER

"Do you hear that?" Marissa asked.

Everyone around us was loud so hearing wasn't so easy. Also my ears were buzzing.

But then I heard a distinct: *WEEEooooWEEEoooo-WEEEoooo!*

"My phone," I said. It was in my back pocket. I took it out and looked at the display, expecting to see DAD, but then realized that it wasn't actually ringing.

WEEEooooWEEEooooWEEEoooo!

"That's not good," Vi said.

The four of us rushed up to the window and peered through the blinds. Indeed, there was a police car driving down the block. It pulled up across the street from our house and stopped.

"Shit," Vi swore. "Shit, shit, shit."

My heart beat furiously against my chest. "What now?" They were going to call our parents. We were going to get arrested.

Vi put down the bottle of schnapps on the counter. "We're screwed."

"Everyone, shut up!" Lucy screamed. "The police are outside! Follow me out the back! Quietly! Single file! We'll cut across from my house and disperse at the end of the block!" She hurried to the back and then waved at the crowd to follow her out. I spotted Noah behind her, beside Corinne and Joanna. Thanks a lot, Noah. I appreciate all your help.

"We should spill out the booze," Marissa said. "Get rid of the evidence."

Outside, a policewoman was getting out of her car. Shit. Shit. Shit.

"What about the huge mess?" Marissa asked, looking around the party. "It's a war zone in here."

"Let's get rid of the booze first," Vi instructed. "We can't get arrested for mess."

I nodded. At least I think I did. My brain was schnapped out. "Someone help me with the punch."

Together the three of us lifted the bowl and carried it

over to the sink and carefully spilled it down the drain.

"April?" Vi asked.

"Yeah?"

"Do you know you're only wearing one earring?"

"Yes. I am aware. Thanks."

"Next," Vi said.

"Peach schnapps."

Vi picked up a leftover shot from the counter and downed it. "One down. Your turn."

I laughed then did as told. It burned. But honestly, if I was about to get arrested, I didn't want to remember it in the morning.

"Guys!" Marissa hollered. "We have to get rid of the bottle!"

"Good point," I said. "More shots!"

Vi poured me another and I downed it. "One more for good luck!" I cheered.

"No," Marissa said, reaching for the bottle. "We should spill the rest down the sink."

"No," Vi whined. "Not the schnapps! Don't kill the schnapps!"

As the two of them had a tug-of-war, I peeked out the window. The policewoman was in front of our house on our side of the street! And she was . . . talking to someone? Hudson. Hudson was here? When had he gotten here? Unless I was imagining Hudson? What did it say about me if I was imagining Hudson?

The policewoman had her hand on Hudson's shoulder.

Oh no.

What if Hudson really was into something illegal? And now he had gotten caught here, right in front of Vi's house? Would he go to prison?

The policewoman stepped back. And turned around. And walked back to her car. She turned off the siren and drove away. What the . . . ?

The doorbell rang.

"We have to spill it!" Marissa hissed, finally wrestling the bottle from Vi. "And we forgot about the beer bottles! And the cups! So many cups!"

"Wait!" I said. "It's fine." I hurried to the door and sprung it open. "How did you do that?"

Hudson smiled. "Do what?"

"Get rid of the police officer?"

He cocked his head to the side. "What police officer?"

"Don't give me that," I said, pulling him inside and closing the door. "I saw you talking to her."

"She had the wrong address," he said, shrugging. "She was looking for a house down the block."

"Bullshit," I said. "She was coming here to arrest us all, and then you talked to her and she—" I froze. "You didn't promise sexual favors, did you?"

He laughed.

Wait. I got it. "Omigod. I figured it out." I leaned closer to him and whispered, "You're an undercover cop."

He laughed. "I am?"

"Yes. Absolutely. That's it. You're investigating some crazy illicit teen ring at our high school! That's why you're always sneaking off at all hours. For stings. And that's why you have so much money. You have an adult-person job!"

"How much have you had to drink?"

"A lot. But that's beside the point."

Vi and Marissa came over. "Is the cop gone?" Vi asked.

"She's gone," I said.

"What did you do, pay her off?" Vi asked.

"Yup," Hudson said. "I slipped her a twenty. Where is everyone?"

"They snuck out the back," Marissa said.

"The coast is clear," Hudson said. "But you should try to keep it quiet here for the rest of the night."

"I'll call Aaron and co. and tell them it's safe to come back," Marissa said, dialing.

I poked Hudson in the chest. "You are undercover! Wait a sec." I circled him slowly. "Are you even a high school student? Maybe your whole life is a cover. I never thought you looked like Dean. Maybe you're like in college or something pretending to be a high school student. How old are you?"

"Eighteen."

"Hmm. Sure you are. And are you really Dean's brother? Maybe that's just your cover."

"All right," he said. "I'll tell you the big secret, but it has to stay between you and me."

"Yes! I can do that!" I screamed. I lowered my voice. "I can do that," I repeated.

"Here it is. You want to know the big secret? Why Officer Stevenson listened to me when I promised her that you'd send everyone home?"

"Yes! Tell me!"

"Okay, but I'm swearing you to secrecy."

"I swear."

"You swear swear? Because my rep is on the line here, April."

"I swear swear."

"I can trust you?"

"You can trust me."

"I'm only telling you because it's your birthday. . . . Happy birthday, by the way. . . ."

"Thank you. And thanks for the beer. Now get on with it!"

"All right then. I babysit her kids."

"You . . . what?"

"Babysit. Max and Julie. Max is six and Julie is three and a half. I sit for Officer Stevenson on Sunday nights so she and her husband can go to the movies."

"You babysit," I said disbelievingly.

"I do. But that's our little secret, right?"

"That's how you have so much money. From babysitting."

"Babysitting is surprisingly lucrative. Fifteen bucks an hour, five nights a week . . . more in the summer and on holidays. I make almost twenty thousand a year."

I almost choked. "That's insane."

"Well. No taxes."

"That's why I saw you at Ms. Franklin's house?"

"Tommy and Kayla are crazy about me. I let them stay up late and watch *American Idol*."

Talk about anticlimactic. "That's it? That's your big secret? You're a manny? Why a secret then?" I threw my hands in the air. "Who cares?"

"It didn't start off as a secret. I just didn't mention it. 'Cause, whatever, I was trying to seem cool or something stupid. Then people started making shit up . . . and I don't know. Dean thought it was funny."

I wasn't sure if I was buying it. "But . . . maybe babysitting is just another lie. I still think you're an undercover cop." Dean chose that moment to return through the back door I waved him over. "Dean! Your fake brother is here!"

"My what?" he asked. Aaron and Brett followed him in.

"Your fake brother. I figured out why he doesn't look anything like you."

Vi shook her head at me.

"What? I did!" I shrieked. "Hudson isn't even related to him! He's just using Dean's family as a cover! That's why he doesn't look like Dean!"

I expected some laughs. Or a "Totally!" Or something. Not the flushed, embarrassed stares that I got in return.

"April, I'm not an undercover cop," Hudson said. Then he laughed. "I'm adopted."

Well. I turned bright red. "Really?"

"Yes."

"I guess that explains it then," Marissa said. She made a "you stuck your foot into it" face at me before deserting me for Aaron.

"No biggie," Hudson said.

I covered my face with my hands and laughed. "Oh God, I'm so sorry. What an idiot. Why didn't I know that? Was that a secret or something?"

"No," he said. "It just doesn't come up often. At a party. Yelled across the room."

"*Riiight*. I am really sorry."

He leaned over to me and whispered. "*I'm* sorry I didn't tell you about being adopted." His breath smelled like mint gum. "I suppose it should occur to me that people would wonder why Dean and I are so different."

"Yeah," I said. "I did wonder. Is it . . . do you know who your birth parents are? Is that a bad question?"

"No, it's fine. I don't know who they are."

"Do you want to know?"

"Yeah. No. Both." He laughed. "I might look into my adoption records next year when I move out." His eyes burned right into mine.

"Wow." I felt like we were connected somehow. We were both missing parents, one way or another. Missing, and not missing at the same time.

"April," I heard. Crap. Noah. Again.

I stepped back and turned to him. "Sorry," I said. And then wondered why I'd said it. Sorry? For talking to Hudson? For talking to Hudson about something real? Why was I sorry? Should I be sorry?

"I'm going to go," Noah said. His face was tight.

I reached for his hand. "What? No."

He pulled away and headed out the door.

"Noah, wait!"

I followed him outside. "What are you doing?"

"Leaving."

"Why?"

"Because you're flirting with Hudson in front of me!"

My cheeks flushed. "Excuse me?"

"You heard me."

"I was just talking to him. Why are you being such a jerk?" I screamed.

"Why are you acting like a slut?" he yelled back.

"What?" Had he really just said that?

"Running around in your underwear, hot-tubbing nearly naked with half the school, chugging schnapps and then holing up in a corner with that douche."

It felt like he'd slapped me across the face. I staggered back, as though he had. "Fuck you," I said.

We'd fought, but we had never yelled at each other like this. And he had never said anything so awful. I had never said anything so awful.

Noah turned and walked away.

I stood on the porch, reeling.

Then I went to find Hudson.

ON YOUR MARK, GET SET, GO

My mom once told me that the first thing a divorced man wants to do is get married again. Immediately.

She also told me that a man never leaves his wife unless he has another woman in the wings. She said people found running *to* something easier than running *from* something.

I guess that's why she had the affair. To have someone to run to. Or to give my dad something to run from.

TEN THINGS THAT ARE CLEAR AT THREE A.M.

1. It's pouring.
2. Hudson's car keys are in Pinky's purse. (Dean's fault.)
3. Pinky's gone.
4. Dean and Vi are in love.
5. Brett is out cold on the couch, still in his wet surfer shorts.
6. I am still missing an earring.
7. Zachary and Lucy—also missing.
8. I am very drunk.
9. Noah is an ass.
10. Hudson is hot.

"Hud, how did you get here?" Vi asked. The four of us were sitting on the couch.

"Got dropped off."

"By?" I asked. My legs were on Hudson's lap. My head was on the couch cushion. The cactus was moving. It had a white bra on it. Was that mine? I felt my chest. Nope. I was wearing mine.

He smiled. "Mr. Luxe."

"Mr. Luxe, father of . . ." I began.

"Leo. Age six."

I rolled my head from side to side. "Adorable, adorable, adorable. What did you do with Leo, age six?"

"Taught him how to play Monopoly. Had pizza. Read him stories."

"I guess you two will have to bunk with us, too," Vi told the brothers.

"I call your room," Dean said. "Unless you're going to be a bitch about it."

Vi laughed and kicked him.

"Hey, where's Donut?" Hudson asked me.

Donut! My sweet little Donut. I loved Donut. And her teeny-tiny cast. I wanted to cuddle with Donut immediately. "Downstairs. Wanna come check on her?"

"Sure."

As we walked down the stairs, I held on to the banister

for balance. Had I really just invited a boy to my room? Yes. A boy who wasn't my boyfriend? Yes. While I was fighting with my boyfriend? Yes. Probably should not have done that. Even if I wanted to. When we opened my door, Donut was curled on my bed. She purred when she saw us.

"Aw, when does the cast come off?" Hudson asked, looking at her hind leg.

"Two more weeks." We should go back upstairs. But my eyes were heavy. My head was heavy too. Like a hundred pounds. Why was my head so heavy? Was Donut on my head? Where was Donut? Where was Noah? Noah Noah Noah. Ass. Douche. I hated the word *douche*. I hated Noah for using the word *douche*. And *slut*. He'd called me a slut! I couldn't believe he'd called me a slut!

"Poor Donut," a guy who wasn't Noah said. He crawled over my covers and scratched under Donut's chin. "You're a little sweetie, aren't you?"

Hudson! It was Hudson. Hudson was a sweetie. No, Hudson was a stud.

"Hi, Hudson," I said, lying across my bed. Now my room was spinning. Maybe it would stop if I put my head on my pillow. No. Still spinning. But spinning more comfortably. Donut rubbed her ear against my hand. My jeans were too tight. I should take them off. But that was definitely an invitation. Was I ready to make that invitation to the guy in my bed who was not Noah? Maybe I could just take them off without him seeing. I got under the covers, unbuttoned them, and kicked them somewhere under the sheets. "Not an invitation," I said.

Hudson had put his head down on the mattress. "I should go," he said.

He was lying in the bed beside me. In my bed. This was wrong. I knew it was wrong. I had no pants. Maybe Noah was right about me.

"Go where?" I asked.

"I don't know," he said. He stood up.

No. Do not go. He could not go. "Stay," I ordered. "You have to listen to me. It's my birthday." Maybe I should make Noah right about me.

He paused over me. "Well . . . let me turn off the lights."

MY MOM'S AFFAIR

I never told my dad what I heard. The dirty talk on the phone.

A year later my parents told me at David's Deli they were separating.

Not long after the announcement, Mom and I were driving home alone. I asked her if she was going to start dating the Other Guy.

She almost ran through a red light. "Why would you . . . how did you . . . did your father tell you about him?"

I felt horrified. "Dad knows?"

She pulled the car over to the side of the road. "He does."

I sank into my seat. "Is that why you're getting divorced?

Because of the affair?"

She shook her head. "No. It's not about the affair. That's over. Your dad and I . . . we just . . . we've been having problems for a long time. I've been unhappy for a long time. And he wouldn't . . . he wouldn't listen."

"How did he find out?" I asked. I hoped he hadn't accidentally picked up the phone. Or walked in on them. Oh God, I prayed he hadn't walked in on them.

She looked at me. "I told him."

Later, I wondered if that's why she'd had the affair: So she'd have to tell him.

NOW OR NEVER

The room got dark, and then Hudson lay back down next to me.

Our faces were a few inches away from each other. I could kiss him if I wanted to. It would be so easy.

Sure, there was Noah.

But he'd been an ass. I could forget about Noah if I wanted to. Hudson could help. I could run from Noah right to Hudson.

Then I would never have to see the big black hole.

But did I want to?

Yes. No.

Noah.

I still loved Noah. I did. I knew I did.

Then why was I attracted to Hudson? Because he was gorgeous. And sexy. And kind. And because I liked being the Hottest Girl in Westport.

But that didn't make what I was thinking about doing right.

I couldn't hook up with Hudson because I was mad at Noah. I still loved Noah. I'd always love Noah. We had been through so much together. I couldn't—wouldn't—throw away two great years for feeling sexy. Being with Noah had saved me from the big black hole. I couldn't forget that. Wouldn't.

I pulled away, and put my head on the pillow.

"Good night, April," he whispered.

"Good night, Hudson," I whispered back, and closed my eyes.

REASONS YOU SHOULD ALWAYS CHECK YOUR FAKE EMAIL ACCOUNT

From: Jake Berman <Jake.Berman@kljco.com>
Date: Fri, 27 March, 8:10 p.m.
To: Suzanne Caldwell <Suzanne_Caldwell@pmail.com>
Subject: Tomorrow

Suzanne,
I wanted to let you know that we'll be stopping by your place in the morning. Sorry for the late notice—I've been swamped. April knows I'll be in New York, but the

Westport visit is a surprise (for her birthday), so please keep it between us. Looking forward to seeing you again.

Best, Jake

Sent From BlackBerry

THE MORNING AFTER

WEEEooooWEEEooooWEEEoooo!

I bolted awake when I heard the police siren, unsure if it was a real siren—or my dad's ring. I felt around the bed for my phone. No cell. And the futon . . . well, the futon was slightly cramped. There was a leg, a guy's leg, a guy's leg that did not belong to my boyfriend, flung over my ankle. Why was Hudson in my bed?

Oh God. Oh God. What had I done?

WEEEooooWEEEooooWEEEoooo! Upstairs. The siren ring was coming from upstairs.

I looked around for some pants. The sole item of clothing in the vicinity was Vi's red dress that I had on last night, which I vaguely remembered stripping off at one point and leaving on the dock.

That dress was trouble.

I ran up the stairs bare-legged.

War zone. Plastic cups! Beer bottles! Tortilla chips! Stains on the curtains!

There was a bra on the cactus.

Brett was in surfer shorts and face-planted on the couch. He was using the purple linen tablecloth as a blanket. Zachary was asleep in one of the dining room chairs, wearing an aluminum foil tiara on his lolled-back head. The patio door was open—and a puddle of rain was soaking into the faded carpet.

WEEEooooWEEEooooWEEEoooo! Louder. Closer. But where? The kitchen counter! Nestled between a saucer of cigarette butts and an empty bottle of schnapps was my cell. I dove toward the phone. There was a text from Noah but I ignored it. "Hello?"

"Happy birthday, Princess," my dad said. "Did I wake you?"

"Wake me?" I asked, my heart thumping. "Of course not. It's already"—I spotted the microwave clock across the room—"nine thirty-two."

"Good, because Penny and I are on our way to see you!"

Terror seized me. "What does that mean?"

My dad laughed. "We decided to surprise you on your birthday. It was actually Penny's idea."

"Wait. For real?"

"Of course for real! Surprise!"

This wasn't happening. It couldn't happen. I would lose everything. If, after last night, I had anything left to lose. I took a step and a tortilla chip attacked my bare foot. *Owww.*

Mother friggin' crap.

"That's great, Dad," I forced myself to say. "So . . . where are you exactly? Did your plane just land?"

"Nope, we just drove through Greenwich. We should be in Westport in twenty minutes."

Twenty minutes?!

There was groaning from the couch. Brett flipped onto his back and said, "It's eff-ing freezing in here."

"April, there's not a boy over, is there?" my dad asked.

I sliced my hand through the air to tell Brett to shut the hell up.

"What? No! Of course not! Vi's mom is listening to NPR."

"We just passed the Rock Ridge Country Club. Looks like we're making better time than I thought. We'll be there in fifteen minutes. Can't wait to see you, Princess."

"You too," I choked out, and hung up. I closed my eyes. Then opened them.

Two half-naked boys in the great room. One in a tiara.

More half-naked boys in the bedrooms.

Empty liquor bottles and trashed cups.

And Vi's mom nowhere in sight.

I was a dead princess.

QUICK

"Wake up!" I screamed at the top of my lungs. "Vi!" My dad was on his way. My dad was on his way! The house was a disaster and my dad was on his way! I had fifteen minutes to get this place into shape. "Code red! Code red!"

Still-shirtless Brett jumped off the couch. "What? What's happening?"

"You've got to hide," I told him. "And you've got to put on a shirt."

He pulled the tablecloth back over his head.

"That is not a very good hiding spot," I said. "But first help, then hide. Slaves, activate! I need you!"

Zachary stood up and the dining room chair he'd been on fell over.

Vi came running from her room. "What's wrong?" She had definite bed head. Definite. Dean came running out after her.

Guess I know what happened to them.

Marissa and Aaron came tumbling out of Vi's mom's room next.

I rubbed my temples. "People. Dad. On his way. Now. We need to make this place look like we didn't just have a huge party. Otherwise . . ."

"Technically, no parties is not one of the rules," Dean said. "At least it's not on the fridge."

"True," I said. "But I think it's implied."

We all looked around, taking in the spilled glasses, the chip crumbles, the many half-naked boys.

"This does not look good," Vi noted.

"No," I agreed. I glanced at the clock. Nine thirty-four. Ahhh! I started picking up cups, pressing them against my body. I needed garbage bags.

"Can you keep him outside?" Vi asked.

Brett stretched his arms in a yawn. "Who are we keeping outside?"

"April's father," Vi explained.

"Does he live here too?" Brett asked.

"No," I said as I crumpled an empty bag of Cheetos. "And I won't either if you guys don't start helping me." I clapped my hands. "Dean, you're on flood cleanup. Vi, get the garbage bags. Get rid of the cigarette butts. And find the Lysol. Who was smoking in here anyway? Everyone else, start cleaning. I'll get the Miele."

"What's a Miele, man?" Brett asked.

"A vacuum," I yelled. "Now go, go, go!"

TEN MINUTES LEFT

I tidied. Vi vacuumed. Everyone else scooped. "I take it April's father would not be cool with last night's party?" Brett asked.

"Not so much," I said. "Keep scooping."

SIX MINUTES LEFT

"My fingers are going to fall off," Dean complained. "Vi, will you kiss them better?"

"Hells no," Vi said.

I'd tell her not to be an idiot, but there was no time.

TWO MINUTES LEFT

Almost done. Rain was gone, tablecloth was back on table, chips were in the belly of the Miele.

"I'll take out the garbage," Vi said. "Now. Boys. You need to leave or hide."

"We have nowhere else to go," Aaron said. "Where should we hide?"

"Hula?" Brett asked hopefully.

"Are you crazy?" Marissa asks. "Maybe we should hide in your room?" she asked me.

"No, too risky," I said. "What if he wants to see it?"

"Go into my mom's room," Vi said. "Go, go, go!" She ushered them all down the hall.

"Make sure the blinds are closed. And keep the lights off so we can pretend she's sleeping. Anyone who talks is dead! Understood?" I ordered.

I pulled the curtains closed to hide Hula. I pulled my dad's list off the fridge. What else? Was that it?

ONE MINUTE LEFT

A shot glass! On the coffee table! I had it . . . I had it . . . I . . .

Crash. Crap. Crap crap crap. There was no time for this. There was no time for this! I took a deep breath and then cleaned it up. The room looked fine. We were fine. I was going to deal with this. And then I remembered. Hudson.

Downstairs. Sleeping. In my bed. Shit. Also—I still needed pants. I threw open the basement door and took the stairs two at a time. Donut, cast and all, tried to take off up the stairs. "No, Donut, stay!"

"Meow!"

"You have to be very quiet," I told her, carrying her back down. "You're supposed to be dead."

"Hey," Hudson said. "Morning."

I wanted to crawl in beside him. "A bit of craziness going on," I said. "My father is on his way over. Everyone's hiding in Vi's mom's room." I carried Donut over to him. "Can you be in charge of Donut?"

"Of course," he said. "Listen, about last night—"

"Nothing happened," I said quickly. "Can we talk about this later, though? My dad is on his way, and if he sees anyone here it's going to be bad news." I still couldn't help feeling guilty. Even if nothing had happened, I shouldn't have let another guy sleep in my bed. Even though I was pissed at Noah. I wouldn't want another girl sleeping in Noah's bed, would I?

"I know," he said quickly. "But I need to tell you something. I—"

The phone rang.

I prayed that it was my father saying he had a flat tire. But it wasn't his ring. Maybe it was Penny?

PRIVATE.

Ah! There was no time for private. But what if it was Penny?

I sat down beside Hudson and motioned for him to be quiet.

"Hello?" I said. Donut tangled herself around my arm.

"April?" a woman's voice said loudly.

"Speaking," I said. I really didn't have time for this. My father was going to be here any minute.

"This is Doctor Rosini. I have some news. Do you have a few minutes to chat?"

"News?" What did that mean?

"Your test for chlamydia came back positive," she said. Loudly.

Donut bit my wrist.

"What?" I asked. Did she just say what I think she did?

"We tested your urine and it came back positive for chlamydia. It's a sexually transmitted disease. We need you to pick up some antibiotics."

My head was ringing. Donut was still biting my wrist. I tried to shake my arm free but she wouldn't let go. Tears were prickling at my eyes but I wasn't sure if it was the news or the little teeth biting through my skin.

"Donut!" I said finally. "Get off!"

"Let me take her," Hudson said calmly, untangling her from my hands.

The cat shrieked.

"Are you okay?" Doctor Rosini asked.

"I . . . I . . ." I looked at Hudson. Had he heard? "No," I said. I stood up, left Hudson and Donut, went into the bathroom, closed the door, and sat on the closed toilet seat. Then

I got up, turned the water on full blast and sat back down. "Can you start over?" I finally said.

"You have chlamydia," she repeated.

"Chlamydia," I echoed.

"Yes."

"That's . . ." My voice trailed off. "An STD?"

"Yes."

"I have an STD."

"Unfortunately, yes."

"But that's impossible."

"Aren't you sexually active?" she asked.

"I . . . yes."

"Then it *is* possible."

I had an STD. An STD? How could I? I felt exposed and dirty and raw and badly in need of a shower. A hot shower. A long hot shower. I crossed my arms in front of my chest but then uncrossed them, not wanting to get so close to myself. "No, but you don't understand. My boyfriend and I have been together for over two years."

"It's possible one of you got it from a prior relationship."

I shook my head expecting her to see. "But there was no prior relationship. We were both virgins!"

"Hmmm. It is possible to transmit chlamydia through oral sex. But it's rare." She paused. "Are you sure about your boyfriend?"

"No, but . . ." I wasn't sure what to say. I just kept shaking my head. Had Noah . . . had sex with someone else?

"We'd like your boyfriend to come in so he can be treated as well."

"Noah needs to be treated too?" I asked. "He has it?"

"It is likely," she said.

"Chlamydia," I repeated.

"Yes."

"But I . . . I don't even know how to spell chlamydia."

"Hard to spell, easy to catch," she said dryly. "That's part of our public service campaign."

I'd have laughed if I hadn't wanted to cry. "Are you sure?"

"We could do another test if you want, but these are pretty conclusive, and I'd still like to get you started on the antibiotics. To avoid complications."

Complications? "What kind of complications?"

"If untreated, chlamydia can cause PID—pelvic inflammatory disease—which could lead to infertility."

All her words were swishing through my brain, like dirty dishwater in the sink. "Infertility?" My heart stopped. "Do you mean I might not be able to have kids?" I thought of Penny.

"Your symptoms weren't indicative of PID, so I wouldn't be too concerned with permanent damage. But it's a good thing you got tested."

"It burned when I peed," I said.

"Most people don't get any symptoms," she said.

Was I supposed to feel lucky? I felt like I'd been kicked in the stomach.

The doorbell rang. My father. My father was here and I had chlamydia. Hi, Daddy! How are you? Good? Great! I'm fine too. Except for the chlamydia.

Chlamydia, chlamydia, chlamydia. Hard to spell, yes, also hard to say. How much wood would a woodchuck chuck if a woodchuck could chuck chlamydia?

"April?" the doctor asked. "Can I get your pharmacy information so I can call in the prescription? It's a one-day dose of antibiotics."

"Yes. Um . . . can you send it to the Walgreens on Saugatuck?"

I heard footsteps above me. My father's footsteps. I needed to go upstairs. I also needed pants. I turned off the water, and ran into my room.

"April?" Vi yelled. "Your dad and Penny are here!"

"Hi! Coming! I'll be two seconds!"

"So I'll see you in two weeks?" the doctor was saying. "And we'd like to see your boyfriend as soon as possible."

"Yes. Great. Can I call back to schedule?" I spotted my jeans, tangled in my covers, and pulled them on.

What kind of girl takes off her jeans when she's sleeping next to a guy who is not her boyfriend? Oh! A girl who gets chlamydia!

"Hey," Hudson said. He was aiming for eye contact, but I wasn't going to let that happen. No sirree. "You okay?"

"April," the doctor continued. "I'm sorry you have to deal with this, but I'm glad we caught it."

301

Caught it. Like a rat. I imagined a rat running through my body, gnawing on my ovaries. I wanted those antibiotics. Now. Hey, Dad, before breakfast can we make a pit stop for some rat poison?

After the doc and I hung up, Hudson reached for my arm. "April?"

"No, I'm not okay," I said, now avoiding his touch as well as his eyes. I buttoned my jeans. "Did you hear that whole conversation?"

He didn't answer.

Awesome. My cheeks burned. Urine and cheeks. Even awesomer. "Bet you're counting your lucky stars that we didn't hook up last night, huh?"

"It's not that big of a deal," he said.

I looked into my full-length mirror. There I was. I looked the same. No different than I had looked pre-chlamydia. Or at least pre-knowing I had it.

I needed to tie my hair back. It was a mess.

"It is a big deal," I said. I picked up an elastic and pulled my hair into a ponytail. I turned to him. "Do I look diseased?"

We locked eyes. "No," he said.

"Keep Donut quiet, 'kay?"

He nodded.

I hurried up the stairs and closed the door, praying my dad wouldn't ask to see my room.

Game face. I definitely needed a game face. Even though all I could think was chlamydia, chlamydia, chlamydia. I had to stop the word from flashing through my head. I had to. I had to stop it. I had to stop it and I had to go say hello to my father and I had to hope that the house was clean and that my father did not see the evidence of last night's party and that he would not realize that Vi's mom didn't live here or that we had lied to him or that I had chlamydia.

Because if he realized that I had chlamydia I would have to go to Ohio.

Yup, that I was sure of. He would not let me stay here if he knew that. He would not want me living in a pool of disease and grossness. He would want to protect me and love me and keep me safe and clean.

I blinked away tears. I could not cry now. I could not think about this now. I could not, I could not. I opened the door handle and burst into the living room.

"Hi, Dad," I said.

number ten:
got caught breaking and entering

THE VISIT

My dad and Penny had made themselves comfortable on the couch that twenty minutes earlier had been Brett's bed, but they sprang up as I walked through the basement door.

"Happy birthday," my dad said, hugging me to him. "I missed you." He smelled like Dad. Warm, and musky.

"You too," I murmured, and let my head rest against his shoulder. And then I thought, don't get too close. I might be contagious. I pulled back. "Should we go?"

"Actually, we thought we'd wait for Suzanne to get out of the shower. Say hello."

"I've never even met her!" Penny exclaimed, looking around. "Can you believe it?"

The shower. They thought Suzanne's mom was in the

shower. Why did they think that? I listened closely and indeed, the shower was running. What the hell? I gave Vi a look. Whoever had turned on the shower was a dead man. Or woman.

"She's dying to meet you," Vi said smoothly. "I hope she gets out soon. She takes ridiculously long showers. Let me go tell her you guys are here." Vi disappeared down the hallway, closing the door.

I sat down across from them and smiled. "So," I said. "You have a wedding tonight."

"Yup," Penny said. "Tricia's wedding. Did you ever meet her? An old friend from work."

"I was going to take the train in tomorrow to see you," I said.

"I know, but we wanted to surprise you today," my dad said.

"Right." I forced a smile. "Who doesn't like a good surprise?"

Vi reappeared. "My mom locked the door. So sorry. Hopefully she'll be out soon." Then she mouthed at me, "Dean. In shower." She made a throat-slashing motion with her hand.

Fifteen minutes later the water was still running.

"You know what, Dad?" I said. "Why don't you say hi to Suzanne when you drop me off? I'm sure she'll be done by then."

"Yeah," Vi said, standing up. "That's a better idea. She

uses the shower as a steam and it can take forever. She thinks it makes her lose weight. Ha, ha, ha."

Weight–loss obsessions. Must run in the family. I squeezed my eyes shut. Couldn't worry about Vi now. Too many other things to worry about.

TABLE FOR FOUR (DAD, PENNY, ME . . . AND MY STD!)

My father's and Penny's mouths were moving, but I was having difficulty processing their words.

Hello. Hello. Chlamydia. Chlamydia. Question number one: How did I get you, chlamydia? From Noah. Obviously. Since he was the only person I've slept with. Wrong! The only person I had ever *had sex* with. These days, I *slept* with guys all the time. Ha-ha. But I had only had sex with one. He was the only person I had done *anything* with.

The answer: Noah gave me the chlam. Yes, I was calling it the chlam for short. I was allowed to give my STD a nickname since we knew each other so intimately.

Question number two: How did Noah get it?

The more complicated question, clearly. He couldn't have gotten it from me, if I got it from him. Which meant, he had to have gotten it from someone else. As far as I knew, I was his first. And he had never done *enough* with anyone else to give him the chlam. So. There it was. Noah cheated on me. No. I took a sip of coffee. Yes. He had to have. When we'd first started dating, he told me he'd never had sex. Unless he'd lied. He either cheated on me or he lied. As I debated the options, I dribbled coffee down my shirt.

Penny leapt into action, and pulled a wipe from her purse. I wondered if I could use one to wipe my body clean.

"So how's my birthday girl?" my dad was saying, a big smile on his face.

"You look great," Penny said. "Your skin is just glowing. Are you using a different soap?"

No, it's the chlam! It does wonders for the ovaries *and* the complexion. "Thanks," I said instead. "Maybe it's the water at Vi's?" It was probably the birth control pills, actually.

"How's school going?" my dad asked.

"Fine." I pretended my face was Silly Putty and stretched it into a smile. "Everything is fine." Absolutely friggin' fine.

"We wanted to talk to you about next year," my dad said.

"Okay." Next year? First I had to get through this year.

"We're very proud of you," my dad said, beaming.

"You've kept your grades up," Penny said.

"And you've been very responsible," my dad added.

In what world am I responsible? What is he talking about? I haven't crashed the car? Or burned Vi's house down? "Thanks," I said.

"We know Vi is going away to school . . ."

They looked at each other, then my dad turned back to me and said. "We think you're ready for your own apartment next year."

"My own apartment?" I repeated in shock.

"Yes," Penny said. "I was thinking a one-bedroom in town. Something with a doorman. So we know you're safe.

We'd rather you come to Cleveland, but since this is what you want . . . What do you think?"

"Wow," was all I could say. My own place.

Just me.

That was what I'd wanted.

My own place. At seventeen. That's what I'd asked for. My own dishes and laundry and bills and TV and oven. I could handle it too. I wouldn't have been able to back in January, but now I could. But is that what I wanted? To live on my own? My own place so I could have Noah come over whenever? Noah, the lying bastard? What I wanted was to stick Noah's head in the oven à la Zelda.

I forced a smile and said, "Sounds great."

CAR TRIP

I called Vi from the backseat of my dad's car. "Hi!" I chirped into the phone. "How's it going?"

"They all left. Thank God. It's just me and Donut. Safe to bring Papa Bear back."

"What?" I said extra loudly. "Your mom had an appointment?"

Penny spun around to face me and frowned.

"Oh, she does," Vi said. "An appointment with her pillow most likely. Or a bottle of Merlot. She loves those appointments."

I made an exaggerated shrug. "That sucks! My parents

are dying to say hello!" I looked up at Penny. "Sorry. She's at . . . the hair salon."

"Oh really? Which one? I have an appointment too!"

Hmm. "Vi," I said. "Which salon is your mom at?"

"Um . . . Salon of *Mary Poppins*?"

"She's not sure," I told Penny.

"Wouldn't it be funny if you ran into her?" my dad asked.

"If you do," I said, "tell her I say hi."

WE NEED TO TALK

When my dad dropped me off, I waved from the doorway. When he drove away I closed the front door and went to my car.

That was it. Dad's visit over. Parental crisis averted. Must now focus on the crisis in my pants.

Vi opened the door and stuck her head out. "Where are you going?"

"Errands," I told her. I would talk to her about everything. After. First I had to go to the pharmacy. And I had to talk to Noah.

Funny how life messed with you. This morning when my dad called I thought a disaster was about to run me over. And I'd been right—but it hadn't been the disaster I'd seen coming. That disaster had fizzled. This disaster had blindsided me.

"I'll be back soon," I said. I closed the car door and

backed out of the driveway. Vi stood in the doorway making a "What's going on?" motion with her arms.

My prescription was waiting for me at Walgreens. Zithromax. One dose. I wondered if the pharmacist knew what it was for. I didn't look her in the eye. I also bought a water. I sat in my car in the Walgreens parking lot and took it immediately. There. Do your work, Zithromax! Now what?

I knew what. I had to talk to Noah. I checked the text he'd sent this morning.

Noah: Are you up? I can't sleep. But I don't want to call in case you're still sleeping . . . Sorry about last night. I love you. Happy birthday.

I should call him.

No. I didn't want to call him. I didn't want to speak to him.

Because once I spoke to him, he'd have to answer.

I did not want to hear the answer.

Shit. I had to go to his house and talk to him in person.

I put the car in REVERSE, and my phone rang.

"Hey," Noah said.

"Hey." I shifted back into PARK. I didn't know where to start.

"Did you get my text?" he asked.

"Yes."

"About last night . . . I'm sorry for being a jerk. I guess I just don't like seeing you with that douche. And about the earring. Did you find it?"

"Huh?"

"The earring?"

The earring. He was talking about the earring. It felt like that had happened ten years ago. "Noah."

"Yes."

Where to start? A joke maybe? What do you get if you scramble a *Y, C, H, L, M, A* . . . "Did you cheat on me?"

"What? What are you talking about?"

"Did you sleep with someone else?" The words were coming out of my mouth but I felt like someone else was saying them.

"Why would you think that?"

Because I had proof. Unfortunate proof. But—

"Did you?" I asked.

"No," he practically screeched.

He was lying. He had to be lying.

"I swear," he said. "April, no."

My head hurt. "I have chlamydia."

"What?"

"A disease. I have a disease. A sex disease. That I had to have gotten from you."

No comment.

"Hello? Can you explain?"

Still no comment.

I closed my eyes. It was sunny out. Too sunny. "Noah? Are you still there?"

"Yeah."

"Well, did you hear what I said? I have it. Which means I got it from you."

"How do you know that?"

I banged my fist against the steering wheel.

"Did you go to the doctor?" he asked.

"Of course I did! It's not a home test!"

"When? You never told me you were going to the doctor."

"I didn't want—" Wait. "Who cares if I told you? I went."

"Is it possible it was a mistake?" he asked. "Or maybe you got it from somewhere else."

My chest felt tight. "Like where? Are you asking me if *I* cheated?" Now was not the time to mention the Hudson incident, although I'm sure he was thinking about Hudson.

"I don't know," he said. "Like a toilet seat or something?"

Now I banged my head against the steering wheel. "I didn't get it from a toilet seat."

"What about your hot tub? I knew that thing was a bad idea. It's gross."

"It wasn't from the hot tub. You have to go to the clinic. And get tested."

"But nothing's wrong with me. I feel fine."

"Most people don't get symptoms."

"I don't have an STD," he said, his voice incredulous.

"Yes, you do!" I yelled, and before I knew it tears were

rolling down my cheeks. "If I do, you do. Even if you didn't give it to me, then I gave it to you so now you have it. We both do." He was really pissing me off. Why did he have to make me feel like I was in this by myself? I didn't just magically get it. No matter what, we were in it together. I was not alone in this. It was physically impossible.

"You're right," he said. "I'm sorry. Fuck. This whole thing just came out of nowhere."

"No kidding," I said, wiping my eyes.

"I'll call my doctor, okay? And I'll get checked. But I bet it's all a mistake. It has to be."

"So you didn't cheat on me?" I asked, my voice filling with hope.

"I love you. I wouldn't do that. I would never do that."

"But what about Corinne? Did you sleep with her? Maybe she had it."

"I never slept with Corinne."

"What about before Corinne? Before me?"

"No! No one. And I never cheated on you with Corinne. You know that. You can't keep bringing that up."

"I know, I just . . ." My head was spinning. "I'm confused, okay? And upset."

"Don't be. Everything will be okay. I promise."

Was it possible? If it really wasn't from him and I was blaming him . . . I wanted to believe him. Maybe it was from Hula. Or a toilet seat. Or maybe the results were wrong.

"Okay," I said.

Anything *was* possible.

BACK HOME

"So," I said, tossing my purse on the floor. "Are we alone?"

Vi was sitting on the couch holding a jar of peanut butter and a spoon. "Yup. Where did you disappear to before?"

I stood in the middle of the room and put my hands on my hips. "Walgreens. I needed antibiotics. For my chlamydia."

Her jaw dropped. "Holy shit."

"No kidding. And FYI—burning pee? Not always a urinary tract infection." As awful as all this was, it felt good to talk about it.

"Oh. My. God. April. I'm so sorry."

"Me too. Antibiotics taken, though. So hopefully it is gone. Or almost gone."

"Jesus. I can't believe it. But how did you get it? Weren't you using condoms?"

"I . . ." The words didn't come out.

THE ELEVENTH TIME NOAH AND I HAD SEX

"Uh-oh," he said. "I think we finished the condoms."

"We did? All of them?"

He laughed. "Yeah. I forgot to get more." He was lying on top of me.

"Oh."

"Yeah. Whoops."

"Well . . . I am on the pill."

"Yeah. You sure?"

"Yeah."

"Okay."

"Okay."

"I love you," he said.

"You too."

GETTING YELLED AT BY VI

"April," she asked again. "Weren't you using condoms?"

I didn't answer.

"Oh God, come on. You slept with him without a condom? Are you an idiot?"

My head hurt. "I don't know."

"What were you thinking?"

"That he's my boyfriend."

"That's why I don't want a boyfriend," she said angrily. "You can't trust them. You can't trust anyone. You have to look out for yourself. You have to respect yourself."

"I really don't feel like a lecture right now," I said. "We used condoms but then they ran out and we just felt so much closer. And I'm on the pill."

"The pill does not protect against STDs! Or HIV!"

"Stop sounding like a public service announcement!"

"You obviously need to hear it! You got chlamydia from your boyfriend!"

"Probably . . ."

"Wait. What? Did you sleep with someone else? Hudson? Please tell me Hudson didn't do this."

I shook my head. "It wasn't Hudson. *Nothing* happened with Hudson. And, I haven't been with anyone else."

"Then what?" she asked. "You can't get it from a toilet seat."

I shrugged. "You don't know that."

She snorted. "Yeah, April, I do. Who do you think wrote the STD article for *The Issue*?"

"Well, maybe it's from Hula."

She closed her eyes and rubbed her forehead. "You did not just say that."

"It's possible," I squeaked.

"No, April, it's not. Is that what Noah said? That you got it from the hot tub?"

I didn't answer.

"He's full of it."

"He's not," I said. "It is a germ-fest in there. We never remember to check the pH levels and—" What the hell was I talking about? Was I really repeating what Noah had said?

She kept shaking her head. "First of all, even if it were a germ-fest, even if you did catch it from the hot tub, which, for the record, is totally impossible, Hula wouldn't have spontaneously produced chlamydia. You would have gotten it from someone in the hot tub. Are you saying you got it from me? Now I have it too?"

"It was a *used* hot tub. Maybe it wasn't cleaned properly." I knew it sounded moronic but I couldn't stop myself from saying it.

"You're being stupid."

"Don't tell me I'm being stupid!"

"But you are being stupid. Your boyfriend is lying to you. He slept with someone else, caught something, and gave it to you."

"No. There has to be another way."

"I know it's hard for you to let go of him. He was there for you after your parents got divorced. And when your mom left. But you can't stay with him because of that. You can't be afraid to move on. He's an asshole dragging you down. Clearly you're attracted to Hudson—"

"This isn't about Hudson!" I said. Yes, I was attracted to Hudson. But I loved Noah. Didn't I?

"Stop. You're lying to yourself. You need to open your eyes."

I crossed my arms tightly. She had no right. "What, like you're so perfect?"

"I never said I was perfect."

"You're a total control freak! You fixed up the guy you like with someone else so you don't have to commit to him! You work out in the middle of the night! You won't let me drive! You follow me around turning off lights! It's worse than living with Penny. And let me tell you, being a control freak isn't going to change the fact that your mom is a total flake. And you know what? I could have just stayed in her room, because she's not coming back."

Vi visibly flinched. Then she turned around and stomped over to her room, slamming the door and leaving me alone.

My chest tightened. Had I really said all that?

Never mind. She had been acting like a bitch. Just when I needed her to coddle me, she attacked me. Telling me I was stupid. Accusing Noah.

But then. What I'd said was pretty awful.

Now what? I needed to get out of here. I needed to be with someone who would sympathize with me, not scold me. I needed to vent and to hear an "everything's going to be okay" from someone who wasn't Noah. I needed my mom. I wanted to put my head in her lap and let her play with my hair, like she used to. I wanted her to tell me everything would be fine. But she wasn't here. As usual.

I grabbed my purse off the floor, walked out the front door and got back into my car. I'd go to Marissa's.

I called her from a red light. She didn't answer.

"Hi," I said. "It's me. I need to talk to you. Call me when you get this?"

I kept driving. Going nowhere. I needed to figure this out. Did he cheat on me? Would he? Yes. He must have. He must have slept with Corinne. I needed proof. Who would know? Corinne. Corinne would know. Yes. I would go to Corinne's. I made a U-turn and then a left and a right and then I parked in front of her house.

As I got out of the car, I felt sick. And excited. Not happy excited, just incredibly wound up. Colors were brighter. Sounds were louder. I had known about Corinne and Noah all along, hadn't I? Yes, I had. Of course Corinne and Noah were sleeping together. She wanted him. She always did. And someone had given her the nasty disease and she had given it to Noah and now I had it. It was all her fault.

Heart pounding, I stomped up her stairs and rang her doorbell. Maybe Noah was here now. Maybe they were having sex and laughing at this very moment.

There was rustling behind the door. I could feel someone looking at me. And then— "April? What's up?" Corinne, in jeans and a white tee, her red hair in a bun. Then she bit her lip. She did not look surprised to see me.

"We need to talk," I said gravely.

She nodded. Nodded! Obviously she was guilty! She came outside and closed the door behind her, even though she was barefoot. She sat down on a step, bracing herself.

I walked to the bottom of the steps. No way I was sitting down for this. I put my hands on my hips and glared at her. "I know," I said.

Her shoulders sank. Her head dropped. She looked like a scared turtle. "I'm so sorry."

Oh my God. She admitted it! She actually admitted it! "Sorry's not good enough," I spat out. "What you did was so wrong."

She burst into tears. "I know," she sobbed.

She knew hooking up with *my boyfriend* was wrong. But did she know about the chlam? Did she do it on purpose? Did she try to get me sick?

That seemed a little far-fetched, I realized. So maybe she didn't know. Maybe she had it and had no idea. Maybe I shouldn't tell her. Let her find out on her own. One day. In ten years.

Oh God. No. I was not *that* girl either.

"You should know that you gave him something," I told her. "You might want to go to the doctor."

She looked up at me through her tears. "Gave him what? Mouth to mouth? I couldn't have. I didn't get out of the car."

Huh? "What does that mean? You guys only did it in the car? What, did you drive around the city finding abandoned parking lots?"

Her eyebrows were knotted in confusion. "It wasn't a parking lot. It happened right in front of your house."

How awful could she be? "You hooked up with Noah in front of my house? Were you just trying to spite me?"

She blinked. Then blinked again. "What are you talking about? I didn't hook up with Noah. I mean, I kissed him, a million years ago, you knew about that."

If she didn't hook up with Noah . . . "Then what are you so sorry for?"

She burst into tears again. "For running over your cat!"

I took a step back. "You ran over Donut?"

She nodded.

"Why did you run over Donut?"

320

"I didn't mean to! Honestly! I was driving down your street and I didn't even see her in front of me."

This made no sense. I thought back to the night of the accident. Vi and I had been in the hot tub. I'd left the door open. Corinne hadn't been over. "But why were you in front of my house?"

"I was just driving by," she said, playing with her fingers.

"Corinne, I live on a cul-de-sac. There is no reason to drive by. And your lights were off."

She closed her eyes and I watched tears stream out of the corners. "I was at Joanna's."

"You were at Joanna's? I didn't even know you were that good of friends with Joanna."

"I'm not," she said quickly. "I mean . . . I am." She turned bright red.

I realized what was going on.

"You mean you're *dating* Joanna."

"Oh God, please don't tell anyone."

"Wait, hold on. I'm not going to tell anyone." I sat down beside her. "But I had no idea. When did you start seeing Joanna?"

"I'm not *seeing* her. I'm just figuring things out. I don't know. After the Noah thing happened I realized that maybe guys just aren't for me. Oh God. I can't believe I just said that."

"But you are always flirting with Noah."

"Not really. Well, maybe a little. But just for show. Because I'm not ready for anyone to know about me and

Joanna. And girls. Whatever."

"I thought you were trying to—"

"What, steal him?"

When she put it like that it sounded stupid.

We sat in silence for a moment.

"Can we get back to the running-over-my-cat part?" I finally asked.

She nodded. "I turned my lights off when I drove by so you guys wouldn't see me. And after I heard the crunch—"

We both winced.

"I should have gotten out of the car. I wanted to. But I couldn't. Then I would have had to tell you why I was driving by your house and . . ."

"Why didn't you call someone? The animal hospital?" If I hadn't noticed Donut was missing she would have stayed outside all night.

"I didn't know it was your cat. I didn't know you had a cat. I kind of hoped that maybe it was a branch."

"Right."

"I'm sorry. I didn't know until later that week when I heard about it from Noah in class. And I felt sick. So sick. I'll pay you back. I can't believe how expensive it was. I bought half the punch at your party to try and pay you back!"

"Thank you," I said. And realized I meant it.

And I thought she had been there to hit on Noah.

Noah.

What did all this mean about Noah? Did this mean . . .

could he have been telling the truth? That he never cheated on me? But then how did I get the chlam? My cell rang and the call display said MARISSA.

"Corinne, I have to go. But I promise not to say anything about what you told me," I said gently. "Even about the cat part. It's between us."

"You're the best. Thank you. Thank you so much. And I will pay you back. I promise."

"Donut's fine now. Don't worry about it. The party raised enough money." I waved good-bye as I answered the phone. "Hey," I said.

"Hi! Happy birthday! Omigod, this morning was crazy. But it was so good to see Aaron! I'm so bummed we won't be spending the summer together. But I had a great idea. I was thinking that maybe the two of us should spend the summer in—"

"I have to talk to you," I interrupted. "I'll be outside your house in two minutes."

"Hey! What happened? Did your dad find out? What's going on with you and Hudson?"

"Nothing," I said. "Just come outside."

"Are you okay? You sound weird."

"Yeah, well, I feel weird. I need to talk. I need advice."

"I'll be right out."

She was standing in the driveway by the time I got there.

"What's up?" she asked, sliding into the passenger side. She looked at my face. "What's wrong?"

323

I put the car into PARK and turned off the engine. "I have chlamydia."

Her jaw dropped. "Shut. Up."

"I know, huh?"

"How do you know?"

"I went to the doctor to get tested for a UTI. And they found it."

"Did you talk to Noah?"

I turned to her. "He said . . . he said he's never cheated on me. I don't know. Vi said he's lying. I had to have gotten it from him, right? He's the only guy I've ever done anything with!"

"Yeah," she said slowly. "It had to be him."

"Vi says he cheated on me. But . . . I don't know. I can't believe he would do that. I just can't. We've been so good. Like a real couple. We talk every night. We spend all day together. He couldn't have done it. Where would he have found the time? If he did give it to me . . . I'm thinking it must have been before. When we weren't together. Maybe when we were freshman? I know he said he had never done it but . . . you'd think if he had sex when he was a freshman he would have told someone. Everyone. I mean, what guy wouldn't?" I knew I was rambling but I couldn't stop. I didn't want to stop. If I kept talking, then I wouldn't have to think. "Maybe he got it then," I continued. "I thought he could have slept with Corinne but I really don't think that happened anymore so I don't know—"

"April," she said. She looked down at her lap.

"I'm rambling right?"

"I heard a rumor."

"Huh?"

"I heard a rumor about Noah."

My heart stopped. "What?"

"That he hooked up with someone else. That he cheated on you."

I closed my eyes. "Really?"

"I didn't believe it," she said, her words coming out in a gush. "You guys were the perfect couple. But now . . . I don't know."

Everything froze. "With who?"

"Not Corinne. Some chick he met on vacation. I thought it was a stupid rumor."

"When did this happen?"

"Over Christmas break. In Palm Beach. On New Year's."

"This Christmas?"

"Yeah."

I remembered this Christmas. I had told him about the move. And then he had cheated on me. Guess he was not a fan of me staying around after all. Or maybe he'd been pissed that I'd postponed our big night of sex because I was stressed about my dad moving. "He cheated on me before we slept together."

"Yes."

"So he slept with someone else and then he slept with me."

"I guess. But it's just a rumor. It may not even be true. That's why I didn't tell you. I didn't believe it. You guys were like the perfect couple and he made you so happy."

"Where did you hear this rumor?"

"She's camp friends with Brett's girlfriend, and Jane asked Aaron if I knew her, and . . ."

They all knew. The whole Aaron crew. Jilted Jane. Who I'd pitied. Jilted me. "What's her name? The girl."

"Lily," she said. "Lily Weinberg."

Lily. Stupid Lily. Disease-ridden Lily. Whorish Lily. "I can't—wait, when did you find all this out?"

She shrugged, not looking at me. "A while ago."

"How long ago?" My voice tensed.

"A couple months. I don't remember."

"Are you joking? You knew that he cheated on me a few months ago? And you didn't say anything? How could you not say anything?"

"I didn't want to upset you. And it was a rumor."

"I don't care if it was a rumor! You should have told me!"

She burst into tears. "I'm sorry! I thought about it but—"

"Did you hear about it before I slept with him?"

She didn't answer.

"You did! How could you not have told me? Why didn't you stop me?"

"I tried to stop you! At the movie theater! But you wanted to do it. You were obsessed with doing it."

"I was not obsessed. I wanted to have sex with my

boyfriend, who I was in love with. And who I thought was in love with me too. I thought you were just being prudish. I thought you just didn't want me to do it if you weren't."

"April, come on."

"I might kill you," I snapped.

"You're not really pissed at me," she said. "You're mad at Noah and you're taking it out on me because I'm sitting here."

"No, I'm mad at you because you're a bad friend."

She flinched. "I'm sorry. I should have told you. I was just . . ."

"A bad friend?"

"No. Yes." She wiped her eyes with the back of her hand. "And afraid. I was afraid if I told you you'd break up with him—"

"Yeah."

"—and then you'd move to Ohio."

Great. Just terrific. Did everyone think I stayed just because of him? "So you tricked me into staying."

"I'm sorry," she said again. Her shoulders sagged.

"Me too," I said. "Can you get out now?"

"April—"

"I'm serious. Get out. I need to call Noah."

"I'm here if you want to talk. And I'm sorry. I love you, you know that. And I swear—I didn't think it was true. I didn't think it was possible. Noah's an ass."

She got out of the car and gently closed the door behind her.

Instead of waiting for her to get back to her house, like I usually did, I sped off.

THE TRUTH

Five minutes later I was outside Noah's house. I parked the car and walked over to the park across the street.

I called him and asked him to come outside and meet me. I hung up. I couldn't believe he hadn't told me the truth today. How could he lie to me like that? He'd lied during the I Never game too. Never had sex? Please.

Am I the only one who told the truth during I Never?

Noah could have told me. Maybe not then, in front of everyone. But later.

Or before we'd had sex.

I knew he was acting weird. Hadn't I asked him what was wrong? He could have told me then. I'd given him an opening. A wide, big-assed, we-haven't-had-sex-yet opening. Jerk. Liar.

I wasn't facing him, but I heard his shoes on the pebbles behind me.

"Hey," he said.

I was sitting on the green bench. I didn't turn around. He walked in front of me.

"I have to tell you something," he said.

"You think?" I crossed my arms across my chest and

then wondered if I should punch him instead.

"I slept with someone else."

Everything ached. I nodded. "Go on."

"Over Christmas."

I wanted to dig myself under the grass, but I tried to stay upright. "And a few hours ago, you lied because . . ."

"Because I was freaked out. I don't know. I shouldn't have. I just did."

"And you slept with someone else because . . ."

He didn't say anything.

I kicked my foot into the ground. "Say something! I don't understand! Explain it to me!"

"It just happened," he said softly.

"That's such bullshit!" I yelled. My voice carried across the park. "Sex doesn't just happen. You make it happen." I thought of the night before with Hudson. It could have happened then. Easily. But we hadn't let it.

He was quiet for a second and then he said, "I'm an idiot. It was only once. I was drunk."

"That is not an excuse."

"I'm not saying it is!" He rushed to say. "I'm just telling you the truth."

"A little late."

His cheeks were flushed red. "I know. I should have told you."

"You should have told me. You should have worn a condom. With her. With me."

"I know! But I hadn't planned on it . . . on anything." He

slammed his fist into his palm.

"So did you know this girl well?"

"Yeah, her grandfather lives next door to mine in Florida."

"So where were you guys? On the beach?"

He looked down at the ground. "You don't really want to know."

Now I really wanted to punch him. "Now you're going to tell me what I do or don't want to know? You do not have the right to do that. You have no more rights. I want to know the details. Every detail. Go."

He took another breath. "We were on the beach. And we just . . ." His voice trailed off.

"Hooked up," I spit the words out.

"Yeah."

The whole scene was playing in my head and I couldn't make it stop. I could see his eyes, the way he looked at me just before he kissed me. The way he touched me—he had touched her. This random girl. Why had I asked for details? I didn't want them. Hadn't I learned my lesson last time?

I felt sick. Dizzy. Empty. Off-kilter. Drunk. Punched. Raw.

"If you didn't want to get caught you should have worn a condom. And at least told your slutty friend not to blab to all her friends. Yeah. It's a small world. And I know all about Lily."

He winced as I said her name. "I'm sorry, April. Really. I do love you."

"Save it. I don't understand," I said again. "You couldn't wait? You only had to wait a little longer."

"It wasn't about waiting," he said.

"I thought things were good with us," I said quietly. "Weren't they good? Why would you sleep with someone else?"

"They were good. They *are* good."

My head hurt. "You wouldn't have slept with her if they were good. That's not the way it works."

"I guess . . . I was just freaked out. Your parents were moving. And you decided to stay. Again."

"So?"

"It was a big deal. And it just . . . I don't know. Your mom moved to France. You stayed. Your dad moved. You stayed. It was a lot of pressure. On me."

"Wait, wait, wait. I didn't do all that for you!" My head was spinning.

"Oh, come on. Why else would you have stayed? When I asked you why you weren't moving to Ohio you said it was because of me!"

I thought back to our conversation that night in the car. I'd kept repeating how much I loved him because I thought he was upset about us not having sex. But the whole time he was freaked out about how much I supposedly loved him.

I'm all yours, I'd said.

Oh God.

"I was trying to make you feel good." I had said what I'd said because I was trying to make him feel needed, to feel loved. "It wasn't about you."

It was about everything. School. Him. Marissa. Vi. My life. Moving to Ohio meant saying good-bye to everything and I hadn't been able to do that.

Leaving Westport was scary. Everyone else had moved away and moved on. But I couldn't.

"It wasn't *only* you," I said. "I think I was afraid to move on."

As I said it, I realized it was true. Maybe being afraid to leave wasn't about Noah or Marissa or Vi or school. Maybe it was about everything that had happened over the past few years. Maybe it was about me not wanting anything else to change.

"I thought it was because of us," he said. "And I wanted you to stay. I wanted to be with you. But it just felt . . . big. Heavy. I felt trapped. If you were choosing me over your family . . . I had to be worth it."

I looked at him. "So you chose to prove your worthiness by sleeping with someone else?"

"I just freaked out. With Lily there was no bigger meaning. I should have told you before you and I slept together. I kept wanting to tell you. But then things were so good with us and I thought I could just forget it ever happened."

"If only you hadn't given me a disease."

"It was stupid. I don't know why I did it. Things with us felt complicated and this was just easy."

"She was easy," I said, and then wished I could take it back. It wasn't her fault. It was, obviously, but she's not the one who owed me anything. She owed me nothing. He'd owed me more. "No, I take that back. It wasn't her fault. It's yours."

"I know it's my fault. Can you ever forgive me?"

I looked up at him. The guy I had loved. Loved more than anything. He'd freaked out. Felt cornered. Reacted. Could I forgive him? Then nothing would have to change.

His cheeks were bright red. His eyes were wet.

Maybe if he'd told me after it happened. Before we'd had sex. But it was too late. "No," I said. "I can't."

I got off the bench and walked away.

ON THE ROAD

I put the key in the ignition and drove. And turned. And then turned again. I stopped the car in the middle of the street. Where the hell was I supposed to go? My boyfriend was a cheating bastard. My roommate thought I was an idiot and a bitch. My best friend lied to me.

I had nothing here. Nothing left.

How was I going to go back to school? How could I face any of them? Hudson knew about the chlamydia. Corinne probably did too now, after putting together the pieces of what I said. I wished I had moved to Ohio.

Maybe I was wrong all along.

Maybe I should have moved.

Maybe I would be better off in Cleveland.

I stared at the stop sign in front of my car. Yes. Cleveland. That's what I had to do. Move. Move right now. I didn't even have to say good-bye to anyone. I'd just go. I'd fly back with my dad tomorrow. I could start school there on Monday. Who needed Westport? I didn't.

My heart started to flutter. It wasn't even *that* crazy. Most of my classes were AP classes. They'd be easy to transfer.

I took out my cell. "Dad," I said. "Daddy, I have to talk to you. It's important. Where are you?" At least someone will be happy with what I have to say. He'll want me. I'm wanted in Cleveland.

"Hi, Princess! I just dropped Penny off at the salon. I'm going to do some Westport errands before picking her up and driving back to the city."

"Dad. Listen. I changed my mind. I want to move to Cleveland."

He laughed. "What?"

"I want to come. Now. Tomorrow. I don't want to be in Westport anymore."

I waited for the joy. "April. You're almost done with the year."

What? That wasn't joy. "I know. And I want to finish the year in Cleveland." My voice felt strange.

"But you're so happy at Suzanne's! I don't understand."

"I'm not happy at Suzanne's," I said. "I'm not. I want to leave. I need to leave."

"Come on. You can't move *now*."

"Why not?"

"It's the middle of the semester!"

"But you wanted me to move in the middle of the year a few months ago!"

"January is not the same thing as April. You only have two and a half more months of school."

What was his problem?

"Look, Princess, this is a big decision. Why don't you sleep on it? I bet you'll feel better tomorrow."

My head started to spin. Why did my dad sound like he didn't want me? I gripped the phone tighter.

Because he didn't want me.

He was happy with his new life. Just him and Penny. No sullen teenager to ruin the mood, or share a wall with. He finally had a clean slate.

And I spent the last three months trying to stop him from dragging me to Cleveland . . . when he never would have.

Well, happy birthday to me.

"I don't understand," I said, my voice breaking. "I thought you wanted me to come."

"I do want you to come. Of course I do. But Penny just turned the second bedroom into a studio. She's painting again, you know."

I couldn't move in with them because my stepmom needed her art studio. "Don't you have three bedrooms?"

"Yes, but the guest bedroom just has the pull-out couch and all our gym equipment. . . ."

"Where's the canopy bed?" I asked.

"We didn't have a place for it. So we gave it to Penny's niece." My father coughed. "April, we're getting you your own apartment. That's what you wanted."

"I did," I said. I had wanted it. Hadn't I? I didn't know what I wanted. I knew that I didn't want to feel like this.

Abandoned.

Dirty.

Unwanted.

Left behind.

Like everyone had their own lives—lives that didn't include me.

"So you don't want me to move to Cleveland," I said.

"Of course we want you to," he said. "But right now . . . it's just not practical."

My cheeks were wet. I didn't want him to be practical. I wanted him to say he wanted me with him. I wanted him to say he couldn't live without me. But I knew he wouldn't. He could live without me. He could live without my mom. My brother. Me. Everyone could live without me.

"If you still want to live with us after the school year we'll figure it out."

Honk!

"Uh-huh," I said, choking on my tears.

"Maybe we can get Penny a separate studio. Or we've been

thinking about renovating the basement."

Honk, honk, honk!

"I have to go." I hung up and hit the gas. I didn't know where to, but I had to get away from here.

HOME, AGAIN

The key was still under the mat. Was it considered breaking and entering if I used a key? Also, if no one was living there? I had driven around until almost seven and then somehow ended up here. The FOR SALE sign was still displayed on the front lawn.

So what if I had nowhere else to go? I was going to live right here. The one place I felt right. 32 Oakbrook Road. I turned the key in the door and opened it. "Hello?" I said, just in case. My voice echoed through the house. No one answered. The den looked smaller than I remembered it. Once upon a time the four of us had sat here on a green couch covered in stitched white circles and watched TV. Now the room was empty.

The walls were a pale yellow. Had they always been yellow? I didn't think so. I couldn't remember. I went upstairs to my room. My empty room. My cherry wallpaper was gone. My bed was gone. My carpet had been replaced. But it was still my room, damn it.

I sat down on the floor, and leaned my head against my wall and looked out my window.

My cell rang. I glanced at the caller ID.

My mother. Fantastic.

"Happy birthday to you! Happy birthday to you! Happy birthday, dear April—"

"Mom. Just stop."

"Why? What's wrong? It's your birthday!"

"It's been a bad day."

"Why? What happened?"

"I don't want to talk about it."

"*Okaaaaay.* April, have you looked at dates for the summer? We need to get you a ticket before they—"

"I am not coming to France!" I yelled. My voice echoed in my empty room. Even though I had nowhere to go, I would still not go to France.

Silence. "You mean this summer?"

"I mean ever."

"You're being crazy."

Maybe. But I was still mad at her. "It's not like you really care if I come."

"Of course I care!"

"If you wanted me there you would have made me move in the first place."

She took a breath. "You didn't want to come. You wanted to stay with your friends. With Noah. I wanted you to be happy."

"Yeah, right."

"You were already so mad at me . . . what was I supposed to do? Force you to come?"

Yes. No. I didn't know what I wanted. I wanted her to say I had to come with her no matter what. That she couldn't live without me. I wanted to be with my dad. I wanted to be with my friends. With Noah. With Hudson. I wanted to be with Matthew. I wanted my mom here. In this house. I wanted to be with them in France. I wanted a million things that were all jumbled together.

"Maybe that's what I should have done," she continued softly. "Forced you to come."

"Better than leaving me by myself," I snapped.

"I left you with your father. You were supposed to be with your father." She sounded like she was crying. "I just wanted you to be happy," she repeated.

"I'm not happy."

"Then come. Please. I love you. I'm sorry."

"It's too late," I said. "I have to go." I hung up. I turned the power off and threw my phone across the empty room.

ANOTHER BREAK-IN

It was two in the morning. I was in a strange house, lying on my old floor, staring at the ceiling. After I'd explored the house, I'd returned to my room and stared at the ceiling and cried. Then I'd fallen asleep.

I hadn't eaten since brunch, but I wasn't hungry. I was tired. Bone tired. And sad. And depressed. The bottomless black hole was lurking. And I really, really had to use the bathroom.

But what if it burned when I peed?

I knew I was being stupid sitting—lying—here, but I wanted to see how long I could stay. If I could do it. If I could just disappear. Sink into the black hole. Some real estate broker would find me next month, nibbled on by mice.

Knock. Knock, knock, knock.

Was that someone at the front door? Obviously I couldn't answer it. But why would someone be knocking at the door of an empty house in the middle of the night? It was probably a branch. Or a cat. Maybe it was my imagination. Stop imaginary knocking, stop!

It stopped.

Now it was just me and my house. All alone. The way we liked it. I tried to close my eyes again. But I really had to pee. The moonlight had lit up the room, but the rest of the house would be dark. Would I still remember the way? And did I have tissues in my bag? I stood up, stretching my arms above my head. When I reached my doorway, I felt the walls in the pitch blackness and moved down the hallway. As I moved deeper in, the darkness enveloped me. I held my purse close to steady myself. I think the bathroom was just a few steps up. . . . There was a window in the bathroom, wasn't there? There'd be moonlight?

There was another creak from downstairs. And what sounded like a door opening. Was someone else in the house? How was that possible? Did someone else know about the key? No. The key was in my pocket. But had I locked the door behind me? I couldn't remember. I definitely didn't remember locking it. Oh, jeez. My heart started to pound.

Did other people use this house as a free place to crash? Had a crazy person seen me come in and was now going to kill me? There were whispers. Whispers everywhere. I had to be imagining it. Houses made noises. Especially old houses. I just wished it wasn't so dark in here.

Creak. More whispers. If only I hadn't watched so many episodes of *Vampire Nights.* Maybe it was Zelda. She had followed me here. Hi, Zelda!

Clearly, I was losing my mind. Didn't chlamydia make you go crazy? I remembered something about that from health class. No. I think that was syphilis.

Maybe I had that too.

Now the stairs were creaking. What was I doing in an abandoned house in the middle of the night? Asking to be murdered? If only I had a flashlight. But who carried a flashlight with her? There was one in my car. But what good would that do? Thanks a lot, Dad. You almost had my back. My cell. I had my cell! I would turn on my phone and there would be light and the noises would stop. I reached into my purse and pressed the ON button. Ta-da!

A face lit up in front of me.

I screamed.

She screamed.

"Jesus Christ," the voice said. "It's just me."

Vi.

The downstairs lights turned on. "Hey," Marissa said. "That's better."

I blinked. "What are you guys doing here?"

"Finding you," Lucy said, coming out of the kitchen.

"But . . . but . . . how did you know where I was?" I sputtered.

"You're not that complicated," Vi said, and rolled her eyes.

GROUP HUG, LUCY TOO

We sat in my old room, eating donuts. Mine had sprinkles. I hadn't realized how starving I was until I'd bit into the gooey deliciousness.

"I broke up with him," I told them. "He admitted it. He slept with someone else. And lied about it. My birthday was officially the worst birthday ever. How about that? I discovered the only thing worse than crappy things happening the day after your birthday—crappy things happening on your birthday."

"True," Marissa said. "But you know what that means?"

"What?"

"That the day-after-birthday curse has been broken," Lucy said.

I shrugged. "But today isn't over yet. It just started."

"No," Vi declared. "The curse is over."

"I agree," Lucy said. "You're in the clear."

I took another bite. Maybe they were right. "I can't believe you guys found me."

"Vi and I both thought of it at the same time," Marissa said.

"But why were you awake?"

Vi snorted. "We weren't going to go to sleep with you missing. We almost sent out an AMBER Alert."

"I went over after you left my house but Vi said you weren't home," Marissa said. "So I decided to wait for you."

"We called you a million times," Lucy jumped in. "Hudson and Dean came over too. They think Noah is a total tool."

"I think they always did," Vi said.

Marissa nodded. "Well, Hudson looked like he was ready to drive over to Noah's and run him over."

"Dean heard the rumor at the party," Vi said. "I guess Brett told someone who told someone who . . . anyway. Dean kept muttering how Noah didn't deserve you, but I assumed it was because his brother had the hots for you. I tore him a new one for not informing me immediately, but he didn't want to ruin your birthday."

I remembered how Hudson had been interrupted this morning. "I think Hudson was trying to tell me."

"Hudson was *very* worried about you," Vi added. "He really cares about you."

"We all do," Marissa said. "Your mom was really worried too. She called the *house* phone five times."

She had?

I turned on my cell. I had many messages. Including texts from Marissa, Hudson, and Vi.

I looked up at Vi. "You were right this morning. I *was* lying to myself. And I'm sorry I said what I said."

She shrugged. "Yeah, well, you were right about me

343

too. My mother is a flake." She looked at Lucy and then at Marissa. "And I need to stop playing games with Dean. Before I lose him for good. And I *am* a control freak."

"Can we talk about the workout DVDs in the middle of the night?" Marissa asked. "Because I think that needs to be mentioned."

Vi banged her head against the wall. "I'm full of crazy, huh?"

"We're all full of crazy," I said. "I broke into my old house and almost peed on the floor. But I do wonder why you feel the need to do HardCore3000 at three in the morning."

"I don't know," Vi said, shrugging. "It makes me feel less anxious."

"So would sleep," Lucy said.

"I think you should talk to Lucy's mom," Marissa said to me and Vi. "Both of you."

Lucy groaned. "Seriously? My mom?"

"She *is* a social worker," Marissa said. "I'm guessing she knows how to deal with all this stuff."

"She does," Lucy said. "She's just so . . . earnest. And annoying."

"No kidding," I said. "She got me a ten o'clock curfew." I pointed at Lucy. "You got me a ten o'clock curfew."

Lucy hid her face in her hands. "I know, I know, I'm sorry about that. I was a complete ass, but I wasn't trying to rat you out. I was trying to persuade her to move

344

back to New York. She was so convinced that kids here were clean-cut and perfect so I took the video to scare her into going back to the city. Which did not work. Obviously."

I thought about how Lucy's mom had done exactly what my parents hadn't. Dragged her along. Sorry you're not happy about the decision, but tough, I'm moving to Westport and that means you too, kid.

I thought back to my conversation with my mother. I kind of wished my parents had said that to me.

I looked over at Lucy and swallowed hard, feeling ashamed. Maybe I'd been left behind, but she had lost her father. That was loss I couldn't even imagine. I let my head fall against the wall. "I'm sorry I thought you were a psycho."

"I'm not psycho," she said. "I just wanted to move home."

"What about the blackmail?" Vi asked. "Let me Hula with you or I'll tell my mommy on you. That was borderline psycho."

Lucy waved her hands in the air. "You had a freaking hot tub! I had to get in somehow! And you guys seemed cool."

"We are cool," Vi answered.

"I'm sorry," Lucy said, biting her lip.

"And I'm sorry I didn't tell you about Noah," Marissa said to me. Her cheeks were red. "I should have."

"I'm sorry I took it out on you," I admitted.

"There's a whole lot of sorry going on here," Vi said. "Let's play I Never with 'I'm sorry.' If you are sorry about something, you have to take a bite of the donut."

We all laughed.

I picked up a donut. "I'm sorry Noah cheated on me. After I . . . after I stayed in Westport."

"Twice," Vi said.

"That means two bites," Marissa said. "Big ones."

"Did you really stay for him?" Marissa asked.

"A little bit for him. And for you guys. And I was afraid to try something new."

"But why didn't you go with your mom?" Lucy asked. "Maybe I wouldn't have come here if I'd had a choice but . . . she's my *mom*."

"I didn't want to leave my life. Or my dad. And I was really mad at her. I guess I'm still really mad at her."

"She was really upset when she called," Vi said. "She misses you."

"I know," I said. I thought about me and Vi and my mom and Marissa and Noah and my dad. No one was perfect. But we all did the best we could. I guessed you had to forgive when you could, move on when you couldn't, and love your family and friends for who they were instead of punishing them for who they weren't. "I miss her too," I said.

"Do you know what would be awesome?" Lucy said, picking up another donut.

"What?" I asked, still thinking of my mom.

She took a large bite, and then chewed and swallowed. "Finishing this conversation . . . while Hulaing."

HE RETURNS

We soaked and watched the sunrise. The Long Island Sound turned white, then yellow, then pink, then blue. When our stomachs started to rumble we made omelets. At about eight A.M., we called it a morning. I was just about to crawl under my covers when—

WEEEooooWEEEooooWEEEoooo!

I thought about letting it ring. What was the difference? What would happen if I didn't answer? Clearly, he was not going to make me move in with him.

WEEEooooWEEEooooWEEEoooo!

Aw, hell. "Dad."

"Hi, hon. Did I wake you?"

"Nope." At least this time I wasn't lying.

"Good. I'm outside Vi's house. Can we talk?"

I sat back up. "What about your out-of-towners' brunch?"

"I'm skipping it. I wanted to see you."

"Oh. Sure. Gimme a sec."

A few minutes later I was opening the passenger door to his rent-a-car.

A bouquet of tulips was on the passenger seat. "Are those for Penny?"

"For you," he said.

"Oh!" I picked them up and put them on my lap. "What for?"

"They're an apology. For what I said yesterday. I'll always have a room for you. If you want to move in the middle of a semester—then you can move in the middle of the semester."

My eyes filled with tears. "That's not how you felt yesterday. You made it sound like you didn't want me at all."

"I . . . you surprised me. And I was just so proud of you. About how you made a life for yourself here. I was thinking about logistics. Which was dumb. If you're not happy here, then come live with me. We'll figure out a way. And if there's no room in our house, then we'll move somewhere else. There's always room for you and Matthew."

I nodded. "Thanks, Dad."

Yesterday, I'd wanted to run. But today . . . well, my friends had found me today. And anyway, I didn't know exactly what I wanted, but I knew that if I left Westport, I wouldn't be running *to* Ohio, I would be running *from* Westport, and for me, that wasn't the right reason to run.

"Dad? Are you happy?"

He blinked. "What do you mean?"

"After everything that happened with Mom. You got through it, right? You're happy?"

He nodded. "I'm happy. Very happy."

I was thinking about lightning, but I didn't want to bring it up.

But he answered me anyway, as if he could read my mind. "You know, April," he said. "Sometimes you don't need lightning to start a fire. Sometimes, it builds on its own."

I nodded. My throat hurt.

"I'd love to have you if you want to come to Cleveland," he said. "But I won't be hurt if you want to stay."

I nodded again. "For now . . . I think I'm going to stay here."

He kissed my forehead. "Stay for now, think about things, and let me know what you want to do next year. If you want to get an apartment. Or move in with us. Or if you want to stay at Suzanne's. No rush."

"Vi's finishing school this year," I admitted.

"I know. But Suzanne doesn't mind you staying. She wrote me this morning saying so, actually."

Ha. Did she? I contemplated telling him the truth. Telling him that the emails from Suzanne were actually from Vi.

But . . .

No rush.

ONE MONTH LATER

I knocked. Twice. My heart fluttered with the sound.

"Who is it?" the voice said.

"I heard you were having a party," I said. My heart fluttered again. Was I really going to do this? Was I really going to try something new? Trust someone new? I straightened my shoulders and tried to channel Vi. If she could trust someone new, so could I.

Hudson opened the door and smiled. "How did you know where I was?"

"Dean is over at our place. I beat it out of him."

"Dean is always over at your place," he said, stepping onto the porch.

That was true. Dean and Vi had been locked in Vi's room for the last month, since my birthday. And it didn't look like they would be separating any time soon. Vi had gotten a full scholarship to Columbia, and Dean had decided to go to NYU. "New York girls are the hottest," he'd proclaimed. "Someone should write a song about *them*."

"Welcome to Ms. Franklin's," Hudson said. "I'm glad you finally made it."

"Me too."

"I hope you know that the reason I haven't been by in the last month is because I wanted to give you some space."

"I know," I said. "Thank you. All is settled." Noah was history. There had been lots of crying, lots of Hulaing, and a follow-up visit to Rosini. But it was done. He was done. "And I know we have a lot to talk about."

"Since the kids are in the living room, can I just do something before we go inside?"

I nodded.

His hand cupped my cheek and he leaned toward me. As our lips touched, my whole body sizzled.

It was lightning.

what i did
(and probably should have done earlier)

GOT ON A PLANE

The three kids in row fifteen were moving like glaciers. I'd be a hundred by the time they were done. And we were back in row twenty-four.

What time was it anyway? Poor Donut. Stuck with the bags. The amount of paperwork required to get her here had been insane, but worth it.

I switched on my phone. Seven A.M. local time. A text popped up:

How's the hottest girl in Paris?

Hudson. I smiled. Typed back:

She's still on the plane!

Marissa grabbed my hand. "Movement! Are you ready?"

I nodded. Yes. I felt ready. To explore Paris. To see Matthew. To work on my relationship with my mom. I stuck my phone in my purse and felt my heart leap. I gave Marissa a huge smile. I had her with me for the whole summer. And then . . . I was staying for senior year.

I was a little nervous. I was a little scared. But it was time to be a little gutsy.

"This is going to be awesome," she squealed. "Can we go to the Eiffel Tower today? And then the Seine tomorrow? I definitely want a baguette. And an espresso." She squeezed my arm. "You *are* going to come back for college. Right?"

I nodded. Probably. I skipped in my spot. Row twenty-three was on its way. I picked up my bag. Pulled it over my shoulder. I was ready to explore.

"Let's go," I said. And I went.

TOLD MY DAD THE TRUTH

"So are you up to anything fun today?" I asked my dad one night in November. I was sitting on my favorite spot on the couch, chatting with him on the phone, while Matthew did his homework on the living room floor and my mom and Daniel made dinner in the kitchen. It was already evening here, but only noon in Ohio. I had just gotten off the phone with Hudson at Brown. We had been planning his trip—he was coming to spend New Year's with me.

353

"Penny got us tickets to see *Mary Poppins*! It's a national production that's in Cleveland for two weeks. It was her favorite movie as a kid and the play's gotten rave reviews."

I almost dropped the phone. I swallowed a nervous laugh. What was he going to do? Set a nine o'clock curfew? "Dad? Um, listen. I have kind of a crazy story for you. . . ."

fifty-eight people
i'd like to thank
(and probably a few I'm forgetting)

Laura Dail, my incredible agent.

Tamar Rydzinski, the queen of foreign rights.

The most excellent gang at HarperTeen: Farrin Jacobs (still brilliant), Kari Sutherland (thank you thank you thank you, Kari), Elise Howard, Catherine Wallace, Allison Verost, Christina Colangelo, Kristina Radke, Sasha Illingworth, Melinda Weigel, Amy Vinchesi, and Rosanne Lauer.

Joel Gotler and Brian Lipson for all their hard work in Hollywood.

Elissa Ambrose, my mom, for her love and willingness to read, edit, and discuss on command.

Lauren Myracle and E. Lockhart: I have no idea how I ever did this without you two. You are my cheerleaders, my editors, and my co-conspirators. Thank you for everything.

Emily Bender for her terrific suggestions.

Tricia Ready for her fantastic help.

Jessica Braun, as always.

Bennett Madison for helping me shape and title this book.

Alison Pace for her notes and friendship.

Little Willow, aka Allie Costa, for her awesome insights.

Veterinarian Lindsay Norman for all her suggestions about Donut. (Of course, any mistakes are all my own.)

Pierrette C. Silverman from Planned Parenthood of Southern New England for taking the time to chat and explain. (All mistakes, also my own.)

Susan Finkelberg-Sohmer for her medical expertise. (Mistakes—mine.)

Targia Clarke for taking such great care of my little one.

Ronit Avni, who took me in and housed me in her basement when I was seventeen.

Shobie Riff and Judy Batalion for being my friends and saviors during the year of the futon. (Todd too, but more on him later.)

Aviva Mlynowski, my little sister, for introducing me to all the movie people (and because I love her and am very proud of her).

Larry Mlynowski, my dad, for his constant support and for always trusting me (even when he probably shouldn't have).

Love and thanks to my family and friends: John & Vickie Swidler, Louisa Weiss, Robert Ambrose, Jen Dalven, Gary Swidler, Darren Swidler, Ryan and Jack Swidler, Shari and Heather Endleman, Leslie Margolis, Bonnie Altro, David Levithan, Avery Carmichael, Tara Altebrando, Ally Carter, Maryrose Wood, Jennifer Barnes, Alan Gratz, Sara Zarr, Maggie Marr, and Jen Calonita.

And, of course, a million thank-yous to the loves of my life, my husband, Todd, and our daughter, Chloe.